ONE FALSE MOVE

Out of the corner of his eye Overstreet saw the lithe young woman reach into a slat bonnet that hung from the wall. She swung around with a gun in her hand. It was an old-fashioned horse pistol like Overstreet had used so many times as a boy.

"Now, you thieving *tejano*," the girl snapped at Hatchet, "you put down that box."

Hatchet's stubborn, bearded chin was low. "You ain't got the nerve to shoot anybody. But I'd break your arm." He turned toward her.

"I told you to stand back, Hatchet," Overstreet said again. "That's an order."

He stepped toward Hatchet. The girl swung the pistol around to cover him, too. "You promised us, Lieutenant. I'd just as leave shoot you as anyone of your sticky-fingered renegades."

Overstreet stopped. So did Hatchet. The lieutenant swallowed hard. One nervous twitch of her finger could kill either of them as completely as a Yankee cannonball. And the fire in her dark eyes showed she would do it...

—From *Long Ride, Hard Ride*

THE WAY OF THE WEST

ELMER KELTON

COTTON SMITH

MAX BRAND®

LEISURE BOOKS  NEW YORK CITY

A LEISURE BOOK®

Published by

Dorchester Publishing Co., Inc.
200 Madison Avenue
New York, NY 10016

ISBN 10: 0-8439-6163-5
ISBN 13: 978-0-8439-6163-8

Printed in the United States of America.

First printing: October 2008

10 9 8 7 6 5 4 3 2 1

Visit us on the web at www.dorchesterpub.com.

THE WAY OF THE WEST

Table of Contents

Long Ride, Hard Ride

I
"The Wagons of Munitions"

There could be no doubt about the sudden volley of gunfire that echoed from the ragged mountain pass to the south. For more than an hour the sixteen soldiers in gray had watched the mirror flashes on the high points. They had seen the blue-clad Yankee cavalry patrol trot into the defile.

The rattle of gunfire tapered off. For a terrible ten minutes there was silence, a quiet as awesome as had been the screaming sound of death at Valverde on the Río Grande, or Apache Cañon in the Glorietas.

Lt. Miles Overstreet, Confederate States of America, unfolded his spyglass with trembling hands and trained it on the pass. He stood tall, a lean, angular man in dusty gray, with futility weighing heavy on his shoulders. His hand-sewn uniform was frayed and stained from a thousand miles and more of riding and fighting and sleeping on the ground. A thousand miles since San Antonio. A thousand miles of sweat and thirst and blood.

The Indians came then, fifty-odd of them, riding northward in single file. The clatter of their ponies' bare hoofs on the rocks came clear as a bell on the sharp morning air. Exultant yelps ripped from red throats like the cries of demons in a child's nightmare. Behind them the red men led a dozen riderless horses, not wild mustang Indian ponies, but well-bred mounts of the U.S. cavalry.

Overstreet's leathery skin stretched even tighter over his jutting cheekbones. Despite the knife-sharp chill left from the night air, a trickle of sweat worked its way down through the streaked dust and the rough stubble of whiskers. He lowered the glass and looked at the remnant of his command. Fifteen men, flat on their bellies in skirmish line.

"Load up," he said. "We're next."

For this was New Mexico Territory in April of 1862, torn by civil war, with white man against white man, and red men against them all. Less than a year ago, fiery Col. John R. Baylor had led his 2nd Texas Mounted Rifles up from captured Fort Bliss to take New Mexico for the newly formed Confederacy. Then had come Gen. Henry Hopkins Sibley and his huge brigade. These men were ill-clothed, ill-fed, poorly armed, but through eight months of struggle and privation they had ridden to one victory after another—Fort Fillmore, San Augustine Springs, Valverde, Albuquerque. At last, they had raised the Confederate flag over Santa Fé itself and envisioned a daring sweep across to California, to the gold fields, to the open sea.

Then came disaster in one flaming day at Glorieta Pass. Grim men in tattered gray turned their faces southward toward Texas, the sweet taste of victory now bitter ashes in their mouths. Men like Miles Overstreet, who had known the dream and now stood awaiting the futile end of it, had been wasted under a savage onslaught that no one had even considered.

He listened to the click of captured Yankee single-shot carbines as his men prepared for a battle that could end but one way. He saw one soldier flattened out in fear, without a weapon.

"Vasquez," Overstreet called to a dark-skinned trooper from the brushy cow country below San Antonio, "give Hatchet back his gun. His little mutiny is over."

His men! The thought brought an ironic twist to his cracked lips. The sorriest soldiers in Sibley's Brigade, and Major Scanling had saddled him with them. A thousand times he had cursed the day he stole a victory right under the pointed nose of the glory-hunting major. Scanling's lips had smiled as he read the communication. But his eyes never masked the anger that simmered in him. Scanling transferred Overstreet then. Gave him these men, prisoners all, to relieve their guards for action.

"We need a good officer like you to handle them," he had said, his yellow eyes gleaming. "Take them. Delay the federals long enough for the main body of troops to get away. Hold every pass as long as you can, then drop back and hold another. We're buying time with you . . . with you and these miserable scum who call themselves soldiers. Go on, Overstreet. Go on and be a hero."

He had hated the major then, and his hatred swelled a little more every time he'd been forced to use his own gun to keep half the men from running away. Now, this looked like the end of it.

Beside Overstreet, young Sammy McGuffin rose on his knees and lowered his head in prayer.

"Better flatten out there and spend your time getting ready for those Indians, son," the lieutenant said curtly.

The boy looked up in surprise. "You don't believe in prayer, sir?"

"I believe in a man taking care of himself."

The Indians stopped three hundred yards short of the Confederates' position. They shouted defiance and waved muskets and Yankee guns and showed the fresh scalps that dangled beneath the firearms. Then they wheeled their ponies and galloped away into the morning sun, shouting their victory to the mountains.

Overstreet stood watching open-mouthed, hardly believing, hardly daring to believe.

Sammy McGuffin's high-pitched voice spoke out, almost breaking. "They're leaving. They're letting us live. But why?"

The answer came in a gravel-voiced drawl from a thick-shouldered, middle-aged Texan with a stubble of black beard coarse as porcupine quills. Big Tobe Wheeler said: "That's the way with Indians, boy. To them killing is a sport, kind of. Without they really got their blood hot, they'll generally kill just enough to satisfy their appetite. They'll count a few coups and have them a victory to brag about in camp. They'll pull out before they start to taking a licking themselves. Maybe tomorrow they'll get the itch again and come looking for us. But not today."

The trooper named Hatchet was already on his feet and making for the horses. "Well, they ain't going to be finding *me* here."

Overstreet yelled at him, an edge of anger in his voice. "You hold up there, Hatchet. You'll ride out when the rest of us do."

Hatchet turned and glowered at him with eyes the light blue of a shallow stream, disturbing eyes that never stopped moving. As was his habit when he was angry, he gripped his right arm with his speckled left hand. The faded gray sleeve showed where a sergeant's chevrons had been torn away. Hatchet was a thief. He had lost his rank after he had left a battle to hunt for loot in a bullet-scarred town.

"Look here, Lieutenant, you know we're whipped. Between them damn Yankees and the redskins, we ain't got a chance. Now let's hightail it like the rest of the brigade and get back to Texas with our hair."

Overstreet's long back was rigid, and his lips were tightly drawn. "We're heading for Texas like the rest, Hatchet. But we're going like men, not like whipped dogs. Any time we get a chance to take a lick at the federals, we'll do it. Try to run away again and I'll gun you down."

Deliberately he turned away from Hatchet's silent fury, half expecting a bullet in his back. One day the bullet might come. And if it did, he knew that probably every man in the outfit would swear he had died by enemy fire.

"Mount up," he ordered his scalawag band. "We're moving south."

He rode out in the lead, tall and straight in the saddle, just as he had once ridden with the Texas Rangers, before secession. He held his shoulders squared. But within him was a certainty that Hatchet was right. Wasted, gone for nothing, were all those hard miles they'd fought. All those days they'd ridden until their tailbones were numb and their dry tongues stuck to the roofs of their mouths. All those men they'd lost. Good men, fighters. They'd died bravely, most of them. But they'd died for nothing.

A dull ache worked through his shoulder, and for the hundredth time his mind dwelt on the angry words of that girl in the makeshift hospital in Albuquerque. Shafter, her name had been, and she was a Union supporter all the way. A refugee from farther south, someone had said. Her name was American, and so was her speech. But proud Spanish flowed in her raven hair, her piercing brown eyes almost black, her oval face in which even her hatred pointed up her strong-willed beauty. She was helping in the hospital only because wounded Yankee prisoners were being treated there along with the Texas soldiers.

Always he remembered the sharp odor of the nitric acid before it was swabbed onto his wound to cauterize it, and he remembered the caustic words she had spoken after he had half fainted from the searing agony.

"Remember this well," she had said. "It wouldn't have happened if you *tejanos* had stayed home. This is Union land. Maybe you've taken it, but you'll never hold it. You were beaten before you started."

She was right. They were beaten. It was a painful thing to run away, leaving so much unfinished, so much hope unfulfilled. Yet it might not be so bad, he thought, if they could win just one more victory, one more triumph as a final gesture. With all his soul he longed for that one last chance.

Out of his fifteen men there were two whom he trusted more than the rest. Before riding into the pass, he sent Vasquez and big Tobe Wheeler up on either side to scout for ambush. When they hipped around in their saddles and waved their hats, he moved on in.

They found the Union soldiers heaped like rag dolls, scalped and mutilated. At a glance Overstreet knew the Indians had stripped them of guns and ammunition. A few months ago the sight would have made him turn away, sick to his stomach. Now he only grimaced and rode on in.

His gray eyes sought out the body of the commanding officer. Spotting captain's bars on the shoulder of a bullet-torn uniform, he swung down and knelt beside the dead man. There might be papers.

Inside the coat pocket he found an envelope, the corner stained a sticky red. Opening it, he became aware of the onetime sergeant methodically searching the pockets of the Union soldiers. "Hatchet," he thundered, "do you even have to rob the dead?"

The trooper's pale eyes flitted over him, then away. "They must've been trading-post Indians, Lieutenant. Leastways they knew what money's for. They ain't left a two-bit piece in the whole bunch."

"Get back on your horse, Hatchet," Overstreet ordered.

He took the letter out of the envelope. Reading it, he felt his heartbeat quicken. There was a sudden eager tingling in his fingertips.

He had hoped for another chance, all but begged the devil for it. Now here it was, delivered by a bloody band of paint-smeared savages. He read the letter again, half afraid his imagination had run away. But it hadn't. This was an order for the Union captain to take a detail of cavalry and proceed to the Walton Shafter ranch west of the Río Pecos. There he was to prepare for shipment a store of rifles and ammunition that had been hidden by Union forces fleeing northward from Fort Stanton the year before.

A train of ten wagons will be dispatched on the 10th instant, and should reach the ranch within two days after your arrival. Shafter, his daughter, and household should also have returned by this time. The family abandoned the ranch and took away the cattle upon the approach of the secessionists.

You will render all possible service and show utmost courtesy to them. Shafter was a loyal scout for the forces of General Kearny fifteen years ago. The family has been of much aid in this campaign.

I do not have to tell you how badly any and all munitions

are needed if we are successfully to push the rebellious Texans from our borders.

Martin Nash
Colonel, Commanding

Overstreet clenched his fists, crushing the order. Ten wagons of munitions. Not enough to wage much of a war, but enough for one good battle, if judiciously used. And who could say? It had taken just one battle, that awful fumble at Glorieta Pass, to turn back the gray tide that had all but engulfed New Mexico. Ten wagons of munitions. Pitifully little, but who could say they might not halt the retreat, and launch the gray legions on a new drive that could carry all the way to California?

II
"The Gun"

A quivering trooper named Brinkley spoke up and penetrated the spell.

"For God's sake, sir, can't we get out of this place? My flesh is crawling like a barrel of snakes."

Overstreet led the men on beyond the grisly scene in the pass. He reread the letter, as he rode, and wished the Yankee colonel had been more specific in locating the ranch. But probably the captain had known.

A name leaped out at him. Shafter. *Shafter, his daughter . . . should have returned.* He remembered the dark-haired, dark-eyed girl in the hospital. Shafter had been her name, too. The same? It couldn't be. The haunting beauty of her face had been with him ever since he had left Albuquerque. But he knew he would never see her again.

South of the pass they stopped to breathe the horses. Trooper Brinkley took off his coat, a worn gray coat with a big blue patch on the right elbow. "How long to Fort Bliss, sir?" he asked. "A week? Ten days?"

Overstreet fingered the letter. This was as good a time as any to break the news. Watching sullen anger swell in many of the men's eyes, he told them about the Yankee colonel's order. He had expected some trouble, but he hadn't expected it to come so suddenly. Eyes wide with fright, Brinkley swung into his saddle and started backing his horse away.

"Not me, Lieutenant. I wouldn't stay in this country for ten wagons of gold."

He touched spurs to his horse's sides. Another soldier leaped into the saddle and clattered after him.

Overstreet reached for his holster and brought up the Colt Dragoon he had used with the Texas Rangers. He fired the shot, just over the men's heads.

The two soldiers hauled up short. They came back, their faces sickly pale even beneath the dirt and whiskers.

"Take their guns away, Vasquez," Overstreet ordered the dark-skinned trooper. "They'll go to Fort Bliss when the rest of us do."

He felt Hatchet's washy eyes upon him. "You're a long way from home, Lieutenant," the trooper said casually, so casually that Overstreet felt a chill work down his back.

He remembered a hellish afternoon a week ago when they had turned back a Yankee troop in a rock-strewn cañon. A bullet had whipped by his ear and into a boulder, burning his face with rock dust. It hadn't come from Union guns. He had whirled and seen Hatchet lowering a carbine. But with all that shouting around them, what could he ever prove?

The coldness still on him, he cut short the rest stop and pushed the men on. They rode in stolid silence, the talk long since burned out of them. Before sundown they stopped to cook a light supper, then moved on a few more miles to a dry, fireless camp.

A pink tinge was creeping over the east when Tobe Wheeler shook Overstreet's shoulder. "Two men gone, sir."

The lieutenant leaped to his feet and quickly looked around him in the cold semidarkness.

Wheeler rubbed his bushy jaw. "Brinkley and Thallman, sir. Short-handed like we was, we had to let Brinkley have a gun to stand guard last night. We put Thallman with him to see he didn't run away. By the way she looks, I'd say he talked Thallman into going with him." Wheeler's rough face twisted in a scowl. "Worst of it is, sir, they took a lot of our rations along with them. And we got little enough as it is. You want to trail them?"

Overstreet clamped his teeth together and choked off an oath. "Let them go. If we caught them, we'd have to waste two more men on guard duty. Get the men up and let's move out."

He drove his right fist into the palm of his left hand. What else could he expect from the men Major Scanling had given him?

So the troop moved on, riding from the time the peach color broke in the east until the last red had faded from the western sky. Every time they passed a settlement or ran into a brown-skinned settler, Overstreet sent Elijah Vasquez to inquire in Spanish about the Shafter Ranch. For three days the answer was only a shrug of the shoulders.

Then one day they came upon a Mexican herding a small band of sheep. Vasquez turned away from the man, his weary face split by a gleaming smile.

"He say it is to the south, not far from the Río Pecos. He say Shafter and his herd have pass this way, not many days ago."

Overstreet saluted the herder and headed south, his men behind him. The herder never gave the soldiers more than a passive look, such as he might have given a freight outfit with a string of mules or a line of ox-drawn *carretas.* War was an old, old thing to these people.

The troopers quartered east. Watchfully they crossed cañon after cañon, ravine after ravine that snaked out in search of the alkaline flow of the Pecos. At last the men drew rein and looked out across the turbulent brown water that etched its way between the mountains and the dreaded Llano Estacado, the Staked Plains.

There had been considerable Indian signs, so the detail sent its outriders far to the flanks, and Overstreet allowed no hunting for fresh meat.

Presently Wheeler came riding back in. "Settlement ahead, sir. Trading post seems to be all there is to it. Looks more like an Indian camp than anything else to me."

Overstreet climbed upon a low point and unfolded the spyglass. No sign of Yankee troops. There was only one long, L-shaped adobe building, with a small storehouse behind it. Out to one side was a brush corral with a number of Indian ponies in it. Scattered all about it was the litter and filth of years of careless camping.

More than once along the border Overstreet had gotten the sudden sense of dread that crept over him now. Frowning, he folded the glass and rejoined the command. "Vasquez, you and I will go in alone. The rest of you men will stay out of sight. If you have trouble, come on the run. If you don't, come in ten minutes."

As an afterthought he handed Wheeler the spyglass. Then the two men in dusty torn gray rode into the settlement. A wariness kept stirring in Overstreet. He could see it in Vasquez's face, too. Vasquez had nerves like the steel in the long-bladed knife he wore in his belt and that he had plunged hilt-deep into the shoulder of another trooper at Albuquerque because that trooper had molested a girl whose skin was brown like that of Vasquez.

A dark, portly man stepped out of a middle door and stood hesitantly in front of the rude adobe building. Hands shoved into the waistband of incredibly dirty trousers, he studied the men in gray. Then he looked at their horses. Overstreet knew the man would give his eyeteeth for the two mounts.

"Ask him first if there've been any Yankees around here yet," the officer said to Vasquez. The soldier spoke in quick, fluid Spanish. The trader's reply came back in chopped Spanish, accentuated with hand signals and a quick shaking of the head.

Vasquez turned to the lieutenant. "He say no, no Yankees. He say the men in gray are always his friends. Also he ask if we are alone."

Overstreet realized suddenly that something in the man's face wasn't Mexican at all. The eyes were blue. And now that he looked closer, he could see the sun strike a reddish tinge to the matted beard and the hair that showed under the broad-brimmed sombrero. The discovery set needles pricking his skin.

He became aware of almost a dozen dark men stepping stealthily out of doors all along the lengthy adobe building. A few were Mexican, but most were Indians. They were armed, and they formed a wide, tight circle around the two soldiers. Overstreet fought back a panicky urge to draw his gun. It would never clear the holster.

One of the Indians was wearing a soldier's gray coat with a blue patch on the right elbow. Short hair rose on Overstreet's neck. Brinkley's coat! The two deserters had not gotten far.

The trader switched to English. "Ain't no cause for alarm, Lieutenant. All of us here are good friends of the South."

As he talked, his mouth broken in a mirthless, yellow-toothed smile, the trader was walking toward the two soldiers. Suddenly he reached out and caught the reins of both horses, right before the bits.

Vasquez whipped out an oath and grabbed for the knife at his belt.

"Hold it, Vasquez!" Overstreet barked. He could see the yawning chasm of death in a dozen gun muzzles.

Still talking, now triumphant, the trader said: "If I was you, I'd step down easy. Was I to give the signal, my boys'd cut you in two. They like to see the blood run."

Anger and fear mixed in the blood that pounded through Overstreet's veins. Throat dry, he started to obey. Just as his right leg swung over his horse's rump, he saw sudden excitement hit the Mexicans and Indians like a cannonball. The trader's smile vanished. He let go of the horses.

The Rebel soldiers had ridden in quietly and ringed the post. All of them had guns in their hands. A quick murmur rippled through the motley trading-post bunch as they weighed the proposition, whether to drop their guns or stand their ground. At last one wrinkled old Indian lowered the ancient muzzle-loading pistol he held, and the others followed suit.

Relief washed through Overstreet as his men rode in. The scare had left him momentarily weak. The black-hearted Wheeler was in command, sitting his horse with all the pride and arrogance of a Yankee general. He saluted the lieutenant, then motioned for the Mexicans and Indians to line up.

Overstreet turned to Vasquez, who seemed to have taken a quick grip on his nerves. "Call everybody out of the building into the yard. Tell them any man who hesitates or runs will get a bullet through him."

Three more Indian bucks, a couple of slatternly squaws, and a disheveled Mexican woman came out of the building and joined the line.

"All right, men," the lieutenant said with vengeance in his voice, "search every room. If anything goes wrong, don't hesitate to shoot."

It was then that Sammy McGuffin pulled his horse up beside the Indian wearing the gray coat.

"Look," he shouted, pointing his finger. "He's got Brinkley's coat on."

Evidently thinking he was being pointed out for death, the Indian desperately lunged at Sammy's horse. He grabbed the carbine from the boy's hand. It exploded, and the kid jerked, crying out in pain. Dalton Corbell shot the Indian.

Tobe Wheeler grabbed the boy and held him in the saddle until two troopers jumped down to ease the whimpering lad to the ground. The wound was a raw, gaping hole well inside the left shoulder.

Watching the wound being bandaged, Overstreet asked Wheeler: "Think he can ride?"

Wheeler nodded. "He'll have to, I reckon. A couple of them redskins slipped away during the excitement. Even afoot, it ain't going to take them all week to find help."

Searching the post, the soldiers found only a couple of cases of old muzzle-loading guns, a little gunpowder, a roomful of Indian trade goods, mostly rotten whisky, and a nose-pinching stack of buffalo robes.

Overstreet nodded toward the hides. "There's no buffalo here,

Wheeler. I'd bet these were traded from the plains tribes across in Texas."

The thick-bodied soldier drawled: "If you was to ask me, sir, I'd say this is what they call a Comanchero post. A dirty bunch of Indian traders that'll swap guns, whisky, captured women and children, or anything else, long's there's a profit in it. It'd suit me fine to cut the throats of the whole bunch before we leave here."

The lieutenant caught a short, banty rooster of a trooper named Duffy gulping a long swig of the trader's whisky. The little man choked, and tears welled up into his eyes. "Terrible stuff, sir," he wheezed, the whisky still searing his throat. "Should be against the law, the making of it. Will you have a drink with me?"

Overstreet shook his head. "No. And if I catch you taking another drink of it, I'll make you walk till your drunken brain explodes. Dump that stuff out, all of it."

The soldiers piled up all the guns, powder, and trade goods. Overstreet told them to take out what they could use.

"Then set fire to the rest of it."

The fat trader's mouth dropped open. His hands began gesturing violently. "For God's sake, Lieutenant, you wouldn't go and leave us here unarmed, would you? We got enemies."

Overstreet gritted: "From the looks of your red-skinned cronies here, I'd say you ought to have friends enough to protect you." He frowned at the trader then, and an idea came to him. "What's your name?"

The red-edged eyes smoldered. "Howden Tate Bowden. What difference does that make to you?"

Overstreet reached forward and grabbed the man's dirty collar. "Do you know where the Walton Shafter Ranch is?"

The fat man nodded. "I ought to. What few troubles I had, that's where they come from."

Overstreet snapped: "Then get your saddle. You're riding with us."

The trader started to argue, but Wheeler poked him in the belly with the muzzle of a carbine. Bowden turned to obey.

As he saddled a fat pony in the corral, he flicked his hate-filled eyes at Overstreet. "I promise you this . . . you won't get far . . . my friends'll be on your trail before the dust settles . . . your scalps will be drying on a pole by this time tomorrow."

Overstreet angrily grabbed the man by the grimy collar again, and shoved him roughly back against his horse. "If you think you're going to lead us into an ambush, you'd better forget it. You'd die with us, because we'll slit your throat like we'd butcher a beef. Remember that. Now let's go."

They put the wounded boy into his saddle, and one trooper rode beside him to give him support. The detail moved out. Three soldiers rode ahead, pushing all the Indian ponies before them. Overstreet turned back once to look at the dark smoke that curled upward into the hazy sky. He got a grim satisfaction from the dismay on Bowden's greasy face.

He knew the trading post Indians wouldn't follow afoot, and they certainly wouldn't go to the Yankees. But they might bring another kind of help—dark-skinned savages with paint-smeared faces, muskets and short bows, lances and scalping knives. The thought made Overstreet spur harder.

Far into the night they rode, then slept in a fireless camp with no warm rations. All night Sammy McGuffin whimpered in painful half sleep. Before daybreak the troop was up and moving again, watching the back trail for any sign of pursuit.

It was a long ride, a hard ride. Sitting wearily in the saddle, Overstreet let his mind wander back through the years to other rides he had made. They had been long rides, too, and he had made them stirrup-to-stirrup with his father. The distance hadn't mattered much to him as a boy, for always there had been something new to see. And always there had been that commanding fire in old Jobe Overstreet's eyes.

Jobe Overstreet had been a circuit rider, with a black coat over his shoulders and the book in his pocket, and he had ridden the length and breadth of the frontier to bring the word to scattered settlers who hadn't seen a church in years. It had been a hard life, one that would have left a weakling of a boy by the wayside. But it had been worth all of it to thrill to that grand fever in his father's voice as he would stand above the gathered crowd in a clearing or on a hillside or along a creek bank.

But gradually, somehow, there came a change. Young Miles Overstreet found other activities more to his interest. He made fewer and fewer of those long rides beside old Jobe. That impassioned voice no longer sent a thrill tingling down his spine, and doubts began to crowd out the faith that had dwelt so long with him.

He would never forget that day he rode up to the little log structure that passed for a home and told his father that he had joined the Texas Rangers. It had been painful to watch the bitter disappointment etch itself into his father's lean, brown face.

"Don't be too soon making up your mind, son," Jobe had said with patience.

Not until then had Miles noticed how completely gray his father had become.

"'Tis a sad thing to see a man turn away from the Book and take up the gun. The gun brings misery and death to the body. But the book, boy, the book is food and drink and life for the soul."

But Miles had been young and bold and high of heart, and he had ridden away. The quick glance he took over his shoulder was the last look he had ever gotten at his father. That look was burned into his mind, his father standing like a great oak, his broad shoulders sagging a little, his head bowed in prayer.

Soon afterward Jobe Overstreet had gone down toward the coast to give comfort to the dying in a yellow fever epidemic. But the fever fastened itself upon him. And as the epidemic itself died away, Jobe Overstreet died, too.

The news had struck Miles like a thunderbolt. That a man who had spent his life serving the Lord should have to die in suffering when he had been on a mission of mercy. . . . Miles Overstreet's faith had ebbed away, and it had never returned.

III
"The Girl from Albuquerque"

In mid-afternoon he began to notice that Bowden was leading them slightly to the east again. Worry began pulling at him, and he sent outriders a little farther away to watch for signs that anything was wrong.

It wasn't long in coming. Vasquez spurred in, waving his hat excitedly. "Indian camp, sir," he shouted breathlessly. "About a mile ahead. Forty men, maybe fifty. This man"—he motioned toward Bowden—"he try to make us ride right into them."

Fury pulled Overstreet around in the saddle to face the trader. "You misled us, Bowden. You remember what I told you?"

The pudgy cheeks drained of color, and the blood-rimmed blue eyes widened. Suddenly Bowden spurred the pony and clattered down the rocky slope, trying recklessly to make the Indian camp. Half a dozen troopers raised their rifles.

"Don't shoot!" Overstreet yelled. "You'll have the whole camp on us."

He spurred after Bowden. The fat Indian pony wasn't much match for a well-bred cavalry mount, even though the bigger horse was tired from day upon day of riding. Overstreet reached his long arm around the trader's neck and pulled him out of the saddle. Then he dropped him and watched him roll and thrash among the sharp rocks. He swung down and jerked the trader onto his feet, drove a fist into the wide mouth, and sent Bowden rolling again.

Out of the corner of his eye he saw Vasquez catch the trader's horse and start bringing it back.

Overstreet stood with fists doubled and watched blood trickle down the fat chin. "I meant what I told you back at the post, Bowden. You're going to lead us to Shafter's. I'll tie a rope around your neck and drag you through the rocks if I've got to. But you'll lead us, and lead us right."

No words passed from Bowden's bruised lips, but his blackening eyes told of the hate that seethed in him. Stiffly he mounted the pony and headed out again, a little west of south.

They had to make another dry, cold camp. Lying rolled up in his dirty blanket, sleepless, Overstreet let his thoughts wander again. They dwelt mostly upon the girl in Albuquerque. There was pleasure in remembering her dark eyes, the beauty of her face. In his imagination even the harshness was gone from her words, the only words she had spoken to him. Strange how it was that sometimes even the thought of a woman could bring comfort to the worry-crowded mind of a man.

They came in sight of the Shafter place the next morning. The ranch headquarters had been built along a creek that evidently ran at some times of the year and held water in deep holes the rest of the time. In a small, irrigated patch stood traces of last year's corn crop. Last year had been a dry one in New Mexico, poor for forage and poorer for crops, unless they had had some irrigation.

All the buildings were of the inevitable adobe, set close together as in a fort, with open space all around and a stout cedar picket fence on all sides to slow up any attack. The main building was in a hollow square, with a Mexican patio in the middle. All rooms evidently opened into the patio, for there were only windows along the outer walls. Out back was a cedar thicket. Nearby, but outside the fence, were the small adobe outbuildings and pole corrals.

Overstreet noted with satisfaction that there were only three or four horses around. Scattered up and down the creek were cattle grazing upon the short green grass that had begun to rise.

"No sign of Yankees, Wheeler," he said.

At his signal, the men moved into double file and struck up a trot. At the rear was Vasquez, acting as guard for Bowden.

"Straighten up in those saddles, men," Overstreet ordered. "At least we can *look* like soldiers."

Wheeler spurred to the front and opened the gate that led through the tall picket fence.

Three men stepped out of the archway that led into the patio. They stood waiting, regarding the soldiers in quiet hostility. Two were Mexicans. Warily Overstreet watched the rifle one of them held in his hands. The third man stepped forward into the yard with the dignity of a soldier proud of his service. He was not a big man, but Overstreet got the idea he was as sturdy as an oak.

He wore an old deerskin shirt and plain black trousers. Overstreet noted that the man's right arm hung stiffly at his side.

The stiff-armed one spoke quietly, and the Mexican reluctantly laid down the rifle. The lieutenant raised his right hand to salute. The man at the archway raised his left in the sign language signal for peace.

"Mister Shafter?" Overstreet asked. The ranchman nodded his gray head, his sharp eyes never leaving the officer's face. "Lieutenant Miles Overstreet, sir, presenting his compliments."

The ranchman's tone was civil but not friendly. "Get down, Lieutenant, you and your men. I reckon you're hungry. We ain't got much, but what's here, you're welcome to it."

"That's kind of you, sir," said the lieutenant. "But first, we've got a wounded man here. We don't have any medical supplies. We'd hoped maybe . . ."

The old scout had taken two long steps toward the boy, McGuffin. He saw the blood on the lad's uniform and called without waiting for Overstreet to finish speaking.

"Linda! Linda! Come out here. There's a man needs help."

A girl stepped out into the patio and through the archway. Overstreet blinked and stiffened in the saddle; words stuck in his throat. It was the girl from the Albuquerque hospital!

Quickly she moved in beside the tanned scout who was her father. She looked at Sammy and said impatiently: "Don't all you *tejanos* just sit there like a bundle of feed. Somebody help me get this boy inside."

Woodenly the lieutenant swung down from the saddle. Wheeler and another man lifted Sammy off his horse. The girl led them into the patio and through a big door to the left. Overstreet watched her, hardly conscious that his mouth was open, and that he held his hands stiffly in midair. Shafter had to speak twice before the officer caught his words.

"My daughter, Lieutenant."

Overstreet nodded and tried to force his startled mind onto something else. He let his gaze sweep over the buildings. "How many people are there here, sir?"

"No Union troops, Lieutenant. You don't have to worry about that."

"How about your own people?"

"A handful. My daughter and me. Half a dozen hands and three of their women. We just came back from up north to get the ranch fixed up. We brought a few cattle with us. The main herd won't come till the grass is up good." He shrugged his shoulders in the manner of one who has spent much of his life among the Mexican people. "So you see, Lieutenant, there's not much here to plague your mind. I'll get the *cocinero* to fix some beef for your men, and you can move on."

He led Overstreet into the bare patio and turned back just before stepping under the shady *portales.* He pointed his chin toward the trader Bowden, sitting his horse belligerently at the rear of the troop.

"I don't know why you have Bowden with you, Lieutenant. It's none of my business. But there's one thing I'll ask of you. I don't want that man to set foot under my roof."

Overstreet had to grin. Here was a man he was going to like, even though Shafter was a Union supporter.

"Bowden is our prisoner, Mister Shafter. He tried to get us killed by Indians."

He was pleased by the grim look in Shafter's eyes that said the trader was getting what he deserved. "He ought to hang," commented the ranchman. "He's a Comanchero, and about as bad as the worst of them."

Again Overstreet looked at the closely gathered ranch buildings. "You're a long way from help here, sir. How've you managed to keep your hair?"

Shafter turned and gazed out across the ragged spread of mountains and the valley that was beginning to show a cast of green as the spring sun had edged northward. His blue eyes were proud. "A man this far out can't look to governments for much help, Lieutenant. He's got to make his own treaties. But I've been living around Indians ever since I came West to trap beaver. That's been thirty years ago. I've been making my own treaties and keeping them, even when armies weren't able to."

Overstreet followed him through a thick, adobe doorway and into a parlor. It was a fair-sized room, about twenty feet square, with a big Navajo rug covering the dirt floor. Taking up most of one side of the room was a big, open fireplace upon which this morning's coals still smoldered warmly. Overstreet ran his fingers over a solid, handmade table that must have come from Santa Fé. The other furniture was the same, crudely designed but strong and well-finished.

Through another door he could hear voices. He stepped up to

it and watched Linda Shafter and a middle-aged Mexican woman working over Sammy McGuffin, talking to each other in soft, quiet Spanish.

Overstreet's heart picked up as the girl's dark eyes lifted to his briefly, then dropped again to her task. The same black hair, the same slender, softly rounded form that had quickened his breath in Albuquerque and dwelt in his mind ever since. It was the same beautiful oval face, the skin smooth as fresh cream.

The lieutenant fingered the rough brush of beard on his face and looked regretfully at the dust and grime on his frayed uniform. He wished the girl hadn't had to see him this way.

Presently she was finished. Freshly bandaged, Sammy McGuffin laid quietly, his eyes closed. Overstreet wondered whether he had fainted or gone to sleep. Whichever it might have been, it was merciful.

Overstreet stood before the girl, hat crushed in his hand. "What do you think, miss?"

She was washing her hands in a pottery bowl. "He'll live, if you'll let him rest a few days and get a chance to mend."

He shook his head. "I'm afraid we can't . . . not long. We've got to be moving south."

Her eyes met his. He knew how he looked and knew what she thought of him by the thinly veiled dislike he saw there. "If you don't want to kill him," she said, "you'll have to leave him here."

He stared at her incredulously. "You'd let a Texas soldier stay here, and you'd doctor him?"

"We'll help any wounded man who needs attention. Even a Texan."

Overstreet wondered. But he knew from the look in her eyes that she meant it, and that her father backed her up. That made it harder to do what he had to do.

"I can't tell you how grateful I am, miss. That's why I hate this so much. We've got to search your place."

A thin line of anger momentarily crossed Shafter's wind-cracked lips. Then he nodded and said in the Mexican fashion: "My house is yours, Lieutenant."

Overstreet took a flashing glance at the girl. There was a flush of anger on her face, and her arms were folded tightly across her breasts.

"Mister Shafter," said Overstreet, "please call all your people together outside there, in the patio."

Shafter stepped to the door and spoke in Spanish to the two Mexican hands. They separated and returned quickly with two other men and three women.

"Two men are out on horseback," said Shafter. "They'll be back by noon."

Overstreet stepped in front of his men. "Now search every room of every building. You know what to look for. Bring along any guns you find. But don't touch anything else. Do you hear me? Nothing else."

As the soldiers disappeared into the buildings, Overstreet turned to the angry girl. "I hope you'll understand, Miss Shafter. In war we have to do a lot of things we hate. This is one of the things I hate most. It embarrasses me, and it humiliates you. But you're on one side of the wall, and I'm on the other. We can't take any chances."

His words did nothing to allay her resentment. So Overstreet tried to dismiss it from his mind. After all, she was a Yankee girl. But the regret stayed with him.

By ones and twos the men straggled back. With them they brought perhaps a dozen guns of all makes and kinds. Anxiously Overstreet searched each face that approached him. But he knew without asking that the gun and ammunition cache had not been found.

Finally all the men were back but one. The missing trooper was Hatchet. Overstreet heard a rattle in a room to his left. He remembered that he had seen Hatchet go into a door on the right.

Fresh color washed into Linda Shafter's cheeks. "That's my room he's in," she said sharply. "I'm telling you, Lieutenant, I will not have him prowling through my things."

She whirled around so fast that her skirt sailed a little and half wrapped itself around her legs as she quickly stepped forward and pushed through a door. The lieutenant heard her gasp, then shout angrily: "Put that down! It's mine!" He heard something crash and heard her cry out in pain.

With two long strides Overstreet reached the room and shoved in. The slender girl was picking herself up from the floor and leaping again at Hatchet. Angry Spanish words were tumbling from her lips. She grabbed for a box Hatchet held behind him.

He pushed her away strongly. "Get away from me, you wench, or I'll really hurt you."

Overstreet barked at Hatchet in a voice sharp as a spur rowel.

"Stand back, there, Hatchet. Whatever you've got in your hand, give it to that girl."

Hatchet whirled on the lieutenant. His wide mouth flared. "Maybe you can tell us what to do in the field, Overstreet, but this ain't the field. What I've found, I'll keep for myself."

Out of the corner of his eye Overstreet saw the lithe young woman reach into a slat bonnet that hung from the wall. She swung around with a gun in her hand. It was an old-fashioned horse pistol like Overstreet had used so many times as a boy. And who'd have thought to look in a bonnet hanging from a peg on the wall?

"Now, you thieving *tejano,*" the girl snapped at Hatchet, "you put down that box."

Hatchet's stubborn, bearded chin was low. "You ain't got the nerve to shoot anybody. But I'd break your arm." He turned toward her.

"I told you to stand back, Hatchet," Overstreet said again. "That's an order."

He stepped toward Hatchet. The girl swung the pistol around to cover him, too. "You promised us, Lieutenant. I'd just as leave shoot you as any one of your sticky-fingered renegades."

Overstreet stopped. So did Hatchet. The lieutenant swallowed hard. One nervous twitch of her finger could kill either of them as completely as a Yankee cannonball. And fire in her dark eyes showed she would do it.

She didn't see Wheeler step up behind her. Like a bullwhip, his hand snaked out and jerked the pistol from her fingers. She whirled on him as if to beat against his big body with her little fists. Then she broke down and began to sob. Wheeler looked down on her in embarrassment and pity and looked as if he wanted to run.

Overstreet snatched the box from Hatchet's hand, put it on a table, and opened it. Inside was a string of pearl-white beads, a brooch that appeared to be of gold, and a couple of sparkling rings.

"They were my mother's," the girl said.

Overstreet handed her the box and put his hand on her shoulder to comfort her. But touching her set his blood to tingling, and he drew his hand away. "My apologies, miss. Whatever else may be wrong with us, we're not thieves."

Outside, he let his anger spill in torrents. "What have I got to do to make you learn that we're fighting Yankee soldiers, not civilians, Hatchet? Every settlement we've been through, you've tried to loot it. I almost wish you hadn't lost your sergeant's rating before you were sent to me. I'd like to have ripped those chevrons off your sleeve myself." To Wheeler he said: "Hatchet's under arrest. Disarm him. Find a good place that one man can guard and put him and Bowden in it."

Later Overstreet faced Shafter and his daughter under the shady patio portals. "I wish I could repay you for the trouble we've caused you."

Linda Shafter's eyes still held a spark. "I wish you could just hurry up and leave."

The lieutenant flinched. "So do I. But first we're going to get the Union munitions that you have hidden here."

Shafter straightened and clasped his stiff arm with his good hand. The girl caught her breath quickly. Then the old scout dropped his hand and said: "Somebody's lied to you, Lieutenant. We don't know anything about any munitions."

Overstreet shook his head. "I don't intend to get harsh now, after what you've done for us. But you know, and I know, that there are ten wagonloads of guns and ammunition hidden somewhere about the ranch. One way or another, we're going to find them."

Shafter folded his good arm across his chest. "Even if there were any munitions, Lieutenant, we wouldn't tell you."

The lieutenant smiled. "If you did, sir, I wouldn't respect you. But we'll find them ourselves."

IV
"Arsenal"

He went back into the parlor and looked around. He knew his soldiers had searched every building. It appeared the cache must be somewhere out on the ranch, not in the buildings. He turned on his heel and felt the Indian rug sink into the dirt beneath his feet. A sudden hunch hit him. He stepped back, pulled up a corner, and rolled away the rug. He saw nothing but the dirt floor.

Impatiently he shoved open a door in the thick adobe wall and went into the next room. He looked under two smaller rugs there. Nothing. But in the third he found what he sought. Half buried beneath the dirt was the knotted end of a rope. He pulled it up until the slack was gone, then began to tug on it. He could see a big block of dirt rise a little. He called for help.

With big Tobe Wheeler and another trooper helping him, he lifted the trap door and set it back on its leather hinges. Even without looking into the musty tunnel, he knew he had found the cache. Carefully he lowered himself through the door, then dropped to the bottom. Wheeler came after him, while the other troopers waited above to help them get out.

"An old getaway tunnel, I'd bet, sir," Wheeler said. "Put there to give folks a chance to light out in case they had to. I'd bet a man a quart of good corn whisky that it comes up in the thicket we seen behind the house."

Exhilaration was in Overstreet like the warmth of Mexican wine. He stood there a moment, almost afraid to look. The dust tickled his nostrils, dust that had lain undisturbed for months, now stirred up again by troopers' boots.

"What I mean, sir," Wheeler called enthusiastically from up ahead, "she's full of powder, percussion caps, and the like. A regular little arsenal, she is."

Overstreet's heart pounded as he worked through the gloom, surveying the huge cache. It was all there, rifle boxes that seemed never to have been opened—keg upon keg of powder—case after case of cartridges and percussion caps. What a battle could be fought with all that. The thought of it prickled Overstreet's skin.

As he stood there, memories came back to him, sobering memories of men he had known, men he had led. Many of them lay dead, way back yonder in an alien land, dead for a cause most of them probably had not even understood. Since Glorieta it had looked as if those deaths had been in vain. Now, maybe they hadn't been.

He knew that this, properly, should be a time for prayer. He wished once again for the faith that had meant so much to him as a boy, the simple but rock-firm faith of his father. But that faith was gone, faded behind the helpless agony of yellow fever, and the sickening glut of war-spilled blood.

He did not bow his head, and he spoke to no one in particular. But standing there in the dusty gloom, he vowed that he would give his own life, if he had to, to insure that those deaths had not been for nothing.

He set up guard posts at each end of the tunnel. Resignedly Shafter watched. He kept his good arm folded across his chest, the fingers nervously tugging at the sleeve of the stiff arm. There was a thin play of anger along his face.

"All right, Lieutenant, so you've found it. What can you do with it?"

"We'll take it with us, if we can. If we can't, we'll touch it off. One thing for certain, Mister Shafter, it'll never kill another Confederate soldier."

A half smile touched Shafter's age-nicked mouth. "You can't pack it out of here on your backs."

Overstreet leaned his angular frame against an adobe wall. "It won't hurt to tell you now, sir. A train of ten Yankee wagons is due here 'most any time, to get all of this. They'll get it all right, but they'll be working for Jeff Davis."

Shafter dropped his arm. Color splotched his face, and his blue eyes hardened.

Linda Shafter stepped forward, her pink lips tightened. "They won't give up the wagons easy, Lieutenant. You know that. Men on both sides will die, fighting for them. Then, if you win, you'll take the munitions and use them to kill more soldiers. Don't you think there's been enough killing already?"

Overstreet shoved away from the wall and stood straight again. He looked levelly into her pleading dark eyes. He could feel regret rising in him, and he fought it. "There's been too much killing, miss. But it's not right to the men who've died if we give up so long as there's a thread of hope left in us." He tipped his hat and started to walk away. He turned back, his throat tight. "I'm afraid we'll have to keep a watch over you from now on. That is, unless you give me an oath that you won't try to get away or send any signal."

The girl's eyes were defiant. "You know we won't do that. If we get a chance, we'll certainly send a warning."

Overstreet bowed gravely. "It's your choice. I'm sorry."

Walking away, he heard Shafter say to his daughter: "He's a soldier, Linda. Secessionist or not, he's a soldier."

A dozen times in the hours that followed, Overstreet walked out to the guard stationed on a rise a few hundred yards north of the buildings. He would take the spyglass he had lent the man and use it to scan the shimmering horizon.

"Haven't you seen anything yet, Tilley?"

"No, nary a sign of wagons so far."

Overstreet would walk back to the buildings, kicking up dirt with the toes of his boots, impatiently drumming his fist against his leg.

Again and again his thoughts turned to the girl, and he found pleasure in them. He told himself she was with the enemy, that he was drawn to her only because it had been so long since he had been near a woman. But he felt again of his scrubby beard, and he went looking for a razor and soap.

Later he visited Sammy McGuffin in the room where the wounded lad had been placed on a rough frame cot and a corn-husk mattress. The thin face was drawn and white. Sammy tried to rise onto one elbow as Overstreet entered.

"Better lie down and take it easy, Sammy," the lieutenant said.

Sammy shook his head. "I'll be all right, sir." He paused, his pained face strained with worry. "About those wagons, sir. Think they'll get here today?"

Overstreet shook his head. "I wish I knew. It'd be worth a ton of Yankee gold to get those wagons here before night. Every hour we have to wait means that somewhere back yonder some Yankee column is getting an hour closer to us."

Overstreet saw how the boy's hands trembled. "It's apt to be a pretty hard fight for them wagons, ain't it, sir?" Sammy was struggling to control his frightened voice.

The lieutenant nodded. "Maybe."

The voice quivered. "If we lose, sir . . . we'll go to some Yankee prison. They'll go and throw us in a dungeon someplace and leave us to rot." His voice broke, and the boy sobbed. "I'm afraid, sir. I don't want to go to prison."

Overstreet put his hand on the slender shoulder. "Don't worry, Sammy. You won't be a prisoner."

Darkly he arose and walked outside. He had intended to leave Sammy here where he could rest and receive attention. But now he knew that, whatever the cost, he would take the boy along.

The sun was slanting down toward the tops of the mountains to the west when the guard came trotting in, sweat cutting streaks across his dusty face. "Wagons, sir. Coming now, maybe a mile out. Counted twelve of them. There's an advance guard of a couple of men, riding this way."

Overstreet started shouting orders, excitement rising in him. "Move all the horses to the thicket, out of sight. Put all the civilians in a room together. Deploy around the building, with guns on the ready."

The civilians were moved into the patio. Overstreet went with them. "We're going to try to work this so there won't be anybody killed," he said. "Best way you all can help is to stay quiet and still."

A glance outside showed him the two Union riders almost at the outside gate. Hands sweaty, Overstreet drew the Colt Dragoon. "Step into the patio gate so they can see you, Mister Shafter. Don't try to make any signals. No use in getting somebody killed."

Shafter stood in the archway. The lieutenant kept back but managed to watch the two federals cautiously riding up. Both drew rein. One, a big non-commissioned officer, held a saddle carbine in front of him. The other, dressed like an officer, had his hand on the butt of a pistol, still in the holster.

Hardly breathing, Overstreet whispered: "Shafter, wave them on in. Tell them it's all clear. Remember, one wrong move and they'll die."

He could see color rise on Shafter's neck. But the ranchman lifted his good hand in greeting, Indian fashion. "Howdy. Get off and come in."

The Union officer's eyes suspiciously roved over the yard and patio. "You're Shafter, I presume."

Shafter nodded.

The Yankee captain finally relaxed and swung down to the sand. The corporal slipped his carbine into its scabbard in courtesy, then followed the officer's example.

Shafter stepped back into the room. For an instant his hot eyes touched Overstreet's, and the lieutenant could see shame and anger in them. Stepping into the room, the officer blinked against the semidarkness. His eyes suddenly widened, and his hand dipped toward the holster as he saw Overstreet.

"Hold it, Captain," Overstreet said sharply, shoving the Colt forward. "You're my prisoner."

The blue-clad corporal was caught right in the doorway. He crouched there, looking out at his horse as if gauging how long a jump he would have to make to reach his carbine.

"Get it out of your head, soldier," the lieutenant said. "A dozen rifles are aimed at you. You'd never make it to your horse."

The soldier stood trembling, more from anger than fear.

Outraged, the captain raised his hands as Overstreet stepped toward him and slipped the pistol out of the holster. "What do you want here?"

"The same thing you do, the Union munitions. We're taking your wagons, Captain. Signal them in."

Already the wagons were in sight. Overstreet could count them.

Red color blazed across the Federal captain's face. "They'll stop out there until I give them the word to come in. I won't do that."

Bluff it out with him, Overstreet told himself. "You will if you don't want to see your men killed, Captain. We're ready to kill, if we've got to."

But the captain didn't bluff. "It would be far better to lose a few men here than to let you take those munitions and kill a lot more."

Overstreet looked at the big Union non-com and knew what he had to do. "Wheeler," he called.

Wheeler entered the room followed by an enlisted man.

"The corporal's about your size," Overstreet said to Wheeler. "Think you could persuade him to lend you his uniform for a little while?"

The Yankee captain bristled. "Listen to me, soldier. If you put on that uniform, even for a minute, it makes you a spy. It makes you liable for hanging."

A half grin appeared under Wheeler's black mustache as he answered in his gravelly, lazy voice. "If you want to hang me, Captain, you'll have to wait your turn. There's folks back home already got first rights on that privilege. That's why I had to leave Texas in the first place."

He led the big Yankee non-com into another room. Overstreet heard the sounds of a short scuffle, then a powerful blow. A moment later Wheeler came back dressed in dusty blue. "Reckon I was a little the biggest."

All of a sudden Overstreet was jubilant. It was going to work. "Now get out there and stand by that gate. Wave them in. If they ask any questions, you're part of the advance detail that got here two days ago. Shut the gate as the last wagon comes through. Then watch out for your neck."

At the gate Wheeler waved the hat he had taken from the Yankee corporal. The wagons had halted, apparently according to orders. Now they began to move.

Overstreet could hear the shouts of the Army mule drivers. His heart was pounding high in his chest as the first wagon came through the gate, then the second and the third. Each wagon had a driver and three spans of mules. They kept rolling. He heard a startled shout behind him, from the enlisted man who had remained after Wheeler had left. "Look out, sir!"

The Union captain had made a quick dash for the door. Hardly having time to think, Overstreet raised his pistol and swung it down at the officer's head. With a sigh the captain sank to the Navajo rug that covered the dirt floor.

Linda Shafter ran to the man. Turning him over, she said something in Spanish. One of the Mexican women quickly brought her a vase of water and a cloth. Wiping the captain's unconscious face with cold water, the girl looked up. Her black eyes leaped at Overstreet in fury. Her lips trembled with words unspoken. The lieutenant knew their meaning even though he didn't hear them, and they brought pain to him.

The twelfth wagon moved into the big enclosure. Overstreet saw Wheeler shut the gate, then sprint away to cover.

Swallowing hard, the lieutenant stepped to the door. "All right, men," he called. "Move out."

The gray-clad Texans stepped outside almost simultaneously. There was a second of shocked silence among the few Yankee horsemen and the teamsters. Then all shouted at once. Carbines and pistols whipped out. A driver popped his whip at his mules and swung them around toward the gate, only to haul up short as he saw it was closed. He jumped down to unfasten it, but was driven back by a whining *zing* from Wheeler's carbine.

Half a dozen wild shots were thrown by the Yankees, but their targets were too elusive. Overstreet's bold voice carried above the confusion. "Throw down your guns. You haven't got a chance. We've got your officer."

Grudgingly the soldiers began to comply. They swung down to the ground and started forming a line, hands held up even with their shoulders. Within two minutes the wagons were taken.

Overstreet wondered about the two extra wagons and found them to be carrying forage and rations for the troops. Pausing now, he realized that his heart was pounding like a steam engine. Somehow, they had done it. The worst scalawag detail in the Sibley Brigade. Hardly a man in it worth his hide and tallow. But they had captured twelve Yankee wagons and a cache of munitions. How far would it be now to safety? A hundred miles? A hundred and fifty? A hard race at best. But the lead had been won.

Quickly he counted the Yankee soldiers. Twelve mule drivers, one for each wagon. A mounted escort of ten men, not counting the officer and non-com. A short detail for such a job. But probably it had been kept short in confidence that the advance detail would furnish escort enough on the trip back. Somewhere, a Union officer had mistakenly discounted the Indian threat.

To his men, Overstreet said: "Half of you take those mule drivers and get the teams unhitched from the wagons. Take them to water. See that they get feed and rest. There'll be little enough of it once we get started."

There was a rattling of trace chains, the harmless cursing of mule drivers as the animals were freed from the wagons and led away in harness. Overstreet turned to the rest of the men.

"Now, you'll line up those wagons by hand, tongues facing out toward the gate. Hurry up. We don't aim to lose any time."

In a quarter of an hour the wagons had been lifted up side by side, the tailgates toward the square adobe main building. Under guard, the mule drivers came back. With the guard detail was Wheeler, still in blue.

"What do you say, Lieutenant, that I take a little spell and get back in some decent clothes? Every time I take a look at the yellow stripe down the legs of these pants, I start seeing red."

The trooper's drawling complaint brought a smile from Overstreet and drained some of the tension. "Hop to it, Corporal. As far as I'm concerned, you're a corporal from now on."

Overstreet took a quick look to the west. The sun had dipped almost to the tops of the mountains, and thin clouds were purple against the red fire of the sky.

"We're going to start loading those wagons now," he said to his own soldiers and to the prisoners. "We'll load all night if we've got to. We'll be ready to pull out of here in the morning, no matter what."

V
"Hostage"

Part of the Union soldiers were put to work lifting the gun cases, the powder kegs, and the boxes of percussion caps up out of the tunnel. Other Yankees picked up the munitions at the trap door and carried them out to load them on the wagons. The only pause was a short mess period for prisoners and guards alike to eat a warm meal cooked out of rations found in the Union mess wagon.

With darkness, the men put up lanterns and candles and worked and sweated and cursed on in their flickering orange light. One by one, the wagons were piled high and the canvas covers laced tightly over the hoops.

Overstreet let the Union captain, whose name was Terrell Pace, watch with him. Pace was fifteen years out of Vermont, ten years out of the Point, and two years in the bitter cold and blistering heat that took their turns in the New Mexico Territory.

"You don't have a chance, Overstreet. You're substituting courage for common sense, and it'll kill you. If you're thinking of heading west and striking your own troops, forget it. Most of Sibley's Brigade is on the other side of the Río Grande, working its way back down to Fort Bliss in Texas. Canby's Union troops are following on this side. Federal soldiers would pick you up before you reached the river."

Stubbornly Overstreet said: "We're going south. We might get help at Fort Stanton."

Pace smiled. "Try again, Lieutenant. There's a good chance Fort Stanton, too, will be in Union hands before you get there."

A new worry gnawed at the lieutenant. He hadn't realized the situation was so bad. There was a chance the captain was lying. But Overstreet knew it was a slim chance, not one he could depend on.

There was only one course, then, he realized darkly. They would have to remain on the Pecos side of the divide and pass Fort Stanton. They would have to try to take their wagons across the Guadalupes and come into Fort Bliss from the east. And in all that torturous route, they could expect no help. No help except from God.

He wondered suddenly why that thought had struck him. It had been a long time since he had even considered asking help from God. He heard a shout from inside the patio. Hatchet's partner, Dalton Corbell, came running out to him, eyes wide with excitement.

"Lieutenant, Tilley's hollering for help. Says one of Shafter's Mexicans is gone."

Keeping Captain Pace in front of him, Overstreet hurried to the building and pushed into the room where he had left the civilians under guard. He found the guard, Tilley, still half in a daze, rubbing the back of his head. Overstreet saw a triumphant gleam in the dark eyes of Linda Shafter. A thin smile crossed the wrinkled face of the old Army scout. Overstreet quickly counted the civilians and found that one was gone.

"I'm sorry, sir," the guard said, pain glazing his eyes. "I thought I'd made friends with Shafter, and I relaxed too much. Somebody hit me over the head. I finally managed to pull up on my feet again, but by then one of the Mexicans was gone."

Angrily Overstreet stepped toward the cripple-armed old ranchman. He saw victory in the squinted blue eyes. Shafter said: "You'll never make it now, Lieutenant. I sent Felipe Chávez, one of the best men I have. You'll never find him out there in the dark. But he can find his way. It won't take him long to catch a loose horse. And as soon as he can locate any Union troops, the Army will be on your tail."

There was a roar from the Texan, Corbell. He was whittled from the same block as his friend Hatchet. Grabbing the scout by the leather shirt, he pulled him off his feet and drove his fist into the old man's stomach.

Overstreet grabbed the soldier's gray coat and tried to pull him back. "Damn you, Corbell, stop it! Do you want me to throw you in the same place I've got Hatchet?"

Corbell's face was red all the way up from his collar. He had a gun in his hand. "We ought to hang him, that's what we ought to do. Just let me go. I'll put a bullet in him."

Overstreet wrenched the trooper's gun away. "It won't do, Corbell. In his place you'd have done the same thing, if you'd had the guts. But you're like your friend Hatchet, and most of the others in this sorry outfit. You've only got the guts when you've got a cinch. Now get out of here. And tell Wheeler I want him."

Corbell paused at the door, his eyes brimming with rage. "Just remember what Chaney Hatchet told you, Lieutenant. You're a long way from home."

With the Union captain's help, Overstreet lifted the old man up and put him on a bed. Linda Shafter glanced at the lieutenant a long moment. He thought he could see a softening in her eyes. "Thank you, Lieutenant," she said hesitantly. "I think he'd have killed Dad." Her lips quivered as she picked up her father's hand.

Wheeler came in. Overstreet said: "We can't waste another minute, Corporal. Speed up the loading of those wagons."

Wheeler frowned. "I'm afraid the men are working about as fast as they can already."

"They've got to work faster. Put all our own men at it, too, except those you have to have for guards."

"Do my best, sir," Wheeler said.

Overstreet motioned to the Mexican men who were still in the room. "You go along with Wheeler. He'll put you to work. And Wheeler, send for Hatchet and that trader, Bowden, too. Let them lend a little muscle."

There was a trace of a grin on the Union captain's face. "Looks as if you outsmarted a whole detail of Federal soldiers only to be defeated by a smart old scout, Overstreet. Why don't you quit?"

A coldness worked through the lieutenant. "We won't give up, Pace, until we're in Fort Bliss, or until we've blown every last pound of powder sky high, so you'll never get a chance to use it against us."

Within an hour the last wagon was loaded and the getaway tunnel was empty. A choking veil of dust hung in it. The men who climbed out were grimy and tired.

Overstreet turned to the east. Not a sign of light there yet. But it wouldn't be long until the sun started pushing back the darkness from above the mountains. He put the Yankee cook to preparing breakfast. He dispatched the teamsters, under guard, to harness the mules and bring them to the heavy wagons. Then he went into Sammy McGuffin's room. Linda Shafter was there. The boy turned his head to look at the officer, but he no longer tried to rise. The soreness had worked all through him.

"Think you're ready to go, Sammy?"

The girl whirled around in protest. "You can't take him out in one of those jostling wagons. You'll kill him!"

Fear rose in Sammy's high-pitched voice. "I'm all right. I can travel. Please don't leave me here for them Yankees to take."

Overstreet tried to smile. "We won't leave you, Sammy."

Outside the room the girl anxiously caught the lieutenant's wrist. Her touch brought excitement to him. "If you're really going to take him, you'd better start praying for him. He'll need it."

"I made him a promise, and I won't abandon him as long as he's so scared of the Yankees. As for the praying, I reckon I'll let you do that. Nobody's ever answered any prayers of mine."

Watching the mules being hitched to the wagons, Overstreet noticed that the short, squatty Duffy was wobbling a little. At first he thought it was merely fatigue and knew there was reason enough for that. But he became suspicious and called Duffy over. The trooper's eyes were glazy, and his breath fairly stank with the smell of liquor. Somewhere he had found a bottle. The lieutenant snatched it from his shaky hand and hurled it to the ground, smashing it.

"Wheeler," he said sharply, "when we start out, tie Duffy's wrist to the tailgate of one of the wagons. Let him walk until he sobers up."

When all the mules had been hitched up and the men had eaten, Overstreet had everyone gather in front of the patio archway.

"Captain Pace," he said, "I'm just going to take along your teamsters. That's as many as my men can watch, anyway."

The captain frowned, as if he couldn't believe it. "You mean you're leaving the rest of us here, free?"

Overstreet nodded. "The rest of your detail, Captain. They'll be afoot. But *you're* going with us." Answering the sudden angry question in the other's eyes, the lieutenant went on: "Without your leadership, I don't think your men will do much to hurt us."

Overstreet stopped next in front of the portly Indian trader. There was an almost unbelievable stench of liquor and tobacco, buffalo hides, grease, and sweat about the man.

"I'd like to hang you, Bowden. Satan himself knows you deserve it. But chances are the Yankees'll hang you soon enough, anyway. I'm going to have to let you go."

A dry grin broke across the man's flabby, bearded face. But there was murder in the evil blue eyes. "Did you ever scalp a man, Overstreet?"

The lieutenant shook his head. A chill played down his back.

"A bloody business," Bowden said. "But you don't know how much satisfaction there can be in it when the man's somebody you hate." He paused to give his words emphasis. "I'm going to get *your* scalp, Lieutenant!"

Even in the near-darkness, Overstreet could see raw hatred burning in the trader's face. That chill hit him again, and he turned away. "All right, men," he said, "mount up."

Captain Pace stepped in front of him. "I'll try once again to put some sense in your head, Lieutenant. The Army will never let you get this train of munitions to your lines."

"They'll never take it," Overstreet said grimly.

"Perhaps not. But if they see they can't, they won't hesitate to blow it up, so you Rebs can't use it. A few bullets in the right place would blast the whole wagon train halfway to the moon."

The lieutenant froze. He realized Pace was right. "Even if it meant killing you and your mule drivers?" But he knew the answer.

"Yes. There are only thirteen of us. But who knows how many would be killed if you got the train to your lines?"

Overstreet rubbed his face hard. If only there were some way . . . Something that might make the Yankees hold back, to avoid a battle with this train.

He looked around, and his eyes rested on the girl, Linda Shafter. Strange that at a moment like this he could think only of her beauty, the warm thrill that had swept over him at her slightest touch. Then the idea came. The only thing that might hold the Union troops back. Under any other circumstances it would have been a cowardly thought, even a despicable one. But this was war. This was a win-or-lose struggle for ten wagons loaded to the top with munitions, worth more right now than his own weight in Yankee gold.

"I'm sorry, Miss Shafter," he said, "but I'm going to have to ask you to come along with us. You'd better get some things together."

She gasped. Old Walton Shafter stormed out of his place like a wounded bear. "She's my daughter, Overstreet. I won't let you do it."

The lieutenant's voice was edged with regret. "I'm afraid you don't have any choice, sir. Neither do I. If I did, I wouldn't think of taking her."

Captain Pace swore. "You intend to buy your protection with a woman's life, Overstreet?"

Overstreet shook his head. "Not my protection, Captain. The protection of the train. Any Yankee troop that catches up with us now will be plenty careful how it shoots at these wagons."

He could feel the old scout's anger upon him like the furnace heat of an August west wind. He turned away to see that his men were on horseback, including Hatchet. The Union teamsters were upon their wagon seats. Sammy McGuffin had been laid carefully on a pile of blankets in the mess wagon. Overstreet pointed to a lead wagon.

"Climb up, Captain."

A moment later the girl came out with a bag under her arm. Old Walton Shafter folded his good arm around her.

"I know there's no use me begging you not to take her, Lieutenant. So I'll just give you a warning. If any harm comes to her, Texas isn't big enough to hide you. Wherever you go, I'll hunt you down. Don't forget that, Overstreet. Because I won't."

The man's eyes were like muzzles of a double-barreled shotgun. They put a chill under the lieutenant's skin.

"No harm will come to her, Mister Shafter, not unless it's from the Yankees. I promise you that. As soon as we figure we're out of the danger area, I'll send her back, with Captain Pace and his men as escort."

Helping the girl up onto a wagon seat beside a middle-aged Union teamster on Sammy's wagon, Overstreet felt the keen throb that passed through him at the touch of her skin. But her stabbing anger was like a whip when she turned her blazing eyes upon him for a moment.

He swung into the saddle, lifted his arm, and brought it down in a forward arc. "Forward . . . *ho-o-o!*"

VI
"Coward"

Mules strained in the traces, and one by one the wheels of the loaded wagons began to turn. In a jangling of chains, a popping of whips, the train moved out of the gate a wagon at a time. Outside, they made a right turn, and the tongues pointed south toward Texas.

As he prepared to follow, Overstreet had all the remaining soldiers and civilians herded into one small outbuilding. He left Vasquez to guard them. "Stay here three hours," he told the dark-skinned trooper. "By that time we ought to be far enough on our way that nothing they can do afoot will hurt us."

Then he turned around and followed in the thin, lingering dust of the wagon train. The sun, just beginning to break through the haze over the mountains, sent long, ragged shadows reaching far out across the broken ground. Sharp morning air brought steam rising from the laboring mules and the nose-rolling horses.

Overstreet felt rather than saw Wheeler rein in beside him. "Well, sir," the corporal said, "looks like we're on our way . . . to hell or to Fort Bliss, whichever comes first."

From the time the light of dawn fanned out across the endless, rough-hewn distance, Overstreet was continually turning in the saddle, anxiously looking over his left shoulder for dust, for horsemen, for men afoot. Each time he faced back toward the moving wagons, a thin smile would come to his lips. But soon the worry was dragging at him again, and he had to look back once more.

Shortly before noon Vasquez caught up, easing his horse along in a sensible, strength-saving trot.

"Any trouble?" the lieutenant queried.

Vasquez smiled, showing a broad row of gleaming teeth beneath his trimmed black mustache. "Only the fat one, the Comanchero, Bowden. He is try to climb out a window. I put a bullet close to him, close like a glove. *Ai,* what *maldiciónes* he heap upon my poor head." The trooper sobered. "I think he is a man to fear, Lieutenant. More *malo* than even the Yankees."

At noon Overstreet halted the train at a little water hole to rest and water the mules and to let the soldiers eat a hasty meal of hard tack and cold Yankee bacon. He detailed Wheeler to check the load on every wagon, to make sure it was riding properly.

From up the line in a few moments came the sharp echo of argument. He saw Chaney Hatchet with his back to the end gate of a wagon, shaking his fist at Wheeler.

"What's the matter here?" the lieutenant demanded.

Hatchet swiveled to face him. There was a flash of defiance in his washy blue eyes as he angrily gripped his right arm with his left hand. "I just told Wheeler I'd already checked the wagon and he could move on."

Instantly Overstreet guessed what was the matter. "What're you hiding in that wagon, Hatchet?"

Splotches of color showed through the dirty saddle on Hatchet's flat cheeks. "Nothing, Lieutenant. I just said everything's all right here, and I don't like being made out a liar."

Lips suddenly tight around his teeth, Overstreet stepped forward. "Move aside there, Hatchet. I'm checking that wagon."

Hatchet caught his shoulder and jerked him back, but not before the lieutenant had glimpsed the little black box wedged between two rifle cases. Flame heat whipping through him, he whirled on the trooper.

"So you slipped back into that girl's room and stole her jewelry box again."

Quick as a jackrabbit, Hatchet leaped upon the wagon and grabbed the box. He jumped down again, his speckled right hand hovering just above the pistol strapped to his waist. "It's mine, Overstreet. I'm keeping it if I've got to blast you to kingdom come."

A shadow of fear lurked in Overstreet, but he couldn't afford to show it. He tried to keep his voice flat as he stepped slowly forward.

"You know you can't shoot me, Hatchet. You'd be stood up against a wall, or hung to a tree limb. Hand me that box and get your hand away from that gun."

The washy eyes reflected indecision. Overstreet tried to take advantage of it by jumping at Hatchet. But the thief darted aside, bringing the pistol up out of the holster and leveling it at Overstreet's body. The lieutenant stopped short, his heart pounding.

But Hatchet wavered, and Overstreet knew the man was not going to fire.

He grabbed the pistol, roughly tearing it from Hatchet's fingers, and hurled it to one side. A sudden, desperate fury exploded in the thief's shallow eyes. With an animal roar of anger, Hatchet sprung upon Overstreet. He dropped the box. The beads gleamed white on the rocky ground, and the rings rolled away.

The first rush threw Overstreet off balance. He fell on his back, knocking some of the breath out of him. Instantly Hatchet was on him, driving his fists at the lieutenant's face. Overstreet threw himself to one side, rolled over, and sprang to his feet. He dodged just as Hatchet scooped up a fist-sized rock and hurled it.

He charged in again, twisting his whole body in a bone-crushing drive at Hatchet's ribs. Hatchet bent at the middle and roared in pain. But somehow he managed to hit Overstreet a hard belt to the side of the head. The lieutenant faltered, blinking his eyes against the spinning flashes of light that exploded in his brain. Hatchet hit him again, and he lurched backward against a wagon wheel.

Braced momentarily, he caught his balance and lunged forward. His drive carried him into Hatchet and on. Hatchet stumbled. Overstreet started plowing hard blows into the man's face and stomach. Fury guided his fists, pounding, crushing, hammering until Hatchet folded and sank weakly onto his face.

Overstreet stood there, breathing hard, his fists still gripped so tightly that the fingernails bit into the flesh. He wiped sweat from his face, and saw the smear of red on the gray sleeve.

"Take his guns away, Wheeler," he said at length. "And see that he never gets them back this time."

He stopped a moment, watching Linda Shafter carefully pick up the jewelry and put it back in the box. Her glance met his, then fell away, and a flush crossed her cheeks. Overstreet swallowed, lurched toward his horse, and fumbled the canteen loose from his saddle. His throat washed clear, he leaned against the horse for support and looked across the saddle. He could feel almost all eyes upon him.

He signaled with his hand and said sharply to Wheeler: "Head them out again. Hasn't everybody seen enough?"

He poured water into one hand and tried to wash his face, but the water trickled out between his fingers. A hammer was driving nails through his brain. He sat down upon the ground and put his wet hand to his forehead.

He heard the canteen lid rattle, then felt the comfort of a wet cloth against his burning face. He looked up at Linda Shafter. She was bent over him, carefully wiping his face with a soaked handkerchief. Her fingers on his cheek brought a sudden warm contentment to him. He watched her, almost forgetting the pain, letting his mind give way to wonder.

She saw the question in his eyes. "I owe it to you, don't I? After you fought for me the way you did?"

He shook his head. "That fight started a long time before either of us ever saw you." He flinched as the cloth touched a cut on his cheek.

"I didn't mean to hurt you," her quiet voice said apologetically. Her dark eyes met his.

"Didn't you?" he asked softly. "You should have after all the trouble I've brought on you."

She didn't answer. She finished washing his face, turned away, and walked back to her wagon. Sitting on the ground, Overstreet watched her, still feeling the stir of excitement she had aroused in him.

The train kept rolling until darkness closed in upon it. It was rolling again by the time the reddening suggestion of sunrise rose in the east. As the hours dragged by, the lieutenant kept pausing to look back over his shoulder. But his eyes no longer spent so much time searching over the broken back trail as they did watching the lithe, slender figure of Linda Shafter, sitting on her wagon seat beside a blue-clad mule driver, or kneeling in the back of the wagon beside the wounded Sammy McGuffin.

Then, in mid-afternoon, a sudden flicker of light snapped his gaze to the top of a mountain far to the left. He reined up sharply and watched. It came again. He looked back and saw an answering flash from behind. Overstreet's mouth dropped open, and a dread chilled him.

Wheeler spurred up beside him, pointing.

"Yes, Corporal," he said. "I saw them."

"What do you think they mean?"

Overstreet bit his lips. "They might mean nothing, or they might mean everything. I'm afraid they mean we've got more than just Yankees to worry about now." He swallowed and looked bleakly ahead. "And only God knows how far it still is to Fort Bliss."

Fatigue rode heavily on his shoulders. His eyes burned from want of sleep. Soreness from yesterday's fight still lay in his bones. He watched the wheels of the wagons turning slowly—Judas Priest, how slowly—their iron rims leaving deep cuts in the earth wherever the ground was soft enough. Then his tired eyes would sweep over the range of hills in the east, searching for mirror flashes, smoke signals, any sign of Indians. A flicker of hope flared in him each time he looked and saw nothing. But always dampening it was the memory of advice a ranger captain had given him long ago: *There's worry enough when you see them, and twice as much when you don't.*

When, at last, he watched the sun bury itself behind the ragged stretch of mountains in the west, he wondered how far the train had gone in two days, and knew it had not been nearly far enough. He looked behind him but knew that in this rocky land there would be little dust to warn of an approaching Yankee column. Again he tried to find some sign of Indians in the mountains, but there was none. Maybe—and he grabbed at the hope like a man in deep water grabs at anything—maybe those mirror flashes hadn't meant anything. Maybe their makers had been only a stray hunting party, now many miles away.

With dusk gathering in, he picked a camp spot near a small stream that flowed through a shallow ravine. "We can't take any chances," he said to Wheeler. "We'll pull the wagons in a circle tonight, and turn the stock loose inside. An Indian's sharp knife on a picket line could leave us all afoot."

He sat his horse a little to one side and watched as Wheeler directed the wagons into a tight circle and had the teams unhitched one at a time.

Just as the last ammunition wagon was started into place, a cry of "Fire!" cut through the sharp evening air. The Yankee driver piled off the wagon and started running. Panic swept through the camp with the speed of lightning, men scattering like quail in every direction. A horrible mental picture flashed into Overstreet's mind—the whole wagon train going up in one huge, ear-shattering blast.

"Get that wagon out of there!" he shouted in desperation. But he knew that not a man would try. Even Wheeler was running. Overstreet spurred forward, fear clutching at his throat. Smoke billowed out from under the blackening wagon sheet, and the terror-stricken mules were fighting in the traces.

Pulling abreast of the wagon, Overstreet braced himself and jumped. He almost missed. Splinters ripped at his hands as he caught hold. Fighting for breath, fear burning all the way down to his stomach, he somehow pulled himself up into the heaving wagon seat. He grabbed at the reins, pulled the panicked team away from the circled wagons and toward the ravine.

His own panic was driving at him. He could feel the heat of the blaze in the wagon bed behind him. The smoke choked him, burned his eyes until he could hardly see. Any second now, flame would eat through a keg and strike the powder. He flipped the reins and yelled like a madman, fighting the team on toward the ravine. There wasn't a chance that he would have time to unhitch that team and save it, he knew. But there was a ghost of a chance he might break the wagon loose.

Almost at the brink of the shallow ravine, he hauled back on the reins with all the strength in him, trying to pull the team sharply to the left, knowing the wagon would never make the turn. The mules pulled back. The iron wheels screamed as they gouged into the bed of the wagon and could turn no farther. Overstreet heard the coupling pole break like the sound of a gun-shot, and felt the wagon heave beneath him.

For a split second he was in the air. Then he hit the ground and was rolling and sliding across the sharp rocks away from the blazing, overturned wagon. He heard the bouncing clatter of the team running on, dragging only the tongue and front wheels of the shattered wagon. Inches ahead of him was the lip of the ravine. In one agonizing effort he threw himself over the edge.

The whole earth seemed to rock with the force of a gigantic blast. Overstreet threw his arms over his head and buried his face as rocks the size of his fist shot out over the edge of the ravine and bounced down upon him. Then there was only the rattle of rolling stones, the easy crackle of flames eating through what little was left of the wagon, and, above it all, the awful ringing in his ears.

A voice reached out to him from the dusk. Overstreet thought he recognized it as Wheeler's. He tried to answer, but his throat was paralyzed, burning from smoke and dust. He heard a horse's hoofs sliding on the rocks above him, and the scrape of cavalry boots running toward him. A strong arm clamped around him. Wheeler's voice called, almost in his ear: "Come help me get him out of here."

Soon he was lying on his back on a blanket, and Linda Shafter once again was washing his face with a cloth. He tried to rise up, but she put her hand on his chest and gently pushed him back.

"Easy now," she said softly. "I don't think there are any bones broken, but we'll have to see. You just lie there a while."

There seemed to be just one big ache through his whole body. But looking up at her, feeling the warm touch of her hands, he didn't care.

"I guess I'm not so patriotic as I thought I was," she said presently. "I should have wished for the whole train to blow up . . . you with it. But I was scared for you. I almost screamed when the blast came. I thought you were caught there."

He smiled. In words measured and slow, he told her: "I don't know why you should have been worried about me. But I'm glad you were."

Her fingers briefly touched his. He reached up and caught her hand. She made no effort to draw it away.

Corporal Wheeler came and knelt beside him. Shame darkened his face. "You better pick you another man to call corporal, sir. The honor's too big for me." He looked down at his huge hands. "I was as close to that wagon as you was. I could've taken it out as easy as you could. But I was scared. I'm a coward, sir. It ain't fittin' for me to be in charge of these men any longer."

Overstreet reached out and put his hand on the penitent trooper's big knee. "You're not a coward, Wheeler. Sometimes a man gets so scared he can't move, and it's not his fault. I was as scared as you were. If I'd had time to think, I'd've run away, too, I guess. So forget about it . . . Corporal."

Linda Shafter watched the corporal walk away, his wide shoulders a little straighter. "That was kind of you, Lieutenant. I think many men would be bitter, being deserted the way you were."

Overstreet shook his head. "It takes a good man to run away, then come back and face up to it like Wheeler did. Next time he won't run."

Back on his feet again, the lieutenant had Wheeler bring him the Yankee who had been driving that wagon. But the Vermont captain stepped up and stood beside the teamster.

"Don't punish him, Lieutenant. He set that wagon afire on my order. I hoped to destroy the train. If you feel that punishment is in order, punish me."

Overstreet wavered. Then he signaled for Wheeler and Vasquez to let the teamster go back to the other Yankees, huddled together under guard well inside the circle. "Punishment won't bring back that wagon," he said. "If I'd been in your place, guess I'd've tried to do the same."

A thin smile broke across the captain's face. "And I'd wager that you'd have gotten the job done, Lieutenant Overstreet."

VII
"Deal with Death"

Darkness dropped over the camp like a blanket, and with it came a nameless dread that Overstreet had felt before while on a ranger patrol along the frontier. It was nothing a man could put his finger on, but it was a strange kind of premonition that frontiersmen had learned to respect and obey. Overstreet sat, leaning against a wagon wheel, in solitary council. Wheeler came and sat down beside him.

Presently he asked: "You got the creeps, too, sir?"

The lieutenant nodded. "Bad."

He noticed a discordant singing across the circle. The voice cracked on high notes and worked its way back down by worrisome trial and error.

"What's that?" asked Overstreet.

Regretfully Wheeler answered: "Duffy. Sneaked a bottle into one of the wagons before we left the Shafter place, I reckon. He'd swap his soul for a drink. You want me to go take his bottle away from him?"

Overstreet shook his head. He had more worrisome problems to ponder. "Let him alone. I hope he gets a hangover tomorrow that busts his head wide open."

But after a while he noticed that the voice was getting farther away. He stood up quickly. "That damn fool's gone clear out past the guard line, Wheeler. You better go drag him back in here."

Wheeler hadn't reached the far side of the circle when Duffy's tuneless song broke off. Overstreet's hair bristled to the terror of a throat-tearing scream.

A guard's carbine barked. From the darkness came the quick clatter of hoofbeats. There were a couple more shots. The whole camp was on its feet at once.

Overstreet's long legs carried him across the circle and out into the darkness beyond ahead of most of the troopers. Wheeler and a guard were standing over the crumpled body of little Duffy.

A long, feathered lance still quivered in the trooper's heart. Beside the dead, contorted fingers lay the shattered remains of a bottle.

After a while fires began to flicker at points all over the mountainsides. Small fires, the kind the Indians made. Overstreet watched, and his blood turned to ice.

Behind him he heard a gloating chuckle. "Better feel of your head, Overstreet, make sure your hair's still on tight. That's Bowden's Indians up there. He told me he'd get you." There was an evil smile on Hatchet's face. "I'll be riding high and have gold bulging in my pockets while the wolves are fighting over your bones."

With cold fury Overstreet whirled toward Vasquez. "Hatchet's known this was coming. Throw him in with the other prisoners. If he even acts like he wants to get away, you put a bullet through him and don't look back."

He went back to his place and stood watching the fires. Impatience began its slow torture of him. He itched to move on, but it was out of the question. Ambush in this darkness would be easy, terribly easy. Besides, the men were dead on their feet, and the teams had to have rest, for even mules can be driven to death.

But there was little sleep for anyone. Lying wrapped in his dirty blanket, tossing fitfully, catching only an occasional tortured nap, he could hear other men tossing, too. From Sammy McGuffin's wagon he could hear an occasional moan. He threw aside the blanket and climbed to his feet.

Linda Shafter was up, too, sitting beside the unconscious young soldier. In her eyes Overstreet could see pain, pain because there was nothing she could do.

"How long has he been this way?" he asked the girl.

Wearily she looked up at him, then back at the boy. "The pain has been getting worse the last couple of hours. It'll get worse still before it gets better, or until he . . ."

Overstreet gently put his hand on her shoulder. "Go get some sleep, Linda. I'll sit by him."

She shook her head. "I can't sleep, thinking about that out there." She pointed her small chin toward the mountain.

The lieutenant bowed his head. His hands trembled. "I'm sorry I brought you, Linda. I never would have, if I had dreamed . . ."

She leaned her head against his chest. Quickly he folded his arms around her and held her. Her body trembled against his. "Oh, Miles," she whispered. "I'm afraid."

For a long time he sat there and held her, comforting her, trying to ease her mind by making her think of other things, and talk about her family. She began telling him things.

"My mother was María Martín de Villareal," she said. "Her family was high in the government at Santa Fé. She died when I was ten. Dad sent me to his family in Missouri then. I went to school there, and stayed with his sister and her husband."

He told her: "I can see the Spanish in your face, especially in your eyes. But I don't hear much of it in your voice."

"You wonder why I have no accent? The children in Missouri picked on me for it, and teased me. I got tired of fighting them all the time, so I went to war on my accent." She relaxed and smiled. "I won that battle."

Pacing the darkness inside the circle, Overstreet knew there couldn't be any turning back. They had to keep rolling south. Trail south and hope for the smile of Lady Luck, hope that by some stroke of fortune they might find other soldiers in gray who would help them fight through with the wagons, all the way to Bliss.

Overstreet heard Sammy McGuffin, begging for water. He held a canteen to the boy's hot lips. He looked to one side at Linda Shafter, lying on the ground, asleep at last. He stopped beside her a moment, knelt on one knee, and pulled the blanket a little higher around her slender shoulders. For a moment the bitter worry faded while he looked down on her face. Lightly he touched her smooth cheek with his fingers, and a semblance of a smile came over his face.

By daylight the men were up, the mules watered, and the wagons ready to go. Overstreet wasted no time in getting them rolling.

"Wheeler," he said, "I want you to flank us on the east. Ride out half a mile . . . farther, if you can. Pick a good man to go with you."

He hipped around in the saddle. "Vasquez, you take it on the west. Pick you a good man, too. And if either of you see trouble on the way, come in on the run."

It didn't take long for trouble to start showing up. Almost as soon as the train was on the move, Wheeler sent Private Tilley back to tell the lieutenant that a band of Indians was paralleling the train's line of march a mile to the east.

"There's maybe fifty of them, sir," the trooper reported nervously. "They ain't made any move toward us yet. Just keep up, like if they was waiting for the right time to jump us."

Soon Forsythe came back from the west flank to make a similar report.

"All right," Overstreet said. "Go on back there with Vasquez. But if you see trouble coming, hightail it back. Don't stay and get yourself killed."

A grave certainty settled over the lieutenant as he watched the flank riders pulling away again. This could be the day. He looked up at Linda on the wagon, then turned away as she swung her glance to him. He didn't want her to see what was in his mind. He knew that dread was stamped in his gaunt face now.

The sun had swung up almost directly overhead when Wheeler and Tilley came spurring in.

"A bunch coming in for a parley, sir," Wheeler said. "That trader, Bowden, is right out in front. He's carrying a white flag."

Overstreet took out his spyglass. With it, he watched Bowden and the painted and feathered Indians top over the edge of a mountain and slant down its side riding in slowly toward the wagons. The lieutenant's hands squeezed the spyglass hard, the way he wished he had squeezed the trader's neck, so that this might never have happened.

"What kind of Indians are they, Corporal?"

Wheeler scratched his black chin. "Comanches, I'd say, sir. Not that it makes much difference."

Overstreet started his ride out to meet the four horsemen. "Wheeler," he said, "keep those wagons moving but be ready for a fight. If I give you the signal, circle them, and circle them fast."

Captain Pace stepped up. "If you please, Lieutenant, my men and I are in this as deeply as you are now. I'd like to ride out there with you, if you'll let me."

Overstreet studied the Yankee officer's face. Funny, the ways of war. Yesterday, enemies. Today, friends with a common enemy. Smiling, he touched the brim of his hat in salute. "I'm honored, Captain. Borrow a horse from one of my troopers."

Halted at the foot of the mountain, the three Comanches sat their horses with the great dignity of a country judge. But Bowden slouched in the saddle, greasy Mexican sombrero low over his gloating eyes. The day was only moderately warm, but sweat trickled from under the broad hat brim and down the flabby cheeks to disappear in the dirty whiskers. There was a filthy smear of dried tobacco amber from the corners of his broad mouth down into the mat of beard. He raised his beefy right hand to the signal of friendship, but a savage gleam in his eyes belied the gesture. "'Morning, gentlemen," he said mockingly. "Glad you accepted council. Wouldn't be none surprised if we was to come to terms." He made a wicked, brown-toothed grin at the lieutenant. "Shoe's on the other foot now, so to speak, ain't it, Lieutenant?"

Knots stood out on Overstreet's jaw, but he said only: "What do you want?"

Bowden spat a brown stream of tobacco juice toward the two men. "I told you once I'd have your scalp. That weren't no brag. I meant it. But I done a heap of thinking since then, Overstreet. I'm a trader at heart. Seems to me we ought to be able to make a deal."

Overstreet looked at the cold, chiseled faces of the three Indians, and a chill settled over him. "What kind of deal?"

Bowden pointed his chin toward the Union captain. "The way I hear it, them Yankees is pushing you *tejanos* back plumb out of the territory. You want to get them munitions back to your own lines to keep the bluecoats from pushing you out. But ten wagonloads won't do you any big lot of good. Why, a bunch of soldiers can waste that much just getting their guns hot. Indians, now, they could make it count." He jerked a stubby thumb toward the Comanches. "Now, I could gather me a couple of hundred good fighting men like them almost in the time it'd take me to send up the smoke signals. Trouble is, they ain't got guns fit to shoot rabbits with. But with good Army rifles, like them in your wagons, they could wipe out half a dozen Yankee towns. And with every town, they'd capture more and more ammunition. Why, just think of it, man. In a month we could have a thousand warriors of half a dozen tribes, armed and ready, men that could sweep over New Mexico like a blizzard and push them Yankees plumb back to Missouri."

An eager excitement gripped Bowden as he talked. His face grew florid, and his voice rose to a fevered pitch. "Then your Confederacy would have the territory. It could push all the way to Californy. You'd be a hero, Overstreet. They'd make a general out of you."

Overstreet's face had drained white, and rage had thinned his lips. "What would you ask in return, Bowden?" But he already knew.

"There's riches in these New Mexico towns, Overstreet. Gold and silver, horses, sheep, and cattle. There's buffalo hides and trade goods. That's what we want. That's all we want. The rest of it belongs to you and Jeff Davis."

Overstreet glanced at Captain Pace and saw the horror in the man's eyes. He turned back to Bowden. "There's one thing you didn't mention, Bowden. Those towns have got people in them, innocent people who don't really have any hand in this war. Those savages of yours would leave a trail of blood behind them that wouldn't wash away in a hundred years. It wouldn't be just men, Bowden. It'd be women and children, too, butchered like cattle." His throat was tight. He felt a hot drumming of blood in his temples. "Sure, we want New Mexico. But we don't want it like that. I'm not giving you the guns."

He glanced again at Pace. The captain said quietly: "Thank you, Lieutenant."

Bowden thundered. "Then there won't be a one of you alive to see the sun rise, Overstreet! And we'll get the wagons anyway." The big trader swept his hand in a wide arc. "I got a hundred warriors out there, Overstreet. They'll wipe you out like a snowball in hell."

The lieutenant's voice was grim. "Not without a fight, Bowden. And if you start shooting bullets into those wagons, you'll set off the powder. The whole train'll go up, and it won't do you or anybody else a bit of good."

Bowden leaned forward in the saddle, triumph in his thick face. "No, Lieutenant, nothing's going to happen to them wagons. These men won't use guns." He pointed to the bow carried by one of the Indians. "These Comanches can take a short bow like that and drive an arrow halfway through a tree trunk. And with a running start, a-horseback, they can shove a lance plumb through a man. You better think it over. I'll give you five minutes."

Overstreet started pulling his horse back. "I don't need five minutes, Bowden. Let's go, Captain."

The trader stood in his stirrups and shook his fist. "I swear, Overstreet, I'll have you roasted alive!" Then, muttering something to the three Comanches, the trader jerked his horse about and spurred across the foot of the mountain. He was waving his hand at someone up on top. Lifting his face, Overstreet saw a mirror flash.

"Get a firm grip on your scalp, Captain," he said, "and spur harder than you ever spurred before in your life."

VIII
"'Here They Come'"

Loping down the rocky slope, Overstreet looked back over his shoulder for pursuit. He could see it coming in a shouting, feathered wave like a tide sweeping in on the Galveston coast. He kept touching spurs to his horse's ribs and fanning the mount's rump with his hat. Stones clattered and bounced from under the flying hoofs.

A few hundred yards ahead of the wagon train he saw a fairly flat open space, cut across one end by a snaking ravine. Down by the lead wagon, Corporal Wheeler was watching. Overstreet waved his hat to signal the train ahead. He had to do it only once. Wheeler swung into action. In seconds the wagons were rolling as fast as the teams could pull them, the canvas covers dipping and plunging over the rough terrain.

The officers spurred into the wagon train just as it reached the open spot. Overstreet waved his hat in an arc, and the wagons rapidly pulled into a circle, the iron wheels screaming on the sliding gray rocks. Shouting men fell into the job of unhitching the teams, turning them loose inside the circle. Then hands grabbed at guns, and men fell on their bellies beneath the wagons, fingering loads into place and trying to catch their breaths before the painted wave swept over them.

Hands trembling with excitement, Overstreet swung down from the saddle, let his horse go, and faced the Union captain. "Will you give me your word that, if I arm your teamsters, they won't use the guns against us later?"

Pace nodded. "You have my word."

Overstreet shouted orders for the Yankees to dive into the wagons and get guns and ammunition for themselves. Then he fell into a brisk trot around the circle, seeing that the men were ready.

Linda Shafter was on a wagon, straining to lift some heavy rifle cases and drop them to the ground. "We've got to build up a shelter for Sammy," she said, her breath short. Overstreet helped her stack the cases on the ground, then lifted Sammy down. The boy was groaning and gripping his fists, now talking deliriously, now gritting his teeth in pain. A pang of sympathy brought a catch to the lieutenant's throat. It looked as if the boy hadn't a chance.

"Linda," Overstreet said, "you get down behind those cases, too."

She did, without hesitating a moment. But she caught the lieutenant's arm and pulled him down toward her. "Miles," she said quickly, tears glistening in her dark eyes, "in God's name, be careful."

He knelt and kissed her. Then he was up again beside the wagons, watching the Indians close in from three sides. He shuddered to the dreadful shouting and the clatter of unshod hoofs on the rocky ground. At first he could make out only the shape of the strong red bodies upon the horses' backs. Then he could see the features on the faces, the open, screeching mouths, the paint-rimmed eyes. And he ordered his men to fire.

The ear-shattering rattle of gunfire made him wince and close his eyes. Then, through the pungent film of gunsmoke, he could see riderless horses racing back and forth in front. The Comanches pulled into their traditional circle, riding around and around the train. Guns roared, and Indians fell. But arrows rained into the circle of wagons like hail from a black cloud. Behind him Overstreet could hear mules scream.

The gunfire went on and on. The ground in front of the circle was speckled with crumpled men and horses. The circling red men began to pull back, stopping to haul their wounded up beside them. Arrows still plunked into the wagons, but no longer did they fall in the same volume as the first moments. Then at last the Comanches reined around and rode away, out of range. Through the settling dust and the rising gunsmoke, Overstreet watched them gather on a rise.

He climbed upon a wagon and counted between fifteen and twenty Indians lying on the ground. For the moment, then, Bowden was beaten. But Overstreet's heart sank inside him as he admitted to himself that the Indians weren't beaten for good. And he knew that they couldn't be.

He climbed down again to check the damage in his own camp. He found two men dead, a Yankee and one of his own. Three others were hit, none badly. Two mules were hit, and three others were so badly wounded that he had to have them shot. Many mules and horses had suffered minor cuts from the rain of arrows.

Wearily Overstreet sat on the ground, watching Linda Shafter dress the wounds of the three soldiers with deft and careful hands. There was little color in her face. He looked away and cursed himself for bringing her out here.

Corporal Wheeler knelt beside him. "Don't reckon it would do us any good to try to move out, Lieutenant. They're scattering all around us again. There ain't a way we can move that they won't be on us like a sackful of cats on a crippled mouse."

Overstreet sat and gazed out across that awful stretch of blood-spattered rock, the heart sick in him, his clenched fist beating in helpless anger against his knee. The cold realization worked around the circle until the lieutenant could see it in the eyes of every man. Fear gnawed at them as they looked at each other, at their officers, and at the gray mountains that stared down upon them in grim and final malevolence.

The lieutenant became aware of a movement among the animals. He arose and saw Chaney Hatchet and his friend, Corbell, mounted. They had guns in their hands.

"Have you gone crazy?" Overstreet demanded. "Get off those horses before some Comanche puts an arrow through you."

"Don't be a damn fool, Overstreet," Hatchet blurted. "Bowden ain't wanting anything but these wagons. Let him have them and he'll turn everybody loose. That's what he told me when we were locked up together at the Shafter place."

"Get off those horses," the lieutenant spoke in measured words.

"Dammit, listen, Overstreet. They'll be on our side, fighting Yankees for us. Think of the glory there'll be in it. And if we string along with them, we'll be rich. There's gold and silver just waiting for us, there for the taking."

A grim smile came to the lieutenant's face. "Gold and silver. That's all you've been interested in since the day you left San Antonio, Hatchet. You haven't cared anything about Texas or the Confederacy."

Hatchet's face twisted. "You're right, Overstreet. I wasn't listening to the bands playing or that fool Sibley talking about glory. I was hearing the jingle of gold in my pockets. Wherever there's war, there's spoils, and I wanted mine. If it hadn't been for you, Overstreet, I could've had it." Greedily he said: "Well, I'm getting my share from now on out. I'm riding with Bowden."

All the soldiers had gathered, facing Bowden and Corbell. The two men swung their carbines.

"Everybody drop their guns," Hatchet barked. "I'll kill any man who don't."

There was a rapid clatter of steel on the rocks.

"We're riding out of here to get on the winning side," he said then. "There'll be gold enough for everybody. Who's going with us?"

The only sound was the soft voice of Vasquez, cursing in Spanish, his blackish eyes fixed in hatred upon the deserters.

"How about you Yankees?" Corbell demanded. "The color of your pants don't make any difference here."

One Yankee stepped out. Corbell motioned for him to grab a horse and a gun. Pace yelled at him, but the bluecoat didn't stop.

Hatchet swung his hate-filled gaze back at the lieutenant. "Just one little piece of business before we leave here. Something I've been owing you a long time, Overstreet. I missed you once."

He leveled the gun. Overstreet's breath stopped, and he steeled himself. He shut his eyes, while the hand of fear clutched his throat.

The booming of a gun crashed in his ears, but no bullet struck him. He opened his eyes and saw Hatchet bend at the middle, then slide out of the saddle. His feet hung in the stirrup. The panicked horse jumped over a wagon tongue and stampeded, dragging the man across the rocks. But Hatchet never knew it, for he was dead before he reached the ground.

Overstreet spun on his heel. Linda Shafter stood halfway across the circle, a smoking carbine in her hands. Sammy McGuffin's carbine, one Hatchet had forgotten about.

Even as the shot was still echoing back from the mountain, Corbell fired a quick bullet into the crowd and yanked his horse around. Elijah Vasquez's hand was a quick blur of movement. Corbell leaned back and fell out of the saddle, the dark-skinned trooper's sharp knife driven halfway through his throat.

In sudden panic, the deserting Yankee spurred away. A crackling of gunfire followed him. His horse dropped beneath him. The blue-clad soldier went rolling, then jumped to his feet and started to run.

Captain Pace took quick aim with a carbine and squeezed the trigger. The soldier sprawled and lay still, his convulsing fingers only inches away from the crumpled body of an Indian.

Corbell's bullet had struck a Confederate soldier. Overstreet knelt beside him but found it too late to do anything for him.

Four men dead, all within little more than the time it takes for two long breaths. Eyes burning, Overstreet turned away from the awful sight before him, turned toward Linda Shafter. He walked to her.

Her eyes brimming with tears, she lifted her trembling hands. Miles swept her into his arms and felt her hands tight upon his back. She buried her face against his chest and sobbed away the terrible shock. He stood clasping her tightly to him. For the moment, then, he was at peace.

From distant protection behind the rocky slopes, the Comanches began a methodical rain of arrows into the circle of wagons. The troopers sought shelter beneath the wagon beds. Overstreet sat beside Linda, watching the feverish face of young Sammy McGuffin, wincing to the pain himself each time the boy twisted and groaned. He beat his fist against his knee and wished to heaven the boy could go ahead and die and have his misery over, or at least lapse into complete unconsciousness that would stop his suffering.

Someone whooped: "They're coming again!"

Out from behind the mountain, swinging down from the hills, surging up out of the ravine, they came riding. Their fiendish cries were an echo from the depths of hell that sent ice through brave men's veins and made strong hands quiver on the wooden stocks and cold steel of cavalry carbines. Once again hundreds of unshod hoofs clattered on the loose stones, and horses and mules inside the circle screamed and stamped under the hail of arrows.

This was to be the charge that would swamp the dwindling force of white men and turn nine wagonloads of death and devastation to the grasping hands of savages. But this time the soldiers were even more ready than they had been. Each man had a stack of rifles and carbines beside him, capped and loaded and ready for a kill. Once again there was the deafening thunder of fire and powder, the defiant shouts of desperate soldiers. Horses plunged to the ground. Indians fell into lifeless heaps or sprawled on the rocks and clawed at air and screamed their last breaths away. But the circling Comanches swarmed in closer and closer to the wagons until it seemed that they would overwhelm them like an angry flight of hornets. Occasionally one broke from the circle and tried to charge in among the wagons, only to be cut in two by a withering blast.

Fearful men cursed and sweated and jammed fresh loads into their guns and swung around to fire again. Here and there soldiers lay still, their lifeless fingers still gripping guns. And, at last, once again, the swarm of Indians lifted and pulled away, leaving more huddled heaps of dead on the barren and bloody ground.

Watching them go, Overstreet rose shakily to his feet. He looked once around the circle and shuddered. Half the command, blue and gray alike, were casualties now. Dead or wounded. Half the mules and horses were dead or lay kicking and screaming until someone mercifully put them out of their misery.

Despair settled over him like a cold, wet blanket. There wasn't enough draft stock left to pull the wagons out now, even if they could get away. But he knew they wouldn't get away. Not now. Bowden wasn't through. He would try again. And the next time, he would win.

Overstreet went back to Linda. His heart swelling, he looked down at her dusty, blood-smeared face, the beautiful black hair that once had been shiny and neat, now windblown and tousled, streaked with dirt. The dark eyes that had been so alive were dull with dread and loss of hope.

He fell to his knees and clasped her to him. "Linda," he cried huskily, contritely, "what have I done to you?"

Later he walked out beside a wagon and leaned wearily against a wheel. Closing his eyes, he conjured up the memory of his father, and he found himself whispering to him. "Pa, Pa," he breathed in despair, "I've led all these people into this trap, and I can't get them out. Isn't there any hope for me at all?"

As if in answer, he remembered tall Jobe Overstreet standing on a wagon bed, the Book in his hand, speaking words of comfort to discouraged settlers who had been hit by an Indian raid. *There is always hope for a man of good heart*, the old circuit rider had said. *The Psalmist said that, though he may fall, he shall not be utterly cast down, for the Lord upholdeth him with His hand.*

Pondering, Miles Overstreet decided that there might be a way. It was a painful one, the end of a dream. He fought against it, rejected it, yet knew it was the only course left to take. Knowing at last what he had to do, he said to Wheeler: "Get all the men over here."

When the men had gathered, he turned to face them. Sadness

was like a cold stone in the pit of his stomach. "We can't save the wagons," he said dully. "We're going to move out of here."

Captain Pace stepped up in protest. "And leave these wagons to the savages, Overstreet? Is that what all these men have died for, what the rest of us are bound to die for?"

Overstreet shook his head. "They won't get the wagons, Captain. Nobody's ever going to have those wagons." He glanced at Wheeler. The despairing look in the big man's brown eyes showed he knew what was coming. "Get every man busy, Corporal. They are to grab all the food and ammunition they can carry. Then spill powder in every wagon, enough to make sure they'll all catch fire. Get moving."

IX
"Last Man"

Watching the sudden hustle of activity, Overstreet felt the warm touch of a small hand on his arm. Linda stood beside him. She said nothing, didn't even look up at him, but he felt the warm understanding that passed between them.

Captain Pace faced them. "Somehow, Lieutenant, I almost regret this. You're my enemy. But I think you deserved a lot better."

Overstreet nodded his thanks.

Wheeler trotted up. "It's done, sir."

"Then take the horses and mules and make a break for that ravine yonder. Take all the wounded with you. And take Miss Shafter."

The girl clung to his arm, her eyes suddenly wide. "Miles," she cried, "what're you going to do?"

He tried to avoid her eyes. "I'll wait till you're all clear. Then I'll set the powder afire. I'll go on to the ravine afterwards, if I can."

The girl still clung to him. "You can't do it. Miles . . . *Miles!*"

Overstreet turned to Pace. "For God's sake, Captain, take her away."

He leaned against a wagon, his eyes closed, listening to the shouting of the soldiers, the pounding of hoofs, the sobbing of the girl. Then he was alone, the last man left with the wagons. Nine wagons of munitions that might have saved New Mexico for the Confederacy. His dreams came back to him in a throat-clutching rush, bitter and forlorn. He tried to shove them away as he drew the Colt from his holster and pointed it toward a black trail of powder that led to a keg dropped beneath one of the most heavily loaded wagons.

He could hear the blood-chilling cries of the Comanches as they started to swarm down again. The sudden exodus of the troops had made them think the train was theirs. Overstreet closed his eyes and squeezed the trigger. The pistol jumped in his hand. Flame leaped up at his feet. A yellow ball of fire darted down the zigzag trail of black powder, dark smoke trailing in its wake. Overstreet turned and began to run, hard as his legs would go. Pounding in his ears were the cries of the Comanches, the sizzling of the burning powder, the anxious shouts of his men urging him on. The ravine was a hundred feet in front of him—seventy-five—fifty.

A terrific blast behind him knocked him down like a giant hand. He jumped up and went on running again, only to be sent rolling once more. Half on his hands and knees, he scrambled the last feet to the ravine, and dropped over the side.

Looking back, he saw that some Indians had been caught in the blast. A hundred yards from the circle, the trader Bowden was down, his horse floundering, the fat man scrambling to get away.

The fire leaped from one wagon to another, shaking the ground with the mighty roar of exploding powder, hurling flames far into the air. A wagon wheel sailed high and came down rolling toward the ravine. Black smoke billowed upward.

The powder all gone, the big clouds of black smoke slowly drifted away. There was only the thin gray smoke rising from the crackling flames that fed on the last wood of the wagons. Soon even that was gone, leaving just the smoldering of ashes, with here and there a burned remnant of an axle or coupling pole pointing like a ragged black finger toward the sky.

Overstreet watched and blinked away the stinging in his eyes and swallowed the last of a great dream. Linda Shafter held his arm.

"I'm sorry, Miles," she whispered.

He heard a voice calling for water. It was a familiar voice that made him whirl. Sammy McGuffin.

"Please," the voice came again weakly. "I'm dryer'n powder. Won't somebody please fetch me a cup of water?"

Sudden joy over Sammy lifted some of the deeper sadness from Overstreet. "He's awake," he said excitedly.

Linda nodded. "Yes, Miles. He was beginning to come out of it before we left the wagons. A lot of the pain has left him."

"What did you do?"

Her dark eyes fastened on his. "The only thing there was left to do. I prayed for him, Miles."

A moistness came into his eyes before he blinked it away. "I'm glad you did, Linda. I'm glad you did."

The Comanches had bunched again not far from the smoldering wagons. There were many less of them now than there had been this morning. Through his spyglass Overstreet watched them argue and gesture among themselves. Then Bowden split away from them and came riding out toward the ravine. With him rode two of the three Indians who had been with him in the parley at the foot of the mountain.

A hundred and fifty yards from the ravine, Bowden reined up. His horse had a decided limp, and Bowden leaned a little in the saddle.

"Overstreet," he shouted, "I want you. Come on out, and the others can go free."

Panic leaped into Linda Shafter's eyes. Corporal Wheeler jumped to Overstreet's side. "Don't do it, sir," he pleaded. "Bowden's lying. He'd butcher you, then finish us off, anyway."

The lieutenant clenched his fists. Fear stalked him. He tried to push it away, but still it was there, lurking in the shadows of his mind, chilling his blood, putting a quiver in his muscles. He called huskily: "Is that a promise, Bowden? You won't hurt any of the rest of these people?"

Bowden shouted back: "I've give you my word. You come out and I'll pull the Indians away."

Still the fear rode him, and Overstreet hesitated. Then, from somewhere back in time, he heard his father's voice again, saying words the lieutenant had heard years ago and forgotten until now. *You can't expect God to make you live forever, son. But if a man believes in Him, he can die in peace.*

Suddenly Miles Overstreet wanted to believe again, as he had so long ago. The fear drew back. He stopped trembling. He faced his troopers, swallowed hard, and spoke to them in an even voice.

"There's one thing I want you men to know. For weeks I hated you, the whole lot of you. I thought you were scalawags, the scum of the Sibley Brigade. A hundred times I wished you were all dead. But in a way I'm glad this all happened. The scalawags and the cowards are gone now. Only the brave men are left. And whatever happens to me, I want you to know that I'm proud to have ridden with you. It's been an honor to serve with soldiers."

He turned and grasped Linda Shafter's arms. He kissed her on her wet cheek, her trembling lips, then gently pushed her away.

"Pray for me, Linda," he said softly. "Pray for me."

He dropped his carbine and unstrapped the Colt. He climbed up out of the ravine and started walking toward Bowden, walking steadily, his shoulders squared.

The voice of his father kept whispering in his brain: *Yea, though I walk through the valley of the shadow of death, I will fear no evil . . . fear no evil.*

He watched the stony-faced Comanches. He watched Bowden. The big man was torn and bruised from being knocked to the ground by the blast. Dried blood streaked the heavy, bearded face. Bowden's hands quivered on the stock of a long-barreled musket. His eyes glowed with hatred. The trader muttered something Overstreet didn't understand and started raising the gun.

The lieutenant stopped and stood at attention. That gray, animal fear was trying to fight out of the shadows again, but Overstreet forced himself to listen to his father. *Fear no evil . . . fear no evil. . . .*

Bowden swung the gun to his shoulder and pulled the trigger. Nothing happened. He tried again and again, cursing and slapping at the gun with the heel of his big hand. Somehow the blast must have damaged the piece. He hurled the musket to the ground, his face crimson in fury.

The Indians watched in stony silence until Bowden stopped cursing. Then one of them pulled a long-bladed knife out of the waist of his leather breeches and handed it to the trader. Overstreet couldn't understand the words the red man muttered to Bowden, but knew their meaning. A gun against an unarmed man was not the way of valor. A man-to-man fight with a sharp blade to strike at the enemy's heart—that was the brave man's way.

But Bowden shrank away from the knife, and Overstreet saw the fear flit across his face. He saw, too, that the Indians had seen it, and they drew back a little from the trader. Indians had an inborn respect for courage, and an everlasting contempt for cowardice.

Bowden realized his mistake. Hands trembling, he grabbed a lance from one of the Comanches. He cradled it under his arm and spurred savagely at the soldier. Miles Overstreet stood still, watching the feathered lance streaking toward his heart. He dropped to one knee and saw triumph forge into Bowden's cruel face.

The horse almost upon him, he threw himself forward, flat onto the ground. Too late Bowden saw the move. The point of the lance drove into the rocks. His reflexes were also too slow. Bowden hadn't let go of the lance. He was jerked from the horse as if he had hit the low branch of a tree.

Overstreet jumped to his feet and grabbed at the lance. He found too late that it was broken. He got the long end of the haft. Bowden's desperate, clawing fingers grabbed up the point of the lance. The big man was on his feet again, holding the point like a knife. His thick lips drew back from his brown-stained teeth, and he looked like a huge animal closing in for the kill. But Overstreet could read fear in the reddened eyes. And now, washed clean like Gulf sand, his own fear was gone.

Bowden rushed, holding the point out in front of him. Overstreet brought up the haft and rammed it into the trader's soft belly. He heard some of the wind gust out of the man. He jumped in to follow up his lead. Grabbing Bowden's left hand to fend off the point, he punched hard as he could into the trader's ribs. But the heavy layer of fat was like a cushion.

With a bear's roar, Bowden shoved forward. Overstreet tripped and landed flat on his back. Bowden dived after him, plunging the lance down. Overstreet rolled away. The point grazed his right shoulder and tore a long hole in his gray coat. He gathered his knees under him and kicked at Bowden. He felt his boot heels grind into soft flesh. Bowden cursed.

The lieutenant rolled over again, sprang to his feet, and leaped at the trader. His fingers closed over the lance point. Bowden was on his back. Overstreet sank his knee on the big man's right hand, grinding the flesh into the sharp rocks. Crying out in pain, Bowden let go of the lance. Overstreet grabbed it with both hands and brought it down with all his weight into the big man's chest.

He stood up, then, and looked away, his stomach drawn up into a knot. The two Indians gazed a long moment at the quivering trader, sobbing feebly against the death that was wrapping around him like a heavy gray blanket. They looked at Overstreet, then wheeled their ponies around, and headed eastward. Overstreet stood there, watching them until the entire band disappeared over the mountain. He knew somehow that they would not return. Finally he faced around and walked back toward the ravine, the sinking sun throwing a splash of red color in his eyes.

Shortly after dawn, Corporal Wheeler came trotting in from a high point where he had been standing watch. "Riders coming, sir, about a mile and a half or two miles to the north. Can't tell anything about them."

His heartbeat quickening, Overstreet followed Wheeler to the point and unfolded the glass. "It could be Indians," he said. "No, it's not Indians. They're riding in a column of twos. Take a look."

Wheeler studied the riders a moment. "It's Yankees, sir. No mistake about it. Old Man Shafter's messenger must've found him some troops."

Overstreet nodded. "Then we've got to be moving out, Corporal. Get the men ready."

In five minutes the men were saddled and ready to ride. All but Sammy McGuffin.

"I'm sorry, Sammy," the lieutenant said, bending over the boy. "We're going to have to leave you. But those Yankee doctors'll have you well in no time."

Sammy nodded. "It's all right, sir. I'm not scared any more. I've found out now there's lots of things worse than a prison. They'll turn me loose, by and by."

Overstreet gripped the boy's hand. "Sure, son, sure."

He stood up to find Captain Pace in front of him, extending his hand. Overstreet took it.

"It's been an honor riding with you, Lieutenant," the Yankee captain said. "We wear different uniforms, and perhaps many of our ideas are not the same, but if we had more men like you on both sides, I'm sure this conflict would not last long. The best of luck to you, sir."

"Mount up," Overstreet ordered his men. Then he turned for the last time to Linda Shafter. He looked for a last time into her shining dark eyes, her lovely face. He held her in his arms, crushing her soft body against his.

"Linda," he said in a quiet, husky tone, "there's no telling what's ahead for us . . . how long this war will last or where it'll take us. But there's one thing certain. Wars don't last forever. When this war is over, I'll come back here, looking for you. Will you wait?"

Her answer was in her eyes. She pulled his face down to hers and kissed him. He felt wetness break along her cheek. Eyes burning, he pulled away from her and swung into the saddle.

Captain Pace had his men lined up. He ordered: "Presen-n-t . . . *arms!*"

The men in blue brought up their guns in traditional salute to seven valiant men in gray. Overstreet looked, swallowing down a lump in his throat.

Ahead of them lay a dozen other battles in places they had never heard of, and would never hear of again. But as he had said, wars don't last forever. Overstreet returned the Yankee salute. Then he reined his horse around and led his six men south—south toward the Lone Star.

Morning War

I

Dawn was fully in control of Torsmill, Texas, when three gunshots brought part-time marshal Jericho Dane running from his blacksmith shop. A marshal badge glittered on his hastily donned long coat as he hurried down the planked sidewalk to determine the reason for the shots.

He hadn't taken time to remove his work apron or put on a shirt under his coat. Instinctively, he felt for the short-barreled Smith & Wesson revolver in his coat pocket as he hustled toward the saloon area from which the shots had likely come. Brown hair bounced across shoulders made thick and strong from wielding six-pound hammers day after day. Coat sleeves strained at the biceps for the same reason. His medium-sized frame was misleading; his strength, built from his work, hidden by his clothes.

Dane's advance was hurried by a fourth shot. He pulled the brim of his misshapen hat to keep it on. So far, no one had come out of any of the three saloons, so he wasn't certain which one was the site of the disturbance. A buggy passed him and he waved at Harold Ringley headed for his bank. Ringley yelled that he thought the shooting came from the Longhorn Saloon; the banker made no attempt to slow down.

Crossing the street strutted Xavier Anthony, dressed smartly as usual and as befitting the town's tailor. Today, the vain, handsome man wore a black, three-piece broadcloth suit with a freshly pressed white shirt and a dark red ascot. His black hat was short-brimmed and cocked slightly on his head. In his right hand was a silver-topped cane.

"Sounds like trouble, Marshal Dane," Anthony said cheerily. "Reminds me of the time we were dug in at Antietam. Those Rebs didn't expect us to charge."

Dane waved his hand. "Thanks, Anthony. Good advice." He didn't stop or pause; the man wasn't one of his favorites. A phony, he sensed. Anthony had returned from the War as a self-publicized hero for the North. On every Fourth of July, the tailor would appear in the full dress uniform of a colonel, augmented with considerable gold braid.

"Any time," Anthony said, frowning and continuing to stroll in the opposite direction.

Farther down the block, a disheveled clerk burst out of the Longhorn Saloon, stopped to determine his next move, and saw Dane coming down the sidewalk. He ran toward the part-time lawman, like a chicken racing away from a determined farmer.

"Marshal! Marshal! There's cowboys in there! They're drunk . . . an' arguing. An' shooting at each other."

Dane slowed and nodded. "Thanks, Jimmy. I'll see what we can do about this."

"You have a gun, don't you?"

"Yes, but I won't need it." The blacksmith-lawman patted his coat pocket and resumed his advance.

Intense blue eyes darted ahead to the Longhorn, noting there were two saddled horses at the hitching post outside the saloon. They carried the Broken E brand, Clell Edwards's ranch, one of the small outfits in the region. Beside them was a buckboard with the two wagon horses showing Cross brands from Rudolph Cross's massive spread. Like many of the smaller ranchers around, Edwards had been in the region since before the War; Cross had come from Louisiana just two years ago with money. Lots of it. And a burning desire to be the emperor of the region.

"Well, there's the problem. I may have to talk with all the ranchers again," he muttered to himself. It was a habit that seemed to have come from working alone most of the time.

As he stepped through the saloon door, an obviously drunken cowboy at the bar swung his long-barreled Colt in Dane's direction. He was taller than Dane, with long sideburns that looked like they had lives of their own, wild strands of hair curled in every direction. His wide-brimmed hat had lost any sense of shape seasons ago. The cowboy's face was nearly square, and he hadn't shaved in days.

Dane didn't know the man, but it was obvious from the bullet holes in the wall that he hadn't intended to kill anyone, just scare them. Either that or he was a terrible shot. Still, this kind of violence was not to be tolerated in Torsmill.

Two other cowhands cowered behind an upturned table at the far-right corner of the room. Oliver Natter, the portly saloonkeeper behind the bar, watched Dane enter; the expression on his round face was a mix of relief and fear.

"Morning," Dane said, walking casually toward the bar with the cowboy continuing to point his gun at him. "Heard the shooting. What's going on? Find a rattlesnake in here?"

The cowboy noticed the badge, grinned and waved his gun in the direction of the men crouching behind the table. "Yeah, two of 'em."

"I see." Dane stepped closer without the cowboy noticing. "Just why are they such, friend?"

After running his tongue along his lower lip, the cowboy declared, "Well, those bastards used the *pond*. Yesterday. They ride for the damn Broken E." He pointed his gun in the general direction of the table and fired again. The slug slammed into the wall behind the table.

"I see. An' your boss, Mr. Cross, sent you after them. To Torsmill. Here."

The cowboy pursed his lips, glanced at his smoking pistol and tried to push his hat back on his forehead, but it was too tight to move. "Well, no, not exactly. No. I came to town to get some supplies. Rope. Coal oil. Medicine. Soap. Epsom salts. Camphor. Flour. Beans. Stuff like that, ya know."

Dane took another step closer to the man. "So you decided to get an eye-opener first."

"Nothin' wrong with that." The cowboy didn't seem to notice the move.

"No. No, there isn't, as long as it's all right with Mr. Cross," Dane said. "But you know the rules. No guns in town. You need to give your pistol to Mr. Natter there. Like those two did. You can get it when you leave town."

The cowboy's face was a snarl. "What the hell do you mean? Give my six-gun to that bastard? I don't give my gun to nobody. Nobody. If *you* want it, blacksmith, you gotta take it." He pointed the Colt in Dane's direction.

Dane raised his hands slightly. "That's your decision, pardner. Makes no difference to me." He made a half-turn to his left as if to leave.

A groan came from behind the overturned table. The cowboy laughed triumphantly and pointed his gun in their direction.

Dane whirled around, grabbing the barrel of the cowboy's gun and slamming down the edge of his opened right hand just below the base of the cowboy's thumb where he held the gun. Both actions were a simultaneous blur. The cowboy's hand popped open with the blow and Dane pulled the Colt away with a grunt.

The saloonkeeper's fat face bubbled with relief. "Came in here quiet-like. I asked for his gun. He wouldn't give it to me. Had a couple of drinks, yelled at those two over there and started shooting." He shook his head.

Still holding the barrel of the gun, Dane pushed the grip against the cowboy's chest. "You're going to jail. For disturbing the peace. Three days or a thirty-dollar fine. Your choice."

"What? Thirty dollars! I ain't got that kinda money." The cowboy tried to pull away from the push of the gun against him, but his back was against the bar. He made no attempt to grab the weapon, not liking the look in Dane's eyes. "If I ain't back today, I won't have a job. Where's Stockton?"

"Should've thought of that before you started shooting," Dane said. "We've got a quiet town here. I have no idea where Stockton is. Doesn't matter. This is a town concern, not a county one." He looked over at the two cowboys who were now standing. "You boys tell Mr. Edwards what happened here. You tell him I said we don't want your argument with Cross in town. You hear me?"

The shortest cowboy nodded, followed by his companion. "Y-yes, suh, we do. Didn't say a word to him. Honest, Marshal. That pond belongs to everybody. No-man's-land, you know. Came to town to pick up some hosses."

"That's fine. Glad to have you. Go on about your business."

As Dane pulled the gun away, the disarmed cowboy asked, "Say, law dawg, you don't have a jail."

"Oh yeah, we do. The shed. Just behind the hotel," Dane said, watching the two cowboys gather their pistol belts from Natter.

"What?"

"You heard me. I'll bring you food and let you go to the outhouse," Dane said, holding the gun at his side. "Three days'll go real fast."

The cowboy grimaced. "Mr. Cross is gonna be damn mad about this. Mad as all hell. You wait, he'll bring in the county sheriff and you'll look real silly."

"You mean his nephew?"

"Yeah, his nephew. Sheriff Turin Stockton."

The two Broken E hands walked quickly to the door, holding their pistol belts at their sides and not looking at Dane.

From the bar, Natter yelled, "Hey, who's gonna pay for these bullet holes?"

Dane turned to the square-faced cowboy, who frowned. "What's your name?"

"Walker. Hollister Walker. Friends call me Holl."

"Well, Mr. Walker, tell you what you're going to do. You're going to fix those holes before you stay in the shed. And you have to fix them to Mr. Natter's satisfaction." Dane motioned toward the saloonkeeper.

"Can I go after that?" Walker asked through clenched teeth.

"No, you'll do three days. If the job's not done right, you'll do three more."

Turning toward the saloonkeeper, Walker pulled his hat from his head. "I'll do a good job. I promise."

Dane slid the cowboy's gun down the shiny surface of the bar toward Natter. "Keep this until I tell you different, Oliver."

"Right, Marshal." Natter caught the sliding weapon and placed it on the back shelf where guns were kept. "Want some coffee? Just made it."

"No thanks. Got to get back to work," Dane said.

Regaining some of his courage as the shock of being so easily disarmed faded, Walker said, "My boss still isn't gonna like this. He'll be sendin' some of our boys in to see what happened to me."

"If they do, I'll make sure they check their guns."

"Yah, sure. You're only one man," the cowboy growled. "Ya cain't sucker-punch all o' them."

Dane smiled, put a firm hand on the man's shoulder. "Be sure to do a good job here, Mr. Walker. I'll be checking." He patted the shoulder. "Remember, I could have arrested you for attempted murder, not disturbing the peace. I'll be back to get you at sundown. If you try to get away, I'll come after you."

"Damn."

"Yeah, damn."

As he emerged from the saloon, Front Street was beginning to believe the shooting was over. Merchants and their anxious customers slowly emerged from hiding. Across the street, a small gathering of townspeople had stopped to watch, uncertain of what had transpired. More bold than the others, Fred Mikman, the town's mayor, was already outside his gun store, looking for signs of further trouble, a new Winchester in his hands.

The livery operator, Lester Wilson, was also patrolling the street, armed with a Henry.

Nearing the gun store, Dane looked over at the German-born gunsmith and waved.

Mikman called out, "How is ze new revolver?"

Dane nodded approval. "Just fine. Thanks for being ready."

This wasn't the time to tell Mikman that he hadn't even taken it out of his pocket.

"Thanks, Lester!" Dane yelled and held up his hand. "Appreciate the support. I want you to take that TJ wagon to your place. Keep it for a few days. You'll be paid."

The livery owner waved his gun and headed for the tied wagon.

Torsmill was a lot smaller when Dane first came, he remembered as he walked back—just a knot of unpainted buildings that had erupted around a year-round well. He hadn't figured on staying. That was four years ago and the town had tripled in size. A Comanche raid on the town in those early days demonstrated to the others how effective he was with a gun—and how cool under the stress of battle.

He was asked to take on the marshaling duties the next day. The town council paid Dane fifteen dollars a month, plus ammunition and one free meal a day at Carter's restaurant. Dane was honest with himself that the extra money had been the primary motive for taking the job while he built up his trade.

In the distance, in all directions, prairie grass sang its endless song. Good for raising cattle. In the hazy distance was a long rolling mass of forested hills that served as a western wall. The buffalo had been killed off years before. Shortly after that, the Comanche were moved to the reservation. In fact, a town baseball team played its games in an area that once was a grazing area for the huge beasts.

"You won't have this job come this time next year, Jericho Dane," he muttered and touched the brim of his hat to a passing couple.

The way the town was growing, he figured a full-time lawman would be needed in another year. Torsmill was a town built by the developing cattle business. There had been several incidents when inebriated cowboys had needed some calming down—and

Dane had done that well, making it look easy even. No shooting. Like now. Just an easy-handed firmness that had impressed everyone, even the cowboys involved.

People here were of good stock, Dane thought as he walked along, waving to merchants and greeting early townspeople; a mixture of immigrants and born Texans. They minded their own business and expected the same from others. They worked hard, raising cattle and some crops, or running a business in town. Everything was fine—and growing, except the biggest ranch pushed for more and more range. Range grass was for the taking and that meant force, or the threat of it. Mostly from Rudolph Cross, the largest rancher in the region. Smaller ranches worked hard to stay alive, fighting to keep access to water.

Even a fool could see there would eventually be clashes over the stream and its mother pond in the no-man's-land five miles from town. Two cowboys had been killed there last year. Area residents had taken to calling it "Kill Pond."

"Good morning, Jed. How are you?" he shouted at the editor and owner of the *Torsmill Times*, a six-month-old newspaper. A sure sign of a growing town. "An interview about this morning? Ah, maybe later. I've got to get back to my shop. Thanks."

Legally, Dane had no authority outside of town; that was county jurisdiction. Or Ranger concerns. But the county sheriff was controlled by Rudolph Cross. In fact, the sheriff was Cross's nephew, Turin Stockton. The rancher had controlled the countywide election through bribes, threats, and simple vote fraud. Stockton had a small office in town, underwritten by his uncle. It had no jail. Stockton was rarely there, or even in town, except to pursue his interest in Mary Tressian, the owner of the Tressian General Merchandise Store.

As far as Dane knew, Stockton had never arrested anyone in the year he had held the job. The previous county sheriff had been mysteriously shot and killed on a trip to Waco. Dane had talked with all the cattlemen anyway, including Rudolph Cross. It hadn't amounted to much, except to keep trouble out of Torsmill. So far. No thanks to the county sheriff.

Impatient to return to his blacksmith shop, Dane walked past a mentally retarded woman of at least forty, stopped and spun around to greet her. Known around town as "Trash Tess," she was constantly going through trash cans. No one knew her last name, or where she had come from. Nor did she. Gossip around town was that she had been left by a wagon train headed for Oregon a month ago. A rider had gone after the group, but he was unable to find anyone in the train who knew her.

"Good morning, Tess," Dane said, returning to where she sat.

At the moment, she was sitting on the boardwalk, eating something that looked like a piece of chicken. Beside her was a huge black purse. He figured she kept what possessions she had in it. Her graying hair was matted and dirty. A tic on the right side of her face appeared regularly—as did an occasional seizure.

"How are you this morning?"

Her dress was actually fairly new; Mary Tressian had given her several garments recently.

Looking up at him, she waved the chicken and blurted, "Wha'sum?"

"No thank you, Tess. That's nice to ask, though." He walked on, telling himself that the town needed to find a place for her to stay.

On occasion, he had let her spend the night in the shed behind the hotel; it served as a jail, mostly to hold drunks who got out of hand. On cold nights, Edward Lindsay, the hotel owner, let her sleep in the lobby, or a room if one was open.

At his blacksmith shop, Dane removed his coat and hat and hung them next to one of the lanterns, where his shirt already hung. The yellow glow from two lanterns hanging on the wall offered supporting light to the new day. Sitting on the edge of his fire was a blackened coffeepot. It was a daily ritual, making and drinking coffee. A foot from the fire, resting on the ground, was his coffee mug. He drank from it regularly throughout the day. Every day.

II

After retying his apron, he poured fresh coffee, took a sip, then began using his bellows to reenergize his fire. Five times he worked it and took silent pleasure in the rebirth of flames.

"Good work, Jericho," he muttered. "How about some more coffee?" He answered his own question with two swallows of the hot brew.

His forge fire was more than a match for the blossoming sun. He liked the solitary nature of smithing; enjoyed, too, the creation of something useful from something hard and strong. The first of four wheel rims was covered with burning wood to generate equal heat throughout the circular iron. He had made the wheels earlier. Satisfied with the rim's temperature, he placed the wheel itself on an adjacent millstone and pushed its hub into the center hole. With the rim held by heavy tongs, he forced it over the wheel, and pounded it with a sledge on his anvil. The wood growled and smoked, but finally accepted the wheel.

"Looks like it's going to be a nice day. Maybe hotter than yesterday. Hard to tell so far," he said to himself and sought his mug for a hearty swallow.

Talking to himself wasn't the only habit produced from long hours of being alone. He also sang quietly from time to time—actually just "Rock of Ages" or "Sweet Hour of Prayer." He considered himself a spiritual man, but not a churchy one. Something about being cooped up and preached to had always bothered him. They were the only lyrics of any kind that he could remember, and then only the first verse of each. Well, he also knew the chorus to "Jimmy Crack Corn." But that was it.

Already sweating in spite of the cool morning, he carried the newly made wheel to the water trough. He turned it in the cool water, tapping it with his sledge as he turned the wheel to complete the adherence. Five taps. He grunted softly as he turned it.

Five had become a significant number to him. The gentle superstition had started during the War; he was down to five cartridges when the Union engagement they were fighting surrendered. Ever since then, he had considered the number five as lucky.

Scooting under the doors, a squirrel appeared and chattered its good morning. Dane turned toward the little animal and smiled. The squirrel had become a regular visitor.

"Well, good morning, my little friend. Are you hungry?" Dane said gently.

The young blacksmith reached into his pocket and withdrew a portion of bread he had brought from his house for this purpose. He tore five small pieces from it. He placed the morsels on the ground just a foot from the squirrel. Unafraid, the little rodent waited patiently, then scurried to the treat and began eating the first.

He always hated to leave his smithing work, especially when he was behind, like now. But his other job as a part-time marshal was an obligation he took seriously. Dane carried a hardened sense of his own capabilities, or lack of them. He'd fought for the South during the Great War and seen more than his share of killing and dying. That's why he had ridden so far away from his burned-out Louisiana homeland, finally ending up here. In Torsmill, Texas.

He was no gunfighter. Being marshal was just something no one else apparently had wanted to do. He was a blacksmith by training and by heritage. His late father had been a blacksmith, a fine one.

After another swallow of coffee, he looked up to see Mary Tressian push through the wide doors of his shop. His feelings for her were hard to hide. He had fallen for the striking general store owner the first time he saw her. But what did a blacksmith have to offer one of the wealthier women in town? He knew Rudolph Cross's nephew was infatuated with her; everyone around knew it, he figured. He shook his head; he couldn't compete with that kind of wealth, that kind of position. Still, his mind-set was hard to evade. He leaned over to return his mug to the ground.

"Well, Marshal Dane, sounds like you've had a busy morning," Mary Tressian said cheerily as she entered.

"Good morning, Miss Tressian. How are you this fine day?" The words seemed stilted to him and he wished they would come easily.

"I'm doing well, thank you. It also sounds like you need to be more careful. Those Cross boys aren't playing for fun, you know."

He smiled. Her voice always made him smile. Trying to think of what to say next, the best he could come up with was, "Are you expecting a busy day?"

She stepped closer and he wished he hadn't removed his shirt and coat. He turned toward the peg to retrieve them.

"That's all right, Mr. Dane. I didn't mean to interrupt your work." Her eyes danced with appreciation at his muscular frame. "Yes, I am hoping for a busy day."

She turned to go, then paused and looked back, seeking his eyes. "Maybe some time, you might ask me to have supper with you." She turned away without waiting for his response and left.

Dane glimpsed her walking across the street as the shop doors swung back and forth until inertia demanded they be still and he could see no more. He jerked his hand away from the fire.

"Man oh man! Be careful, Jericho." He moved to the water trough and shoved his fingers into it, still watching her retreat.

His mind was racing with wonder. Was there a chance with her? Why would she make such a statement if there wasn't? His thoughts began to collect possible ways to invite her—and when. He leaned over to retrieve his coffee mug.

A stumpy, older man in a wrinkled three-piece suit strode into the shop and blurted his intention. "When will my wheels be ready?"

Dane shook his head to clear it of thoughts of Mary Tressian. "Well, they should be done today, Mr. Turner. Probably by mid-afternoon."

"If'n you don't have to run off an' take care o' any more marshalin'," Benjamin Turner said, a smile edging onto the corner of his mouth.

"Yeah, guess so." Dane began covering the tire rim with burning wood.

"I'll check back. Takin' a wagon load out tomorrow."

"Sure."

The day went fast. A full, two-pot-of-coffee day. The sun was disappearing when he finished shoeing the last of five horses. It was a lucky sign, he decided, having five horses to shod. The wheels had been finished a little after the noon hour and Benjamin Turner had been pleased.

At last, he stretched his arms and admitted to himself that he was tired. Very tired. He washed up, using the hand basin inside the small storeroom where he kept his tools, a supply of iron and wood, a sack of coffee and a grinder. The tepid water felt good on his face and chest. A glance at his empty coffee mug told him he had finished all of the brew.

His mind wandered across the street to Mary Tressian. Lights were off in her store so she wasn't there. He wouldn't have gone over there anyway—or would he? He shook his head and began talking to himself.

"Jericho, let's go get some supper. I'll need to get something for the cowboy. Wonder if the restaurant has anything special tonight?" He looked down at his tired clothes and shrugged. A part of him hoped to see Mary there; another part feared it.

III

As expected, the arrested Hollister Walker was quite sober and had done a good job, although reluctantly, on his bullet holes. All were patched and ready for painting. Even in the yellow glow of the gaslights on the walls, it appeared like they were smooth.

"Looks like you've done good work," Dane said as he entered the now busy saloon and spotted the square-faced cowboy sitting quietly in a chair against the wall.

Without waiting for a response, Dane called out to the saloonkeeper pouring whiskey to a full bar of customers. "How's it look to you, Oliver?"

"He's doing a good job, I'd say," Natter said over the joyful noise of the saloon. "Have it finished in the morning, I'm sure. Don't want him painting with a lot of customers here." He poured another drink and added, "Got the paint in the back."

"Good," Dane said and went over to Walker, who slowly stood.

"Whar'd my wagon go?" the cowboy asked.

"It's in the livery. You can get it when you're released," Dane said. "You'll have to pay for it staying there."

"What? I didn't want—"

"That's where we put horses and wagons that are left in town. Like yours." Dane cocked his head.

"I wanna get back to the ranch." Walker's face was like that of a child asking for a cookie.

"Bet you would." Dane shoved his right hand into his long-coat pocket to demonstrate the revolver there. "For now, you're going to jail."

"Damn."

"I'll bring you some supper—after I've had mine."

"Suppose I have to pay for that, too." The cowboy shrugged his shoulders and turned toward the door.

"No. The town pays for that."

Their walk to the shed behind the hotel was a silent one with neither man in the mood to talk. Dane unlocked the shed and swung open the creaky door. "There's a cot and two blankets."

"Damn." Walker pulled on the brim of his hat and stepped inside. He paused. "What if I have to go during the night?"

"You won't." Dane smiled. "When I bring your supper, we can take a stroll over to the outhouse." He pointed to the small building twenty feet away.

"What about a lamp?"

"No lamp."

"Damn."

Dane closed the shed door and relocked it. He shook his head as a soft "Damn" came from the inside. He reminded himself to tell the town council of the need to have a better jail one of these days, entered the busy restaurant and found his worst fear was realized.

Mary Tressian sat at a corner table.

With her was Sheriff Turin Stockton. Although his back was to the entrance, Dane could tell he was talking. She saw Dane enter and her eyes tried to connect with his. Gaslight from the wall caressed her face and danced across her light brown hair, rolled into a tight bun. Her blue eyes glistened with interest in him.

Dane looked away as if seeking an open table. He knew his face was reddening. Everything in him wanted to turn around and run, but he forced himself to stay. He didn't need her pity. That's what her comment earlier today must have been. Pity.

After sitting in the only open table near the door, a bald-headed waiter, with little interest in his supper decision, strolled over. Dane asked for coffee and a steak. Medium rare. And whatever was available on the side. He had decided against asking about the daily special. The waiter nodded and walked away, making no visible note of Dane's request.

He felt silly. Everyone else in the restaurant was with someone else—why hadn't he just chosen to go home instead? He muttered to himself that he could have read one of the two books he had just purchased from her store: a leather-bound edition of Tennyson's poems and a copy of Lewis Morgan's *Ancient Society*. He liked to read; it helped pass the evenings. Usually, he went to sleep after a few pages.

He drank deeply from the coffee as soon as it was poured, trying hard not to glance in her direction. But he couldn't help himself, gazing over the coffee cup held to his mouth. She was looking at him.

She smiled.

Instinctively, he smiled back. How silly, he told himself. She was probably smiling at something Stockton said and tried to return his attention to his coffee.

At the farthest table in the back corner, Xavier Anthony had finished having supper with Edward Lindsay, the hotel owner, Harold Ringley, the town's banker, and Gerald McCormick, who ran the lumber store. All were members of the town council, except Anthony. The three councilmen strolled through the restaurant, acknowledging diners without stopping; they did the same with Dane, and left. Taking time to retrieve his cane, Anthony walked over to Stockton and whispered in his ear. Handsome of face, although thin, with wavy dark hair, brown eyes and long eyelashes, Anthony was admired by many women—and some townsmen.

The powerful rancher's nephew turned in his chair momentarily to see Dane, then swiveled back. Mary's face was taut and Dane guessed Anthony had told Stockton about his arresting the Cross cowboy this morning. Ending his conversation, Anthony patted Stockton on the shoulder and tried to catch Mary's attention. She was looking down at her plate and he walked away, pausing at an occasional table to converse.

Dane's shoulders rose and fell. He hadn't expected the arrest to remain a secret. There weren't any around here. As marshal, he had learned—without interest or attempt—that Mrs. McCormick was having an affair with Xavier Anthony. Dane figured if he knew it, most of the town did—except for Gerald McCormick. He also knew the banker, Harold Ringley, was thinking of selling out and going back east, to teach college. And he knew Randolph Cross was interested in buying the bank. He knew the Masons were talking about building a temple on Main Street. He had also heard the stageline was considering a second run each week to Torsmill, and that a fund-raising to build a school, instead of having it in the old Golligher warehouse, would soon be underway.

He looked up, saw Anthony coming to his table and forced a smile.

"How are you this evening, Xavier?"

"Fine as a fiddle, Marshal," Anthony pronounced, shoving his hands in his pocket. He stood for a moment, expecting Dane to make another comment. When none came, Xavier Anthony pushed his hat back on his head and said in a low voice, "Be careful, Marshal. Those Cross men didn't like what you did today." He shook his head. "It was the right thing, of course."

"Of course," Dane said. "And I'm sure you shared that thought with Stockton."

Anthony's face twisted into anger, then disappeared. "He is a friend of mine. And the only official lawman in the county. The Cross ranch is important in this region, you know."

"I know. So is the law." Dane reached for his coffee cup.

Snorting his reaction, Anthony walked away and left the restaurant, adjusting his hat and tapping his cane on the floor. Ambitious as well as vain, he had run for mayor, but Fred Mikman had won that election quite handily

Dane concentrated on his meal, cutting away the gristle and fat, and enjoying the juicy meat and sliced potatoes. Two different townsmen and their wives stopped on their way out to thank him for the way he had handled the disturbance this morning. In spite of his desire to appear nonchalant, he ate fast. Swallowing the last of his coffee, he ordered a meal for Walker. He stared at the cup and was mildly surprised by a hand on his shoulder. He looked up.

It was J. R. Reicker, an older man with shoulder-length white hair and immense ears. An ever-present, unlit cigar was comfortable in the corner of his mouth. He was the town's judge, trying mostly civil matters. A justice of the peace, really. And the registrar of deeds. His small law office was cluttered with mementos of his life, mostly in Missouri. Prior to becoming a lawyer or a judge, he had been a part of several cattle drives.

Tales of his courageous deeds during the War of Northern Aggression, as part of a Union infantry, were plentiful. As were stories of him fighting Comanches. Unlike Anthony, these observations didn't come from Reicker. Dane liked the man, assessing him as someone who wouldn't talk easily about himself, but who had plenty of backbone. Reicker's evenhandedness, courage and apparent understanding of the law drew him to be appointed judge. His Missouri drawl masked a savvy mind.

"Marshal, ya dun good today," Reicker said softly, pushing his eyeglasses back on his prominent nose, "but ya picked up a nasty enemy. Cross'll have to come to town now—an' it won't be for a church meetin'." He paused, pursed his lips and added, "Ya should'a brought him to me for sentencin'. Not supposed to do both, arrestin' an' judgin'."

Dane looked up and smiled. "Thank you, J. R. Didn't see any need to bother you with this one. I'll remember next time. As far as Cross is concerned, I'm not going to jump to any conclusions. Yet. Rudolph Cross hasn't broken any laws in this town that I know of."

Straightening himself, Reicker nodded and moved the cigar to the other side of his mouth with his tongue. "Be careful, son. Cross is one o' those fellas that figger laws were made for others to worry about." He glanced in the direction of Mary's table. "An' that nephew o' his'n has a real need to prove hisself tough. Tough as his uncle, he wants to be." He shook his head. "Don't see what that thar purty Tressian gal sees in him. Money an' pow'r, I guess. Don't seem the type, tho."

Dane thanked him again for his concern and the old judge left the restaurant. As soon as the meal for his prisoner arrived, he asked to talk with the owner. The waiter's first reaction was to ask if the food was not good. Dane assured him it was and that he wanted to speak with Henry Carter about a city matter.

After the waiter disappeared into the kitchen, Carter burst from it and headed to Dane's table. The engaging restaurant owner was tall, balding and possessed a plump waistline from sampling his own food too often.

"Evening, Jericho. Heard you were busy today," Carter said.

Dane was aware Mary was watching the exchange and it pleased him. "Henry, here's some money to pay for meals for Tess. I know you have been taking care of her, but it's not fair for you to bear that burden alone." He handed folded money to the surprised owner. "I would appreciate it if you see she got fed regularly. I'll give you more when you need it."

Looking at the money, Carter said, "Been trying to take care of her best I can." He handed the money back. "The mayor gave me money for the same thing. Yesterday."

Dane pushed the money back into Carter's hand. "You keep this. Use it when the mayor's runs out. She is the town's concern, I think. I'm going to talk with the town council about it. We need to find her a safe place to sleep. Regularly."

"Well, thank you, Jericho. That's mighty nice of you." Carter nodded to support his comment and shoved the money into his pocket. "She's already come around this evening. Gave her some steak and potatoes." He chuckled. "Said it was good, I think."

They shook hands and Henry Carter retreated to the kitchen.

After eating, Dane waited a few minutes, expecting Sheriff Stockton to come to his table and make some kind of threat for arresting a Cross cowboy. When he didn't, Dane left coins on the table for his meal and left, carrying the covered plate. He usually took noon dinner as his town paid-for meal—and the food for the prisoner was on the town's bill.

He knew Mary was watching him and he was proud of the fact that he hadn't looked at her as he left. The night was cool and it seemed like an ocean of stars had overtaken the darkness. Trash Tess was nowhere in sight. Usually she wasn't at this time of the evening. He hoped someone had taken her in, even if it were the livery.

"I need to talk with Mikman about the town taking care of her," he told himself.

IV

Dane was well into his work by midmorning of the following day. Half a pot of coffee had already been consumed. Earlier he had returned Walker to the saloon, where he was finishing his work under Natter's direction. Dane planned on getting the cowboy at noon and returning him to the lock-up shed.

His squirrel scooted under the doors like clockwork and Dane reached into his pocket for a rolled-up piece of bread. He spread five pieces and said, "There you go, Mr. Squirrel. Hope your night was better than mine."

The blacksmith-marshal had not slept well in his small house at the edge of town. Most of his struggle with sleep came from thinking about Mary Tressian. He was working the bellows to revitalize his fire, after punching holes in a dozen hinges and welding a cracked wagon wheel, when he heard the sound of horses thundering down the main street.

Laying down the bellows, he stepped through the swinging doors of his shop to see what the commotion was about. He grimaced at the sight. It was Rudolph Cross, a massive man with a full beard and a mustache cut so low under his nose that it looked like he was wearing a disguise. Beside him was his nephew, Turin Stockton, almost as big. Dane thought the younger man had a permanent leer. He also wore a star on his coat. Like it was some kind of benighted honor, Dane thought. Behind them were eight riders wearing belt guns with rifles in their saddle sheaths.

Spinning around, Dane went quickly inside to remove his apron, get his shirt and button it on, then pulled free the revolver from his long coat and pushed it into his belt in back and returned to the outside of his shop. It was better to wait for them outside than have them swarming into his shop.

Rudolph Cross reined his big bay hard to stop it in front of the shop and the others swung behind him, spreading out in a line. Sheriff Stockton grinned and tugged on the gun belt at his waist. His blond hair had produced a scraggily beard and his blue eyes looked a little like he had been struck a blow between them at some young age. He was nearly as tall as his uncle, but nowhere near the old man's apparent strength. Rudolph Cross looked and acted like a man who expected his every word to be taken as a need to act immediately.

"Blacksmith, what's this I hear about you sucker-punchin' one of my hands and arrestin' him for defendin' himself against two Broken E men?" Cross snarled. His voice was loud and carried well into the main part of town.

Dane could see a few townspeople had paused across the street to watch this sudden confrontation. One was Xavier Anthony, dressed in striped trousers and a dark cutaway coat. Dane tried to keep his eyes focused on the rancher and not be distracted by the nephew—or the bystanders.

"If you mean I disarmed a man who was firing at two unarmed cowhands yesterday and wouldn't give up his gun when I asked for it, you're right," Dane said, hoping his voice didn't carry any nervous vibration. "I could have arrested him for attempted murder. Instead, he was given the option of three days in jail or paying a thirty-dollar fine. He chose jail." He put his hands on his hips, mostly to be closer to the gun resting in his belt behind him. "He was also ordered to fix the holes he made in the saloon."

"Where the hell's my wagon?" Cross didn't like the response; obviously it wasn't the story he had been told about the incident. Dane guessed Stockton had been the one bearing the embellished news.

"Your wagon is in the livery, where we put horses and wagons left in the street uncared for. Your man will owe the livery for that service," Dane said. "Your nephew there should know that. He's the county sheriff, you know."

Behind Cross, one of his men snickered.

Shoving back his shoulders, Cross bellowed, "The hell he will. I'm taking my man and my wagon—now."

"No, you aren't. I'll decide when he's done his time."

"Who's gonna stop me?" Cross glared at Dane. "You an' your pee-ass badge? I got the sheriff of the county right here."

"Yes, me an' my pee-ass badge. Made it myself." Dane slid his right hand a few inches closer to his revolver. "This isn't the county's concern. It's the town's."

This time all the Cross riders laughed. Stockton looked first at his uncle, then joined in. His laugh was thin, almost feminine.

"I've a good mind to get down an' teach you some lessons, smithy." Cross leaned forward in the saddle.

"Looks to me like you need a lot of backing up, Cross." Dane pointed at the line of riders. "I doubt you do any of your own fighting."

"Let me have him, Unc," Stockton snarled, and started to dismount.

Cross grinned viciously. "All right. Get it done." Waving his hands, he grandly announced, "None of my boys'll bother you, smithy. When it's over, though, we'll piss on your beat-up body."

Dane's only response was to widen his stance as Stockton took off his belt gun and coat and handed them to the closest cowboy, who gave him a pat on the shoulder, supported by a growled, "Take 'im apart, Stockton. It'll be easy."

Nodding and grinning viciously, Stockton sauntered toward Dane with the last comment ringing in his ears. The young blacksmith had heard stories of Turin Stockton beating a cowhand to death, a man he and a bunch of Cross riders had found alone. Stockton's eyes glowed with an evil eagerness as he advanced, opening and closing his fists at his side.

For an instant, Dane wondered if the eagerness to fight him came from jealousy over Mary Tressian. He dismissed the idea as Stockton snarled, "You're gonna wish you kept to shoeing horses, clown."

Dane felt the statement was more for Cross's benefit than to scare him. It didn't matter. Closing fast, Stockton swung a venomous right-hand haymaker at Dane's head. The blacksmith pushed it aside with a well-placed left arm and followed with a right cross to Stockton's exposed chin. The deflected blow was hard enough that it stunned his arm for a moment.

Dane's ability to fistfight came mostly from his father's training; Jethro Dane had won extra money for his family as a bare-knuckle prizefighter in Louisiana, before the War.

Stockton jerked backward and Dane landed a quick jab to his stomach. An eyeblink behind came another uppercut to Stockton's chin. He moved away from the shop doors so he wouldn't be knocked off-balance by being slammed against them.

Staggering, Stockton swung an awkward punch that caught Dane in the side of the head. The sheer weight of his Stockton's dazed him and Dane knew he couldn't let Stockton have many attempts or he would go down. There was no doubt in his mind that the cruel sheriff would kick him when he was defenseless. Maybe putting out his eyes. Or breaking his back.

Fear of that ending drove him.

"Atta boy, Stockton! Take the sonuvabitch apart," one of the Cross cowboys yelled.

Rudolph Cross turned in his saddle and nodded his approval of the comment. Recovering his balance, Stockton swung again, catching Dane's chest and driving pain deep into his body. The blow didn't stop him and Dane closed in, landing a right-hand smash that drove deeply into Stockton's belly, reinforced by his own unintentional grunt, followed by a left that crashed into his rib cage. And a simultaneous grunt.

All of the air left Stockton and he bent over to stop the sudden awful pain.

In a wild fury of blows that followed like wind, Dane's right fist delivered an uppercut to Stockton's chin, followed by a short left cross to the same point. His grunting was like a Gatling gun in support of his efforts. Stockton's right fist bounced off Dane's upper shoulder and Dane landed two blows into the bigger man's stomach.

Stockton stutter-stepped backward, holding both hands to his midsection. Dane rushed into him with a blur of punches that cut open Stockton's cheek, spewing blood on both fighters, and spun his head sideways. A tooth flew from his bloody mouth.

Wild-eyed and badly hurt, Stockton threw a brittle roundhouse that Dane blocked, and stepped into him with another uppercut to his stomach. Stockton wobbled and collapsed. A groan became a whimper. The only reaction was the sound of retching.

Standing over him, Dane looked up at Cross. "How much do you want your nephew to take to satisfy your anger?"

His face filled with anger, Cross ordered the two closest cowhands to get Stockton back on his horse.

"Tell them to clean up the mess. I don't want it in front of my shop." Dane stepped through the doors, grabbed a gray towel lying on a three-legged chest just inside the doors, and returned, tossing it in Stockton's direction. The cloth fluttered and landed on Stockton's heaving back.

A stocky rider with a tied-down hat and knee-length chaps slid from his horse. The man next to him followed, a Frenchman with a thick mustache and striped pants stuck into black boots. They walked over to Stockton and leaned over to help him up.

"*Sacré bleu*. You will be sorry you did this," the mustached Frenchman warned.

"Clean it up." Dane pointed at the regurgitation. "Do it now."

The stocky cowboy grabbed the towel and managed to scrape the mess into the towel with two vigorous swipes. He looked around for some place to put the wadded-up towel.

"Take it with you. I don't want it back," Dane said, watching Cross and sliding his hand to his back to assure himself that his revolver remained where he had placed it.

The gun remained. Unmoved. He was thankful. This wasn't over, he was certain.

"*Quoi*?" the Frenchman asked, anger close to his face.

"You heard me."

The Frenchman muttered something in French that Dane didn't understand, while the stocky cowboy held the balled towel away from his body. It took both cowboys to get the wobbly Stockton to his feet. He nearly collapsed again as they neared his horse, then the stocky rider grabbed Stockton by the belt in back with his free hand and the taller Frenchman grabbed him under his left armpit and almost lifted him into the saddle. The stocky cowboy shoved the towel into Stockton's saddlebags and retreated to his own horse.

Stockton stared vacantly at his uncle and muttered something unintelligible.

"You disgust me. Some sheriff you are," Cross growled, and turned his attention to Dane. "Smithy, do you have any idea of how much money my ranch brings to this pee-ass town? Torsmill exists because we let it."

Dane cocked his head to the side. "Cross, I am well aware of your importance to the town's economy. You and the other ranchers around. We welcome all of you. But only if you obey our laws." He pointed in the direction of Cross's men. "If you and your men are staying, you'll need to give up your guns. The sheriff can keep his."

A thick-chested Mexican called Big Juan, in the middle of the line of Cross cowboys, held up his rifle and snorted. "Come an' git it, *señor*."

None of them saw Dane's hand move until it flashed his Smith & Wesson revolver. "I will. Drop it or I'll drop your boss."

"How long do you think you're gonna live?" the bearded rider beside the Mexican challenged. His frowning eyebrows connected in one hairy line.

"Long enough to kill your boss—and two more of you."

Rudolph Cross held up his gloved hand. "Stop it. We're not staying. That all right with you, smith . . . Marshal?"

"It is," Dane said, his gun still pointed at Cross's midsection. "As long as you leave Walker in the Longhorn to finish his sentence."

"What if he leaves with us?"

"I'll empty his saddle." Dane's eyes studied the cowhands for any signs of movement toward their guns.

"You know, I think you would." Cross studied Dane with a newfound respect.

"Don't try me. This isn't worth blood and you know it."

Cross's shoulders rose and fell. "I'm gonna have my boys get my wagon and buy some supplies. All right?"

"Long as you pay the livery and the general store," Dane said. "Does it take eight men to buy supplies? Just wondering."

Cross actually smiled, then turned in the saddle. "Lecaunesse, you an' Hogan get the wagon an' get what we need from the store. Tell the livery I'll pay later."

"No. You'll pay now," Dane demanded.

"One of these days, smithy, you're gonna get yours," Cross snarled, and reached into his coat pocket and retrieved a small sack of coins. Tossing it toward the derby-hatted cowboy called Hogan, the big rancher bellowed, "Give your guns to the storekeeper." He frowned at the two selected men. "Do you know what I want from the store?"

"*Oui,*" Lecaunesse responded.

"Aye," Hogan agreed.

In spite of their positive responses, Cross rattled off the supplies needed and told them to leave one of their horses for the jailed Walker at the livery. To punctuate his orders, he yanked his reins hard to the left and spurred his horse into a gallop. The other riders followed, with Big Juan riding beside Stockton to make certain he stayed in the saddle.

Dane watched them leave town, noticing Xavier Anthony had left the small crowd across the street. He returned to his work, grabbing the bellows to give the fire on his forge renewed attention. He worked it five times.

Mary Tressian looked up from helping customers as the two Cross riders came into her store. They had secured the wagon and lashed the reins to the hitching rack. Tied to the wagon's back end were their two saddle horses. She was trying her best not to appear nervous. She had seen Cross, his nephew and their men ride into town and knew why they had come. She had heard the egotistical Anthony tell Stockton of the arrest while they ate last night.

Her feelings for the rugged blacksmith were confusing her. Sheriff Stockton was a man many women would be thrilled to have his attention. But she had little interest in him, in spite of his persistence. Their eating together was something she felt pressured into.

Why was she drawn to the quiet Jericho Dane? Why didn't he show any signs that he was interested in her?

A townsman in a too-tight suit entered a few steps behind the Cross cowboys. In a loud voice, he announced, "Marshal Dane backed down Cross and his men. They left town." He paused and added dramatically, "Marshal Dane beat up Sheriff Stockton. In a fair fight. They left that arrested cowboy in the saloon where he's fixing up the bullet holes."

The cowboy named Hogan turned around, his hand resting on the counter displaying rows of branded medicines. "Be careful o' ye words, mister. Rudolph Cross be comin' back and all o' ye will rue this day."

The businessman's face whitened and he stuttered sort of an apology. "I-I w-was only sharing w-what happened. I-I w-wasn't taking s-sides."

Hogan nodded and nudged Lecaunesse with his elbow.

A stray beam of light from the front window accented the collection of patented medicines, along with several kinds of croup syrups and salves for babies, a half dozen bottles of variously labeled female remedies, worm destroyers and stomach bitters, plus containers of Epsom salts, cod liver oil, paregoric, camphor and snake root. The light also caught the handle of the belt guns of the two riders.

"May I help you gentlemen?" Mary's voice refound most of its lilt. She put her hands on her hips. "Torsmill is a quiet town, sirs. A good town. But we don't take well to threats." She folded her arms. "If you want to shop in here, you must first remove your guns."

The customers at the counter quickly moved away, leaving her alone. She glanced at the long-barreled Colt under the counter and wished Dane were here. She almost smiled at the thought. His presence was the first thing she had thought about.

Shifting his weight toward Hogan, Lecaunesse whispered something to the Irish hand. Hogan nodded agreement and said, "Be meanin' no harm to ye, ma'am. We just be here for supplies." He held up the sack of coins. "Payin' cash money we be."

"Pardon, here are our guns, *mademoiselle*," Lecaunesse volunteered, stepping forward with his revolver in his hand, grip held forward.

Hogan watched him for an instant, realized what he was doing, and said, "Oh yes'm. Here be me gun." He yanked free the revolver and followed the Frenchman to the counter.

Both laid their guns on the counter and Lecaunesse picked up one of the shopping baskets.

"Thank you," she said, unfolding her arms. "Do you need any help?"

"*Merci bien.*" Lecaunesse pushed back his hat. "We will need such. Not used to this." He smiled a jack-o'-lantern smile showing two missing teeth. "No offense, *mademoiselle*. But it sure is easy to see why Stockton is sweet on *vous*."

She blushed from annoyance and wished she hadn't. "I'll be with you as soon as I finish helping the Bannons."

A heavyset farmer standing close to the wall waved his arm dismissively. "You go ahead an' help them, Miss Tressian. We ain't in no hurry. No hurry a'tall."

Across the street, J. R. Reicker slipped into the blacksmith shop where Dane was soaking his hands in the water trough.

"Looks like you did a real number of that stuck-up nephew o' Cross's," Reicker said, studying the young blacksmith with newfound interest. "He must've outweighed ya by twenty, thirty pounds."

"Yeah, I reckon he did." Dane pulled his cut hands from the cooling liquid and looked for a towel, then remembered it had been used to wipe up Stockton's vomit. He wiped them on his apron, then his pants.

"This ain't the end o' it, Marshal." Reicker shook his head.

"Probably not, J. R. Probably not," Dane said. "Would you like some coffee? Fresh this morning."

"No thanks, about time fer me to check in with the mayor." The white-haired man left.

V

Dane poured himself a cup of coffee, muttered to himself and began singing. "*Rock of Ages, cleft for me. Let me hide myself in Thee. Let the water and the blood . . . from thy wound side which flowed. Be of sin the double cure. Save from wrath and make me pure.*" That's all the words he remembered. Ever. Then he started over. He looked up to see Trash Tess staring at him. He hadn't heard her come in. He waved the cup at her and she nodded.

He walked over, wondering if she had eaten anything this morning. Her long hair was wilder than usual, like she had just come in from a nasty wind. Her dress was the same one as yesterday—light blue gingham. Down its front was something that looked like manure. It definitely wasn't dirt. A fly seemed interested.

"Have you eaten breakfast, Tess?" he asked, handing her the cup.

She grabbed it and drank of it deeply, then handed it back to him. It was nearly empty. "Yes, I have breakfast."

"Well, when you're hungry, your noon dinner's been paid for. By Mr. Mikman," he said. "All of your meals have. At Carter's place. You understand? Lots of people like you, Tess."

She stared at him for a moment, then grabbed the cup. He thought she said something that sounded like she was grateful. Reaching into her purse, she pulled out a crumpled, brown photograph and held it out for him to examine. He had seen it several times before. His guess was it was of her parents on their wedding day. No one knew who they might be—or had been, or where they had come from, or where they were going when she was left behind. Seeing it always made him sad.

"That's very nice, Tess. They are quite good-looking people. Your mother looks like you, I think," Dane said and held up the coffee cup. "I will keep this cup right here," he said, walking toward the retaining wall. "It is yours. Whenever you want some coffee, you come here. All right?" He tossed out the remains and placed the cup on an upright nail.

He turned around. She was gone.

Dane started to resume work, then decided he would check on the two Cross riders and make certain they weren't causing a problem. That wasn't the reason, of course. He wanted to see Mary; he had made up his mind to ask her out. If she declined, at least he knew.

Splashing water on his face and running his fingers through his hair, Dane took off his apron and put on his shirt and long coat with the badge. He buttoned the coat and adjusted his hat to give him further confidence, then left the shop. He told himself the other reason for going was that he needed to buy another coffee mug.

Hogan and Lecaunesse were loading the wagon as he approached.

"'Morning, gentlemen," he said without pausing.

"*Bonjour*," Lecaunesse said, looking up from depositing a sack of flour in the wagon bed.

"Aye, top o' the morning to ye," Hogan said and grinned.

Mary met him at the doorway with a big smile. "It's good to see you, Marshal Dane."

Touching the brim of his hat, Dane replied, "It's good to see you, Miss Tressian. I, ah, came to see if the two Cross riders were behaving themselves."

"Oh, I hoped you came to see me." Her eyes blinked mischievously.

He swallowed, uncertain of how to respond, and finally blurted, "Yes, ma'am."

"My name is Mary."

His face was a smile. "I know that . . . Mary."

Stepping aside to allow him to enter, she said, "The two Cross men have been very polite. They are nearly finished, I think." She studied him. "Jericho, you must not stand in the way of Rudolph Cross. He is an evil man. He will stop at nothing to get what he wants."

"And his nephew? What does he want?" Dane was surprised at his own response.

Mary frowned. "Jericho Dane, if you mean what I think you mean, you should be ashamed." She placed her hands on her hips. "Just what does a girl have to do to get you to pay attention to her?"

Dane looked at his worn boots for a moment, then looked into her eyes. "Mary, I think you are the most beautiful woman I've ever met. But I can't compete with all that Cross and Stockton have."

Her voice softened. "You silly man. Do you think I care about that? I am interested in you, Jericho Dane. You."

He glanced in the direction of the two Cross riders and found the courage to say what was churning in his mind. "Would you like to go for a ride? Maybe a picnic?"

"A picnic? I would love to. When?"

Swallowing his nervousness, he said, "How about this afternoon?"

She beamed. "Yes. My clerk can handle the store."

"I'll come for you about four. All right?"

"I'll be waiting." She took his hand and brought it toward her. "Your hands are cut and sore. From the fight?"

"Yeah, guess so." His eyes couldn't leave her face.

"Let me get you some ointment. It'll help." Without waiting for his reaction, she hurried to the medicine section.

"Oh, I almost forgot. I need to buy a coffee mug."

VI

Dane and Mary chatted easily as his rented buggy moved across the sweet prairie. He had selected a gentle stream as their picnic location. Ambling water had escaped from Kill Pond long ago, back when the buffalo nation ruled the land.

The string of natural irrigation had worked hard, bringing to life a matching strip of elderberry, live oak, willow, juniper, wild potato and two dominant cottonwood trees along its banks. The stream meandered for a quarter mile, then disappeared underground, but evidence of its presence could be found in a magnificent strand of gramma grass claimed so far by one of the small ranches. So far he had held it. On the north side of the squatty hill that protected the stream was the main pond itself.

Dane couldn't remember being so happy. Mary was wearing a different dress, one with puffed sleeves and a high lacy collar. Her hair was no longer in a bun, but hung loosely with a wide-brimmed straw hat covering the top of her head. He was wearing the best clothes he owned, a dark-blue, pin-striped suit used for his occasional churchgoing. His only suit.

Her smile reminded Dane of a beautiful sunrise. He told her so, surprised at his boldness. She reached over and held his hand resting on the buggy seat. Time passed so fast, they were nearing the pond before either realized it. Only a young deer was drinking at the pond when they crested the hill and it darted away as soon as they headed toward the water. Mary pointed at the swift-running animal, talking about its wonderful freedom.

This was Dane's favorite spot, a refuge from work and worry. He had discovered it upon returning from his visit with the ranchers.

"Oh, how beautiful! I had forgotten how lovely it is," Mary exclaimed as they pulled up alongside the stream. "I used to come here with Dad. He loved this quiet place."

Dane smiled. "Wish I had known him. He sounds like a good man." He jumped down from the buggy and turned to help her.

She melted into his arms. Their lips met and for a wonderful moment everything else disappeared.

Looking into his eyes, Mary said softly, "I've been waiting for this. For you."

"Mary, I can't remember being so happy," he said and touched her face, then ran his finger lightly across her lips.

She kissed them as they passed and they kissed again.

A thunder of hoofbeats broke into their reverie.

"Better get back into the buggy, Mary, until we know who this is."

"Sure."

He helped her into the buggy and headed around the harnessed chestnut horse as seven armed riders cleared the hill behind them. Dane couldn't make out their faces, but guessed they were Cross riders. His hand slipped into his coat pocket and was reassured by the cold steel of his revolver.

As they advanced, he heard one say, "It's that damn blacksmith," followed by, "He's with Stockton's girl."

It was Cross riders. Some from this morning. He recognized the heavy Mexican, then Lecaunesse and Hogan.

"Whatever happens, stay in the buggy, Mary. They won't hurt you." He stepped away from the buggy to meet their advance. His hand moved toward his pocket, then away. To draw a gun now would bring their own weapons into play. There were too many and he had Mary to be concerned about.

"Maybe they're just passing through," Mary said without much conviction.

"Maybe," he answered.

The pockmark-faced foreman leading the Cross band reined his winded horse a few feet from Dane. Winslow Tatum grinned wickedly and pushed back the short-brimmed fedora from his forehead. A shoulder holster, worn over his shirt, held a walnut-handled Colt. His potato-shaped face bristled with uneven whiskers trying to form a beard.

The blacksmith didn't move. The six other riders fanned out around Dane and the buggy, creating a half circle.

"Well, well, ain't this a purty sight," Tatum growled. "The blacksmith tryin' to cut in on Stockton's girl. Think ya had a right after this mornin'?"

"I am not Stockton's girl," Mary blurted. "Go away and leave us alone."

The Cross foreman folded his gloved hands over his saddlehorn.

"Cain't do that, missy. You're on Cross land—an' we don't take to trespassers."

"This is open land and you know it," Dane responded. "Leave."

He wasn't expecting what happened next. Two ropes sailed at him. He slapped them away. A third loop caught him, settled instantly around his waist, pinning his arms to his body. The toss came from the grizzled rider on the far side of the buggy, over the back of Dane's right shoulder. An eyeblink behind it came another loop from the opposite direction. The two ropes held him, unable to move or raise his arms.

A third successful loop found his neck and tightened around it. The hemp rubbed hard against his skin, making it difficult to breathe.

"Now, what do you have to say, blacksmith?" Tatum swung down from his horse, tugging on his gloves and the wide leather cuffs, and handing the reins to the mounted Big Juan. Batwing chaps and worn spurs made brisk music with each step toward Dane. "The boss is gonna be real happy to hear about this."

Dane struggled to free himself, but couldn't. The rope at his neck was making him light-headed and there was nothing he could do about it. He tried to reach the gun in his coat pocket, but he couldn't lift his right hand, trapped against his side.

"Stop it! Let him go!" Mary screamed. "I . . . love him."

"Sure, honey." Tatum walked over, pulling again on his gloves, and opening and closing his fists. "Not too tight, Hogan. I want the sonuvabitch to feel this."

"Aye, boss. Lettin' him breathe a bit, I'll be doin'."

The rope at Dane's neck loosened slightly and he was thankful. As he inhaled, Tatum unleashed a vicious blow at Dane's face. Dane's reflexes were good enough to turn his head and Tatum's fist caught the side of the blacksmith's face, making his teeth crunch together.

As Tatum moved to deliver another blow, the blacksmith kicked him in the groin and Tatum bent over in fierce pain.

"You yellow bastard, give me a chance. I'll take all of you . . ." Dane's words were cut off as the lariat tightened at his neck.

"That be enough, smithy," Hogan yelled.

Straightening himself, Tatum took a deep breath. "You're gonna rue that."

Keeping his body away from Dane's feet, Tatum slammed his fist into Dane's face and followed it with a blow to his stomach. A second blow to Dane's face cut into his cheek and split his lip. Dane grimaced and spit blood into Tatum's face. A third smashed into his face again.

Stepping back, Tatum shook his right fist. "Damn, that hurts."

"*Señor* Tatum, let me have a turn." Big Juan flashed a wide, toothy grin.

"Aye, me be wantin' a turn also," Hogan shouted, grinned and yanked on his rope around Dane's neck for good measure.

At the buggy, Mary grabbed the whip from its stand, jumped down and ran at Tatum, swinging it at him. The whip snapped his face and caught Tatum's cheek, drawing blood.

All of the riders were drawn to Mary's attack. Lecaunesse yelled something in French and Hogan forgot his rope as he leaned forward to add encouragement to Tatum. The youngest rider, a buck-toothed lad not yet eighteen, yelled for Tatum to rip off her dress. With the riders distracted, Dane forced his left hand under the two ropes at his waist enough to push them slightly away from his body with every bit of his strength. Then he edged the ropes upward so that his right hand was free just above the elbow. His right hand reached into his pocket and he grabbed the pistol. He fought the blackness that wanted him.

Swearing, Tatum rushed at Mary, knocking her down and pulling the whip from her hand. At that instant, Dane fired his gun from his pocket at the grizzled cowboy to his left, holding one of the pinning ropes. The man yelped and grabbed his arm, dropping the lariat. Dane spun toward the two men with the ropes around his neck and waist. Just that movement brought another hint of air to his crying lungs.

He fired twice more and Hogan flew from his saddle. The lariat snaked in the air. The third cowboy threw his lariat at the ground and held up his arms. Next to him, Lecaunesse started to reach for his handgun and changed his mind.

Dane spun back to face the stunned Tatum. "If any of your men move, you're dead."

The blacksmith yanked the limp ropes from his neck and body with his left hand. Smoke slithered from the black hole in his pocket. He inhaled deeply, but the fresh air came slower than he wanted. He didn't try to remove the gun from his pocket, not wanting to risk it getting hung up coming out.

Raising his hands, Tatum snarled, "Nobody git stupid. Nobody move."

"*Señor,* you only have three bullets, *sí*?" The Mexican grinned.

Keeping his gun pointed at the wide-eyed Tatum's nose, Dane stepped next to him and yanked the six-gun from its holster with his left hand. He cocked it and said, "Now how many bullets do I have? The rest of you, drop your guns. One at a time. We'll start with you." He pointed at the Mexican rider. "Do it now."

Grinning again, Big Juan eased his revolver from its holster. "*Sí, señor*. I am the peace-likin' man."

"Now you." Dane pointed at the rider to Big Juan's left.

Struggling to her feet, Mary saw the dropped gun of the Mexican rider, retrieved it and joined Dane, waving the gun at the remaining riders. Slowly they dropped their pistols to the ground.

"Now your rifles. Real easy. I'm jumpy right now—and I'm going to shoot if you move too quick." Dane motioned with both revolvers.

"Me too," Mary declared, and looked like she meant it.

Dane watched the men ease their rifles from scabbards and let them fall to the ground. "You, Mex. Get rid of that pistol in your boot. And you, with the red hair, get rid of that gun stuck in your belt in back."

Both Cross men complied with the Mexican snarling through clenched white teeth. "There weel be a next time, *señor*."

He pointed at the downed Irishman who had held the lariat around his neck. Hogan was bleeding at his neck. "Get him back in his saddle. He's not hurt bad." He studied the men for any other signs of hidden weapons. "Clear out his saddle gun and belt gun."

Two riders dismounted and helped the wounded Hogan onto his horse. He was in shock and struggled to stay in the saddle once they pushed him into place. The shorter of the two helpers pulled his horse beside him and reached out to hold the wounded roper upright.

"Turn around and ride out of here." Dane motioned with both guns.

Tatum walked to his horse and swung into the saddle. He made a wave with his hand and they turned and galloped away.

Dane watched him go, feeling the adrenaline leaving his body. He wobbled and went to a knee.

"Oh, my darling Jericho," Mary whimpered, and leaned over to tend to him.

VII

Morning sun woke Jericho Dane from his bed. The brightness of the day told him that it was at least midmorning, maybe later. He slid his feet toward the floor and was startled to see the white-haired judge, J. R. Reicker, sitting in a chair against the wall. An unlit cigar rested in his mouth.

Dane's bedroom was small, one of two rooms in the wood-framed house. The only furniture in the room, besides the chair Reicker now occupied and Dane's bed, was a dresser with one leg propped up with a thick book. Above it was a cracked mirror. The dresser top was covered with a pitcher, small basin and a well-used towel.

"Mornin', Marshal. Glad to see yur back wi' us," the older man greeted him cheerily. "Miss Tressian asked me to sit with you. Make sur ya got along."

Dane looked down at himself and realized he was naked. He looked up with a question on his face.

"I got ya undressed. She didn' think it'd be proper for her to be doin' it." Reicker smiled. "Ya passed out on the way home yestur'day. Took quite a beatin' from those bastards, ya did." He folded his arms. "Heard ya also did some ri't fancy shootin', too. Reckon it saved yur life, boy."

Dane rubbed his jaw where it ached. He felt his lip and recoiled from the pain. His mouth was swollen. His stomach hurt when he moved.

"J. R., what time is it?" Dane slowly got to his feet and tried to clear his muddy head.

"Goin' on noon, I reckon." He pulled a heavy watch from his vest pocket, clicked it open and said, "Make that eleven twenty." He closed the lid and returned the watch to his pocket.

Dane shook his head and the movement hurt everywhere. "What happened to the buggy?"

"Miss Tressian took back the buggy aft'a she got me," Reicker said, cocking his head to the side. "Think she took your picnic basket with her. Not sure, come to think o' it."

Frowning, Dane said, "Dammit, I forgot all about my prisoner! He's been in that shed . . ."

"Nope," Reicker interrupted. "Fed 'im las' night—an' ag'in this mornin'. Put it on the city's tab. Let him do his business. He were real polite."

"I appreciate all you've done." Dane tried to smile, but could only make the right side of his mouth move.

"Think nothin' o' it." Reicker grinned. "Kinda gave me a chance to make it official—ya know, takin' care o' the prisoner an' all."

Moving his arms to determine if there was any pain in them, Dane teased, "Ever do any blacksmithing?"

"No. Cain't say that I have, Jericho," Reicker said. "Oh, I've put on sum 'good 'nuffs,' ya know. Them store-bought shoes fer hosses. But nuthin' like ya do."

Dane smiled. "Shoot. I was going to put you to work at the shop, too."

A knock on the door stopped the conversation.

Reicker smiled and stood. "Ya'd better get yurself dressed. Reckon that'll be Miss Tressian. She takes quite a shine to ya, boy—and she was ri't fierce worried. Came by earlier. Jus' aft'a breakfast. Hope ya don't mind, I fixed myself sum coffee an' bacon."

"Sure. If you'll get the door, I'll get washed up and dressed."

Reicker headed for the front door, paused midway through the main room, and looked over his shoulder. "Why don' I tell her ya'll come by her store in a while?"

Dane smiled and it hurt. "That would be great."

He thought about their kissing yesterday and touched his lips again. It would be awhile before they could do that again. If she was interested. He certainly was. One special moment from that terrible time yesterday resurfaced in his brain. Did Mary say that she loved him? He heard her scream again in his mind: "Stop it! Let him go! I . . . love him." It was probably just the awfulness of the attack and she was trying to get the Cross riders to leave him alone.

Did he love her? Yes. He was certain of it. Spending life with her rushed into every corner of his mind.

Headed for the door, Reicker moved past a handmade table and four mismatched chairs, and glanced at the cold fireplace. It would be like a blacksmith to have a good fire at his working place and none at his house, the old man thought. His own place wasn't much different; he lived alone at the boardinghouse. He liked keeping busy, even volunteering to clerk at Mary's store when legal duties were light; it kept him from thinking about his late wife. She had died only a handful of months ago. Pneumonia. It seemed like she had been gone an eternity. To him.

He opened the door and Mary Tressian greeted him. Her voice at the door was both concerned and lilting. Dane listened without moving. Reicker told her the blacksmith was up and dressing and said he planned on coming by her store soon.

"How is Jericho feeling?" Mary Tressian asked.

The old man chuckled. "Well, he looks like he's bin in a fight wit' a b'ar, but it'd tak' a lot to hold that boy down."

"Please tell him I came by—and I'm looking forward to seeing him."

"Will do, ma'am. That news'll make him feel a lot better."

"Are you coming in today, Mr. Reicker?" she asked.

"Do ya need an ol' man's help today?"

"I always need your help." She smiled. "Unless you've got things that need doing."

"None that I know 'bout. How 'bout I come in after the noon hour?"

"That would be great, Mr. Reicker." She turned away and headed for her buggy waiting at the street.

When Reicker returned to the bedroom, Dane was shaving.

"Have you seen Tess today? Ah . . . Trash Tess?" he asked without turning from the mirror above his dresser.

"Well, now that ya ask . . . no, I ain't," Reicker said, shifting the cigar in his mouth with his tongue. "But she's likely to be close to Carter's place. Gittin' close to noon an' all." He studied the young blacksmith. "Why'd ya ask?'

Dane shook his head. "Oh, I just think the town needs to take care of her. She can't do it for herself. I keep telling myself to ask the mayor about giving her the jail shed to stay in. Never take the time to do it. I'm going to do it. Now."

Reicker scrutinized Dane's reflected face as if truly seeing him for the first time. "Don' know that ever'body thinks along them lines, Marshal. Thar's sum think she's a nuisance. Like they'd think about a wolf—or an Injun." He cocked his head and his large ears wiggled. "If'n ya use the shed fer her, whadda ya gonna do for a jail?"

"Going to use that big tree. Beside my place. Tie 'em to it."

Smiling a wolflike grin, Reicker said, "Well, that oughta make folks think twice 'bout bein' arrested. Might git wet."

"Yeah, they might." Dane finished wiping his face with a towel. "Hey, J. R., I forgot to ask. Would you like to have something to eat come noon? I'm buying."

"Well, o' course."

Dane looked into the mirror and saw a bulge in the judge's coat pocket. "Hey, are you carrying a gun?"

"Yessir, I am. Got me a fine Navy Colt." Reicker lifted the heavy revolver from his pocket. "Did me fine in the Great War. Ya gonna tell me I should'na be carryin' iron?"

"Probably not something a judge should do," Dane said, and chuckled. "But it may be a smart thing to keep it handy. I think Cross is getting ready to take control of Kill Pond. Or try. Might have some spillover trouble between him and the other ranchers. In town. Might."

"Yeah, I were a'thinkin' the same," Reicker said, returning the gun to his pocket. "Cleaned and reloaded it last night. Soon as Cross settles down, I'll quit wearin' it." The old judge adjusted his glasses, rubbed his nose vigorously and pulled the cigar from his mouth.

Dane tried to smile, but it hurt too much. "I'll go see if I can catch the mayor—and I'll meet you at the restaurant. Say, an hour?"

"Ya got yourse'f a deal." Reicker returned the cigar to his mouth. "An' I'll keep an eye out fer Tess." He waved and headed for the door.

"Good enough. After that, I'll get to work at the shop. Afraid I'm behind."

A half hour later, wearing his long coat and hat, Dane walked into the Tressian General Merchandise Store and saw Mary helping a customer. The soreness in his stomach and face didn't care for the walking. It hurt to smile, but he did anyway.

Excusing herself from the older couple, Mary walked through the store toward him; her full skirt was music across the planked floor.

"Oh, Jericho . . . how do you feel?" she asked, stepping close and studying his swollen face.

"Probably about like I look, Mary," he said. "I'm mighty sorry to have taken you into all that."

"Don't be silly. You had no idea. How could you?" She touched his mouth and whispered, "If I kiss it, will it make it better?"

His face reddened and he put his hand to his mouth. "It'd make me feel good." He tried to smile, but it hurt too much.

"I have our picnic basket," she continued. "Maybe we could try that again when you're feeling better." She giggled. "I didn't keep the food."

"Of course," he said and realized everyone in the store was watching them. "I'd better go and let you get back to work."

"They'll wait. It'll give them something to gossip about." She smiled. "You and me."

"I like the sound of that."

"I love it. I love you."

"I love you, Mary." He touched her arm. She asked when they would see each other again and he suggested they have supper together.

She readily agreed.

He murmured good-bye and left the store. Instinctively, he felt for the pistol now resting in his long-coat pocket. He drew the gun and checked the loads. Someone had reloaded it from the ammunition he kept in his pocket—or maybe he had. He couldn't remember. Dane studied the busy street and sidewalks. Townspeople were well into the day. He headed for Mikman's Gun, Knife & Ammunition Shop. His body and face ached with the movement.

Dane pushed open the door widely and saw Fred Mikman. His face was filled with a dark beard and mustache. The bald top of his head was shiny, almost like a mirror. Wide suspenders struggled to keep his trousers in place over an extended stomach. He stood behind a counter displaying an array of revolvers. Behind him on the wall was a long rack of rifles and shotguns.

Born in America of German parents, Mikman was as close to a lifelong resident of Torsmill as there was. He and two other men had settled here and staked out the town when it was just prairie. One, named Torsmill, sold whiskey; the other, Abel Tressian, started the general store that Mary now owned and ran. Both had passed on years ago.

Like Dane, Mikman had accepted the mayor's job when no one else, except Xavier Anthony, wanted it. Oh, there was a town election, but it wasn't close. He worked with a town council of four appointed men and seemed to enjoy the duties. Most of the time.

Right now, he was worried and his large, expressive eyes showed it.

"*Guten Tag* to you, *Herr* Marshal."

"Just plain Jericho," Dane said as he always did.

As usual, the great-bearded gunsmith ignored Dane's offer of informality.

"*Du haff bin* hurt, *Herr* Marshal," Mikman started in. When he was nervous or excited, German words and phrases colored his conversation. "I hope it *ist nicht* of ze serious way."

Dane rubbed his sore neck and licked his swollen lip. "No, had a horse act up when I was shoeing him yesterday, that's all."

Mikman studied Dane for a moment. "*Du ist* many *gut* things, *Herr* Marshal, but *du ist nicht* a *gut* liar." He shook his head to support his statement. "I heard from *Herr* Wilson about vhat happened *vit der* Cross men. That *ist* awful. Awful."

"Well, it wasn't good."

"*Ja*. Let us get a posse *und* go arrest these awful men. That vas attempted murder. *Ja*, that *ist* vhat it vas. Attempted murder." Mikman's face beyond his beard was dark red.

Dane put a hand on the counter, glanced at the guns within. "Thanks, Fred, I appreciate that. I really do. But we have no jurisdiction outside of town. We'd be a lynch mob. No better than them." He looked up. "Might get some good men killed."

"Vell, thar be *nein* help from *der* county law." Mikman's eyes sparkled. "Let us send a vire to *der* Rangers."

"Good idea. Likely be awhile before one gets here, though." Dane folded his arms; the movement hurt his sore ribs.

"Maybe ve get one like this John Checker I *haff* read about in *der* San Antonio newspaper. *Ja*."

Dane smiled, but it hurt too much to become much more than a smirk at the corners of his mouth. "I imagine it's whoever isn't on assignment at the time. Or closest." He looked up at Mikman. "I think Cross is going to try to take over Kill Pond. That'll bring a shooting war. Expected it sooner, with his relative as the county law. Could spill into town."

"*Ja*. I *haff bin* thinking *der* same." Mikman turned his head slightly.

Frowning, Dane said, "Yeah. Might be a good idea to let me appoint a deputy." He licked his lips and felt the swelling around the cut. "If something happens to me, the town still has a lawman. Although Judge Reicker could handle just about anything." There was no bravado in the statement, just the flatness of fact. "He helped me yesterday. I wasn't in very good shape. He and Miss Tressian."

"*Ja*, I know *du und* Miss Tressian." Mikman smiled beneath his mustache, ignoring Dane's last comment. "*Und* I know of *der* beating *du* did give to *Herr* Stockton. *Und* I know about *der* Cross cowboy *du* arrested for disturbance of *der* peace. *Und* I know about *der* shooting *du* did to stop *der* Cross men. From murdering *du*."

Dane wasn't certain where this was headed or if he was going to like it.

"*Herr* Cross *ist* a powerful man." Mikman rubbed his massive beard, then put his hands on his suspenders and pulled on them slightly. "He be *gut* for Torsmill—*und* bad."

Dane nodded and Mikman continued, expanding on Dane's concern that Cross was going to press to control the whole region. After the mayor finished his thought, Dane changed the subject and began his reason for coming in: Trash Tess. He explained that he thought the town should take care of her since she could not care for herself. There should be a place for her to stay, to sleep.

He said that he knew of Mikman's giving Carter money to feed her. He suggested they fix up the jail shed for her. It wasn't wonderful, but it was certainly better than sleeping in the street or in the stable. Or wherever there was room that night. A cot was already there in the shed. It needed some cleaning and a few other items townspeople would likely be willing to donate.

Mikman listened without any reaction, then asked, "Vhat do ve do for a jail? There may be more cowboys coming to town looking for *der* trouble. It vould be awhile before ve could build one."

"There's a big tree outside my shop," Dane replied. "I can tie anyone arrested to it. That'll sure hold them."

"Vhat if it rains?"

Dane smiled, or tried to. "Well, the prisoner gets wet. Might help discourage bad behavior even more."

"I like it, *Herr* Marshal. I like it *var* much." Mikman waved his arms in a circle and said he would call for a quick meeting and get approval from the town council that day.

"Thanks, I appreciate that."

"*Herr* Marshal, *der* council may vant to hire . . . a full-time marshal." Mikman leaned on the counter and looked into Dane's face. "Talk there has *bin*, ya know. Torsmill *ist* growing. Ve *nicht* to vant this trouble *vit Herr* Cross to hurt Torsmill."

"No, we don't. A full-time marshal would be fine with me. These days, I've got more than enough with my blacksmithing."

"Vhat if they vant *du*—for *der* full-time marshal?"

"I would say thanks, but no thanks." Dane turned and headed for the door. "I'm a blacksmith, not a lawman."

"Vait, *Herr* Marshal, there *ist* something I vish to give *du*."

Without waiting for a response, he went to the rack on the wall behind him, lifted a double-barreled shotgun from its rest, and turned around holding out the gun.

"I vant *du* to *haff* this," Mikman declared, pushing the weapon toward Dane. "A marshal should be vell-armed, I think. Especially *vit* this trouble. Around us. *Ja*."

"Let me pay you for it, Fred," Dane said, accepting the shotgun.

"*Nein*. It *ist* gift." Mikman brought out two boxes of shells. "*Du* vill need these also." He paused and added, "I think *der* scattergun vill keep trouble from happening. If *der* cowboys see *du* with *der* gun, they vill . . . be of peace."

VIII

The fire on Dane's forge was winding its way to a dull gold as he finished shoeing a long-legged sorrel. Off to the side, four repaired wheels cooled in the water trough a few feet from his anvil. The friendly squirrel was enjoying the small pieces of bread the blacksmith had brought from the restaurant and placed on the ground.

His face and body ached, but he felt it was important to keep working. His mind was walking with Mary and he mumbled comments to her as he worked and grunted occasionally as he pounded the orange-hot iron. The recollection of her smile pushed him past the pains. A second cup of coffee since the noon meal sat untouched on the stool.

After eating, he and Reiker had brought hot food to the jailed cowboy; Dane told him that he would be released tomorrow morning and that there was a Cross horse waiting for him in the livery. Its time there had been paid for, by the rancher himself. The cowboy seemed relieved at that news. The waiter at the restaurant told him Trash Tess had been there earlier and had eaten only lightly. He didn't know where she went after leaving.

As Dane tapped the last nail in the right rear shoe with his fifth stroke, Fred Mikman knocked on the doors to his shop. Dane smiled. He knew of only one man who would knock before entering his shop.

"Come in, Mayor—and welcome."

By the look on the mayor's face, it was clear he was bringing bad news of some kind.

"Be with you in just a minute, Mayor," Dane said, letting go of the horse's leg, held as he squatted, and stood. "You look troubled, Fred."

"*Ja*, I am so." Mikman wrung his hands together as if trying to cleanse them. "How do I say this?"

Dane patted the horse's back. "I'm your friend. Just say it."

"Ah, *der* council, ah, they *haff* decided . . . to have anudder marshal," Mikman said, looking down at his feet.

He went on to explain the council was worried that Dane's fight with the Cross riders might bring trouble to the town. To quiet the situation, they fired Dane and hired Xavier Anthony as the new part-time lawman. His first task would be to take the arrested Cross cowboy out to the Cross ranch and explain the town was most interested in keeping a good relationship with Rudolph Cross and his men. The council wanted the new marshal to meet with the county sheriff and make certain he held no grudges against the town either.

Laying his hammer against the forge, Dane let the news settle into his mind before responding. He should have expected it, he told himself. Town councils like peace—and they respond to wealth. But Xavier Anthony?

"Does Xavier have the time to do this?" Dane asked, surprised at his first words in response. "With his tailoring?"

"He says he does," Mikman said. "No busier than *du*, he said. In fact, he vere at *der* meeting. Or rather, he vaited to be introduced. Ve had it in *der* hotel, *du* know."

"When does he take over?"

"It *ist* now." Mikman glanced at Dane, then again to his feet.

Dane's shoulders rose and fell. Part of him was relieved to have this responsibility removed; another part was worried about what would happen next. Cross would take the action as nothing more than weakness. Pure weakness. He knew both Cross and Stockton were the tailor's customers, enjoying fine suits. He told himself that wasn't a fair observation; he had done work for Cross, too. But not recently.

He walked over to where his long coat and other clothes hung from the wall. "Let me get the badge. I made it, but it's the town's."

Mikman's face was twisted with agony. "I did *nicht* see this to happen, *Herr* Marshal Dane. I should *haff*. I am so *vehr* sorry. *Vehr* sorry. *Herr* Ringley *und Herr* Lindsay *und Herr* McCornick had already talked to *Herr* Anthony about this. There vas only two votes for *du*. Myself *und* Lester Wilson."

"Don't be sorry, Fred. Really, it's all right. I've got my hands full right here," Dane said, handing him the badge.

He remembered the shotgun and turned to get the gun, resting against the wall. "Let me get the shotgun and shells. I won't be needing them anymore."

"*Nein. Nein.* I vant *du* to keep them. It *ist* gift." Mikman shook his head and waved his hands. "*Ach du lieber,* I do *nicht* like this at all. They are so wrong. *Du* are *der* reason there *ist* peace. *Herr* Cross vill come *vit* guns, I know it."

Dane licked his lips and his tongue ran along the puffy, scabbed wounds. "That is very kind of you, Fred, but you gave it to me as the town's marshal. You should give this to Anthony."

"I do *nicht* like *Herr* Anthony. I believe he *ist nicht* vhat he claims to be," Mikman said, getting red beneath his massive beard. "He vill *nicht* to face *Herr* Cross. He vill run *und der* town vill suffer."

Fumbling in his pockets, Dane finally found the key to the jail shed and handed it to the mayor. "Well, how about turning the shed over to Tess? Did they like that idea?"

Mikman shook his head, before answering. "*Nein.* They decided to leave it as a jail until *Herr* Anthony *und* Sheriff Stockton could decide. They did *nicht* think *der* tree vould be satisfactory. Especially when you are *nicht der* marshal." He pointed in the direction of the large cottonwood.

After a few minutes of disjointed conversation, the saddened mayor left and Dane forced himself to return to his work. He looked over at where the squirrel ate, but the little animal was gone.

"You, too, huh?" he muttered, and looked for his bellows.

After a few minutes of renewing his fire, Trash Tess pushed through the shop doors. She was smiling and immediately told him about a "purty red burd" she had just seen and withdrew a small red feather from her large purse. She pointed to the coffee mug and Dane quickly brought her a filled cup.

"Sugar? I wans sugar this time," she declared.

Dane shook his head. He didn't use sugar and didn't have any at his workplace. "I'm sorry, Tess, but I don't have any sugar."

"Nex' time ya has sugar." She sipped the hot brew, frowning.

"Yes, I will, Tess."

She nodded and took another sip. This time she smiled at him. Sort of a cockeyed smile, but definitely a smile.

"Thank you, Jerr-i-koo," she muttered.

"You're welcome, Tess."

He asked if she was getting enough to eat and he thought she indicated she was, then he asked where she had been sleeping at night. The question annoyed her. He wasn't certain if it seemed to be prying, or if she didn't understand. He tried again.

"Are you sleeping in the alley next to Carter's restaurant?" he asked.

She sipped her coffee and made no attempt to answer.

"You are welcome to sleep here, Tess," he said and pointed toward the storeroom. "I will get you a cot to sleep on. And blankets. What do you think?"

She handed him back the half-drunk mug and shook her head. "Moth'r an' fath'r wou'd miss me."

He took the mug and didn't know how to respond. She waved cheerfully and left. He watched her go; her walk was a lumbering one, stiff and uneven. Her mind was that of a small child's—or was it? He told himself to talk with Mary about getting a cot and fixing up the shed, in case Tess changed her mind. Unless Mary had a better idea.

Later that evening, he and Mary had supper at Carter's, enjoying each other's company. Their eyes engaged each other's and spoke of romantic things to come. Mary couldn't hide her feelings of relief that Dane was no longer responsible for the law enforcement in the town. At the same time, she was incensed that the council had so callously fired him—and hired, of all people, Xavier Anthony.

"What do you think Rudolph Cross will do?" she finally asked, sipping her coffee.

Dane pursed his sore lips. "He's going to take Kill Pond, then I think he'll take control of the town."

"Oh, you can't be serious," she said, louder than intended.

"Oh, I'm serious." Dane took a small bite of his remaining steak. "He'll get rid of Mikman and Reicker." He nodded. "He'll get rid of me. Probably Clell Edwards or one of the other ranchers, too, to scare the others. That would put everything in place. His own cousin as sheriff. Now Anthony as marshal."

Mary's hand sought his. Her face was crumpled with concern. "Don't say that, Jericho. Please. Don't. It should be enough that you aren't the marshal anymore. Won't it?"

Dane started to respond when the restaurant door opened and Xavier Anthony made a grand entrance. A few steps behind him were the three councilmen who voted him in—McCormick, Ringley and Lindsay—looking happy. Anthony held out his cane to reinforce the attention he had already received from the restaurant patrons and grandly announced that peace had come to the region.

"I have Rudolph Cross's word on it," Anthony said proudly

and added, "He was very upset with the way his men had been handled in the last two days, in town and near Kill Pond, by our former marshal." He spotted Dane, who hadn't turned around to watch his performance. "There is a time for violence, and there is a time for making friends. I have made an important friend for Torsmill."

There was scattered applause, along with glances in Dane's direction. The blacksmith resumed talking with Mary as if there had never been an interruption. The topic changed to finding some place for Trash Tess to stay. He told her his idea for giving her the jail shed had been rejected by the town council.

"The mayor liked the idea," Dane said. "He's given Carter money for her meals."

"I hear you have, too."

Dane's face reddened. "And you have given her clothes."

"Haven't seen her today; have you, my love?" Mary asked, noticing the late-arriving foursome was moving through the restaurant to an open table.

Dane nodded. "I forgot to ask if she's eaten here tonight."

"We'll do that when we leave."

"Sure." Dane felt Anthony's presence. The other three men continued to their assigned table.

"Good evening, Jericho," Anthony said loudly. "I presume you just heard my meeting with Rudolph Cross was a successful one. I asked Sheriff Stockton to join me. He was happy to do so. Holds no bad feelings—against Torsmill."

Without looking up, Dane said, "I truly hope that is so, Xavier. I truly do."

"Oh, by the way, he and I wired Ranger headquarters and told them a Ranger was not needed." Anthony held his cane in both hands at his waist. "I understand you had wired them earlier to send someone." His smile stayed with his mouth and didn't reach his eyes. "You seem to see danger everywhere, Jericho. I had a lieutenant who was always seeing the enemy when none was there."

Laying his fork against his plate, Dane started to say something, but Mary spoke first. "Mr. Anthony, you are interrupting our supper. Please find your seat with your friends. We really aren't interested in hearing any of your fairy tales."

Anthony's face turned crimson and he lifted his cane as if to strike her.

"That's the third dumb thing you've done today, Anthony," Dane said. "Put the cane down—and go sit."

Flustered and wary of Dane's reaction, Anthony lowered the cane and spun around.

Shifting his attention, Dane told Mary of his plan to create sleeping quarters for Tess in his small second room within his shop but she hadn't seemed interested. Mary smiled and told him that she had taken Tess into her house. Tess had used it last night for the first time.

"Dad's bedroom hadn't been used since . . . he passed." Her eyes fluttered. "Tess seemed to like it."

Shaking his head, Dane said, "Well, no wonder. Why didn't she tell me that?"

"She likes you, Jericho. She probably didn't know what to say, without hurting your feelings. I'm going to have her do some work at the store. Tasks she can handle, I think." Mary smiled. "But I love you for caring about her."

Dane smiled. "I love you."

"Not as much as I love you, Jericho Dane."

Their long kiss good night outside of Mary's house kept him warm all night long.

IX

Early the next morning, Dane went to the general store. Before he started work. He just wanted to see Mary. And hear her voice. As he stepped inside, he saw Mary—with Tess—in the back of the store. Tess was wearing a freshly laundered dress with her face and hands scrubbed clean. Mary was showing her how to straighten some shelves of canned goods.

He wasn't surprised to see the mentally slow woman there after Mary's comments last night.

"This is Tess's first day working in the store," Mary announced, and stepped back so Dane could see the woman carefully turning cans on a shelf so they could easily be read.

"Good day, Jerr-i-koo," Tess said. "I am stayin' wit' Miss Mary. Is that all ri't?"

Dane bit his lower lip. "Tess, I think that's wonderful."

"Can I still come for coffee?"

"I sure hope you will. I would be unhappy if you didn't."

"Do you haff sugar?"

Dane chuckled. "I'm buying some right now."

Tess beamed, and glanced at Mary, who smiled.

A can spun out of Tess's hand and crashed to the floor. She looked up with a worried look on her face. "I sorry. I can't . . ."

"You're fine, Tess. Just fine." Smiling, Mary picked up the can and handed it to Tess. "It happens to me all the time."

Tess glanced at Dane. "Jerr-i-koo, I didn' mean to."

He nodded. "You're doing a good job, Tess. A very good job."

Mary leaned forward and kissed him on the cheek

Tess watched and giggled. "Mary kissed Jerr-i-koo."

Two customers entered and Dane excused himself, gathered a small sack of sugar and laid coins on the counter. As he paused at the opened door, Mary blew him a kiss and Tess waved.

At his blacksmith shop, he put the sugar in the tool shed, then shed his coat and shirt and put on his apron. Quickly, the fire at his forge took control of the irons he laid there. With his tongs, he carried one iron to his anvil and began striking it with his hammer. Hours passed and only the squirrel interrupted his work—and the occasional cup of coffee. Most of his thoughts were about Mary as he finished a lap weld in a wagon tire and hinges, piled in stacks of five.

He was surprised to see a familiar figure standing a few feet away.

It was J. R. Reicker.

"Need to talk with ya a minute."

"Sure."

"Got a bad case o' the worries," the older man said, sliding into the work area, his face curled with disgust. "That simple fool Anthony. He thought takin' your prisoner back early was gonna turn Cross into his buddy." He took the unlit cigar from his mouth, looked at it and continued, "I reckon he'll just stand 'round smilin' while Cross takes over. Won't know thar's a problem 'til they decide to git rid o' him, too."

"Not much I can do about it," Dane said.

Reicker returned the cigar to the left side of his mouth. "True. But did ya know Stockton an' two of Cross's men jes' rode into town?"

Dane frowned. "He's the county sheriff."

"Well, they dun pulled up in front of Miss Tressian's place. Goin' in."

"Why didn't you say that before?"

"Gittin' to it."

"I'm going over there." Dane rushed toward the doors.

"Figgered."

A few steps from the doors, the blacksmith spun around to take off his apron and put on his shirt, long coat and hat. In minutes, he was at the door to the general store, telling himself that he wasn't looking for trouble, just making certain Mary was in no danger. His hand went to the gun in his pocket, then retreated to his side.

Turning toward the sound of Dane entering, Stockton's face became a snarl as he realized who it was. His cheek and jaw were swollen with streaks of purple and yellow painted across them. His movements were stiff from the beating.

"*Salut*. Look who's here," the closest cowboy, Lecaunesse, proclaimed as he twisted toward the door opening.

The second, stocky man with a tied-down hat and knee-length

chaps, who had been at Dane's shop yesterday, snorted agreement. "The damn blacksmith."

"How convenient," Stockton said, and winced. "After I talked with my girl, I was coming to your shop to arrest you for the attempted murder of two Cross men yesterday. Thanks for saving me the trouble."

Mary straightened; her eyebrows did the same. "The only ones who should be arrested are that awful bunch of Cross cowboys who attacked us, and tried to kill Jericho." Her finger became a negative wave. "And I am certainly not your girl. I am Jericho's."

The customer being helped nervously said he and his wife would come back later and headed for the door, leaving Mary holding the half-filled basket. Dane stepped aside to let them pass, touching the brim of his hat in greeting.

Not realizing what was happening, Tess eagerly brought a can of tomatoes forward and held it out to Lecaunesse. "Do ya wanna can of 'matoes? They be purty."

"*Quoi*? Get away, you worthless tramp!" He backhanded Tess, driving the can from her hand and clipping the side of her cheek with his swing.

She stumbled backward and fell, whimpering. Dane was beside her almost before she fell. He spoke softly to her, asserting that it was all right, that the man was bad-mannered. Mary came quickly to his side and patted Tess's shoulder. Tess stared at Mary with questions in her eyes. Both Dane and Mary helped her stand.

When Dane looked up, Stockton and the two Cross cowboys held revolvers pointed at him.

"Like I said, blacksmith, you're under arrest for attempted murder," Stockton growled. "You're going with us. To that jail shed you like so much."

A slight noise behind them came and went with none of them glancing in its direction.

From the back of the store came Reicker's gruff demand. "What seems to be the problem, Sheriff Stockton?" He had entered through the back door.

His eyebrows arching in annoyance, Stockon glanced in Reicker's direction, as did the other two men. Enough to see the old judge held a long-barreled Navy Colt.

"Oh, glad to see you, Judge Reicker," Stockton said over his shoulder, keeping his attention on Dane. "I was just arresting Jericho Dane here for the attempted murder of two Cross men.

Happened yesterday, near Kill Pond. He wounded them. Luckily, none were hurt bad. The others drove him off."

"I see."

Stockton's smile was gathered at the right corner of his mouth. "Yeah, I'm taking him to the jail shed. Hold him there until the circuit judge gets here. A week or so, I reckon."

Dane was taut; he hadn't expected this. Mary held onto his arm. Tess looked at Mary and took hold of the blacksmith's same arm.

"No. No, ya aren't." The words were like bullets from the old judge.

Stockton spun around and snarled, "What the hell do you mean? I'm the county law here." He remembered Dane and whirled back.

Dane hadn't moved.

"Yah, that ya be. Fer the moment," Reicker said. "Reckon the county'll wise up soon 'nuff. Meantime, we're gonna have us a hearin' on this matter. If the evidence warrants, we'll hold Mr. Dane fer trial. With the honorable Judge Weisner presiding. Whenev'r he gits hyar."

Stockton wasn't sure how to respond. He didn't like knowing the old man's revolver was pointed at his midsection. His shoulders rose and fell.

"All right. A hearing it is," he agreed. "I'll take him to the jail shed and—"

"No ag'in, Sheriff. Mr. Dane'll be allowed to work. On his word that he won't go nowhar." Reicker motioned with his gun. "Do I have yur word on that, Mr. Dane?"

"You have my word, Judge. I'll be here. In Torsmill."

"Good. You boys put away that iron." Reicker swung his gun back toward Stockton, waited for the three men to reholster their weapons, then continued, "We'll have the hearin' at Carter's place. Say, ten o'clock. Tomorry mornin'." He pointed with the revolver. "An' you, Sheriff, you are responsible for bringin' the Cross men who were there. All seven o' them as witnesses."

The stocky cowboy asked, "How do you know it was seven?"

"Shut up," Stockton said, then softened his response to Reicker. "But, Judge, remember, two are wounded."

"Don't reckon their ridin' in a buckboard will hurt 'em none. Ya said yurse'f they weren't hurt bad. Ya bring 'em," Reicker declared.

"If all o' them ain't hyar for the hearin', I'll figger they ain't tellin' it true."

Stockton was unable to speak. He looked at the frowning cowboys, who waited for his direction. None came.

"Reckon ya boys better git to goin'. Wouldn't want to be late for the hearin', would ya?" Reicker said.

"Just a minute, Judge. Please." Dane spotted Tess's fallen tomato can, walked over and picked it up. He took three steps and slammed it into the stomach of Lecaunesse, then dropped the can at his feet. The cowboy bent over and grabbed for the pain.

"Don't ever do that again." Dane stepped back, next to Tess and Mary. "Apologize to Tess."

The Frenchman slowly straightened, tried to take a deep breath, but couldn't. "*Pardon, mademoiselle.*" He bowed slightly.

"Watching you hang is going to be one of my favorite days," Stockton said, pointing at Dane.

The blacksmith stared at him, both hands in his pockets. His right hand was curled around his revolver.

Stockton avoided the glare by heading for the door.

"*Oui*, a favorite day," Lecaunesse said, rubbing his stomach with his hand as he hurried after Stockton.

The second cowboy studied Dane, glanced at Mary and Tess, then at Reicker. He mumbled, "Bringin' 'em in ain't smart." He realized the other two had left, hitched up his chaps and rushed out without looking back.

Dane went to the door and watched them ride away. Mary was quickly at his side, seeking his hand with hers.

"Oh, Jericho. Jericho. This is terrible. Won't it ever end?" she said.

Turning toward her, Dane said, "Not until Cross is stopped—or several of us are dead."

She winced and looked at the closed door.

Tess waddled over, clutching a can of peaches. "Wanna see a purty can?" She held it up for Dane to examine.

Forcing the best smile he could make, Dane said, "Why, sure, Tess. I would like that. Thank you." He accepted the can and studied it. "Oh, you're right, Tess, it is very pretty."

Tess beamed. "Thar is lots more."

"Well, good. I'll buy this one then."

She shook her head in affirmation and looked at Mary for approval.

Walking toward them, Reicker shoved his gun into his coat pocket, then adjusted the cigar in his mouth. "Yur gonna haff to be yur own lawyer, boy. Better talk with Lester Wilson. He'll testify ya were headin' out fer a picnic, when ya rented that buggy from his place—an' how ya looked comin' back."

"I will. Thanks for stepping in, J. R.," Dane said. "That was going to turn nasty."

"Yah. Had me a feelin' ya was never gonna git to that shed."

Dane nodded agreement.

Waving her arms to interrupt, Mary added that she would testify to the whole event from beginning to end.

"Bin a'chewin' on that, missy." Reicker rolled his shoulders as if to relieve an unseen burden. "Ol' man Cross'll figure yur the key to this. If they kin keep ya from testifyin', then it's Dane's word agin' all them." He shook his head. "Not sure I could rule on that thar."

Understood was that Reicker meant he wouldn't be able to declare Dane innocent in that case and he would have to be bound over for trial.

"I will be there, Mr. Reicker." Mary folded her arms defiantly.

After Dane purchased the can of peaches, the rest of the day was a blur to Dane. He had supper with Mary, and Tess joined them. He talked with Lester Wilson, the livery owner, who said it would be a pleasure to tell what he knew, adding that it was time the town stood up to Cross. Sleep didn't want to come and Dane finally gave up and sat at his table, drinking coffee and writing notes.

After washing and shaving, he put on his one suit, now with a hole in the pocket, decided against carrying his revolver and headed out. It was nearly nine twenty. He and Mary had agreed to meet at her store at half-past. For luck, he stopped at his shop, left five pieces of bread for his visiting squirrel, then went to her store. She wasn't there. The store was dark.

At a quarter to ten, he decided she must be waiting for him at the restaurant and walked there. Marshal Xavier Anthony was standing outside Carter's. A table had been set up outside to hold any guns. Twenty or so gunbelts and several loose revolvers rested on its surface. Dane guessed most were Cross weapons.

"Good morning, Mr. Dane," Anthony said. His eyes delighted in the situation. "Sheriff Stockton is already inside—with his witnesses." He cocked his head to the side. "I need to check you over to make sure you're not carrying."

"Do your duty, Marshal," Dane said. "Is Miss Tressian inside?"

"Haven't seen her today, Dane. Why?"

Dane shook his head. "Nothing that can't wait."

X

With no expression, Marshal Anthony advised him that a wagon was waiting to take him to Waco where he would be held for trial. Dane told him to plan to use it for getting cloth and continued inside before Anthony could respond. His mind was whirling with worry. Mary would be here unless something had happened to her.

Everything in him wanted to turn and run to her house, but he knew that would be the excuse Cross and Stockton wanted to hunt him down and kill him. He must prepare himself mentally to go through the hearing without her. With luck, he would look for her later. He had no other choice. His heart was slamming against his chest.

He froze a few steps into the restaurant. *Mary, where are you? Please, God, don't let her be hurt. Please!*

The restaurant was rearranged for the hearing and packed with townspeople; a dozen Cross men had cornered the front tables. The rest of the restaurant was lined with additional interested people, standing and waiting. At the back, one table had been set off by itself for Reicker to preside. One chair was placed for the judge; another at the table's edge for witnesses. Two other tables had been arranged a few feet away, one for the prosecution, one for the defense. Stockton was already sitting at the farthest.

Rudolph Cross sat at the table closest to Stockton. At his table were the two wounded cowboys and others. The grizzled roper had his arm in a sling; Hogan, who had roped him around the neck, was, ironically, wearing a neck bandage. The blacksmith felt his raw neck in reflex. Winslow Tatum completed the table.

At another table, he saw Hollis Walker, the cowboy he had arrested for shooting in the Longhorn Saloon. Walker looked like a boy who had just been told today was Christmas. Sitting beside him was the Mexican rider, Lecaunesse and the bucktoothed cowboy. The stocky man from the store yesterday was sitting at another table with three other Cross men.

Cross saw Dane enter and said something to Hogan, who turned around and met the blacksmith's gaze. Hogan sneered and mouthed, "A dead man ye be."

Ignoring the threat, Dane looked around and saw Lester Wilson sitting with the mayor. Dane nodded and both returned the greeting. Dane took a step forward, then stopped. He needed to talk with Mikman. About Mary. He backtracked and slid between tables, receiving encouragement from various townspeople. He moved past the table with three councilmen—Harold Ringley, Gerald McCormick and Edward Lindsay—and another townsman. None of them attempted to greet him.

Mikman stood as Dane came to his table. "*Herr* Marshal. This is *nicht* a *gut* day for Torsmill. It *ist nicht*."

"Fred, I need a favor."

"Anything for *du*. Anything."

Dane told him about Mary's absence and wondered if he would go to her house and check on her. Mikman quietly agreed and left.

As Dane sat down at the table reserved for the defendant, J. R. Reicker entered from the kitchen and took his position behind the first table. In his right hand was a gavel. He made a simple statement that the purpose of a preliminary hearing was to determine whether sufficient evidence existed for the accused to be bound over for actual trial.

A Cross cowboy at a middle front table yelled, "Hang the no-good bastard. He tried to kill our friends."

At the next table, Lecaunesse grinned and agreed, "*Oui*. Hang thees bastard."

Reicker slammed the gavel against the table. No one saw Henry Carter wince, watching from the kitchen. "One more shout like that an' I'll clear this hyar place. Cross, I expect ya to holt your boys in line."

Cross glared at Reicker, then turned regally in his chair. "All o' you, shut up. This is a courtroom. We are here for justice. For my men."

That brought snickers, but Reicker ignored them. Instead, he withdrew his Navy Colt and placed it on the table. "Let's make real sure we all understand what's goin' on hyar." His voice was strong and confident. "The issue before me—and me alone—is to determine jes' what went on yestiday, out thar near Kill Pond, between these seven Cross cowboys an' Mr. Dane." He paused and fingered the gavel resting on the table. "Thar ain't no argument 'bout a shootin' happenin'—it did—jes' whether or not it were self-defense on Mr. Dane's part, or attempted murder. That's the decidin' part. If'n I decide it were attempted murder, Mr. Dane'll be sent away for trial by Circuit Court Judge Weisner. If'n I decide it were self-defense, he goes free. An' that's it. Clear 'nuff to ev'r-body?"

"Get on with it, Reicker. We all know what the bastard tried to do."

The tables of Cross cowboys shouted their support of Rudolph Cross's statement.

Reicker pounded his gavel again and the rancher told his men to be quiet. The room became very still.

"Sheriff Stockton, is the prosecution ready?" Reicker asked, looking at the county lawman.

"We sure are, Judge. Pretty cut an' dried."

Reicker turned to Dane. "Is the defendant ready?"

Dane took a deep breath and stood. "Not quite, Your Honor."

The restaurant-courtroom wormed with a mixture of gasps, laughs, howls and mumbled observations.

Reicker vigorously pounded the table again. His ears wiggled in response to the pounding. Carter came from the kitchen with a wood cutting board and suggested the judge use it to hit on instead of his table. Reicker nodded without paying any attention to the offering.

"Mr. Dane, please tell this hyar court wha' the problem be?" The judge's face was tense.

"My key witness, Miss Tressian, is not here," Dane announced, looking directly at Cross. "The only reason for that—someone is holding her against her will."

"Cross, jes' what the hell are ya tryin' to pull?" Reicker's face was even harder.

The malicious rancher threw up his heavy arms. His reddening face made his beard look even more like it was a disguise. "Hey, wait a damn minute. I don't know what the hell this blacksmith's talkin' about." He looked around at the men at his table. "Maybe the lady decided she didn't want to be a part of a lie."

"You son of a bitch!" Dane ran at the sneering rancher.

Big Juan jumped to his feet with a short-barreled Colt in his hands.

"Stop, Jericho!" Reicker yelled. "Not here, son. Not in my court. I mean it. Stop."

Dane skidded to a halt; his eyes tore into the cattleman. He hadn't noticed the Mexican with the gun.

Reicker had.

"Put that thar gun down, cowboy. Lay it on the table," Reicker growled. In his hand was the Navy Colt. "I won't say it again."

After a nod from Cross, Big Juan laid the weapon on the table and sat, looking around as if nothing had happened.

"Marshal Anthony, I want this hyar man arrested. He was tolt to come into my court unarmed. That'll be two days in jail or twenty dollars for contempt of court. My court."

Lecaunesse leaned against the Mexican and whispered. Big Juan's eyes widened and he thought for a moment about grabbing his gun, but a glance at Reicker changed his mind. The judge was pointing the big Colt at him.

At the back of the room, Marshal Anthony appeared surprised at the judge's order. He hesitated and looked around, as if expecting it to have been directed at someone else. He swallowed and found his voice.

"Judge, I think that's a bit harsh. The gentleman was only trying to defend his boss against an attack from Dane." Anthony looked only at Cross as he spoke. "I'll not be a party to this."

"No worry, Xavier," Cross's voice boomed across the crowded room. "I'll pay the fine." He reached into his vest pocket, retrieved a twenty-dollar gold piece and tossed it toward Reicker.

The coin bounced on the table and onto the floor, where it spun for a few seconds and settled. Reicker made no attempt to get it.

Instead, he said, "Sheriff Stockton, bring that thar gun to me."

Reluctantly, Stockton shoved back his chair, retrieved the gun and the coin, laid them on Reicker's table and returned to his seat. As soon as he sat, Stockton challenged Dane's delay, noting that he had made the effort to bring all the men involved to the trial on time—even those who were wounded.

Reicker spoke through gritted teeth. "Reluctantly, I dun agree wi' yah. Sheriff Stockton, present yur first witness."

Smiling widely, Stockton announced, "Yes, Your Honor. I call Winslow Tatum, foreman of the Cross ranch, to the stand."

Reicker pointed to the empty chair pushed up against his table and Tatum sat, glaring at Dane. His right pockmarked cheek carried a red streak from Mary's whipping. After Reicker swore him in, he asked the foreman to tell what had happened. His story was that the seven riders were ambushed by Dane when they rode to the stream just north of Kill Pond. They fought back, but two of his men were wounded and Dane got away. He finished and beamed.

"Mr. Tatum, for my understandin', would ya have the six other men who were at the shootin' hold up thar hands, so we kin see who they be?"

Tatum smiled. "'Course, Judge. Hold up your hand if'n you were one of the boys Dane tried to kill. There's the two who were shot." He pointed at the wounded men.

Laughing and chiding each other, all of the riders raised their hands. The grizzled roper held up his left arm, the one not in a sling.

Reicker acknowledged their identification and turned to the blacksmith. "Ya be doin' any cross-examination, Mr. Dane?"

Tatum's expression popped into uneasiness. "What do you mean?"

"Different use of the word 'cross.' Rudolph Cross can't protect you here. The judge means you're going to have to tell the truth, Tatum," Dane said, standing and walking toward the seated foreman. "You gave your oath to that. You realize if you lie in this courtroom you can go to jail."

"I told the truth."

"Really? Let's take a look at it, shall we?" Dane said and stood a few feet in front of Tatum. "I've got a witness who will swear I was out there in a buggy with Miss Tressian. For a picnic."

"Never saw no buggy. No gal with you either." He glanced at Stockton, who looked away.

"Be careful, Tatum. This is a courtroom. You're not back at the Cross Ranch," Dane said.

Tatum's fleeting glimpse at Cross came back to Dane as a frown.

Hogan yelled out, "So what if ye be havin' a buggy?"

Reicker told the cowboy to be quiet and asked Dane to proceed.

"All right, Tatum. If I shot at you boys from ambush, where was I?"

"Ah, behind a tree near the pond. An old cottonwood tree. Yessir, that's it," Tatum hurried his answer. A bead of sweat glistened from his forehead.

"So I opened fire on seven armed men from behind a cottonwood—with a revolver, is that it?"

The room burst into nervous laughter.

Tatum edged forward in his chair. "It wasn't like that."

Dane walked away from him, headed toward where Stockton

sat, then spun around to face the foreman. "How did I know you were going to be there?"

Red wandered up from Tatum's neck. "How the hell should I know? I ain't your keeper."

Chuckles came from the Cross tables.

"Well, that's an interesting response, Tatum. Do you really think a busy blacksmith would ride out there, hide behind a tree, and hope you might come some time, but not knowing when?" Dane's mouth curled into a snarl. "Or isn't the truth that you and your men came upon our buggy . . . Miss Tressian and myself . . . and tried to kill me? Isn't that how I got these cuts and bruises on my face, and this rope burn on my neck? Isn't that cut on your face from Miss Tressian fighting you with the buggy whip? Isn't the only reason I'm alive today because I shot at the men who held me with ropes? Isn't that the truth, Tatum? Tell me. Now."

"I protest, Judge. Dane's trying to badger the witness," Stockton said.

"Didn' sound like sech to me. Answer them questions, Mr. Tatum," Reicker demanded. "Yur under oath, boy."

"While you're at it, where's Mary?" Dane stepped so close to Tatum that their boots touched. "If any of you bastards have hurt her, you'll never have a safe day."

"Hey, that's a threat," Stockton yelled. "He's threatening the witness."

Dane spun and walked over to Stockton's table. "No, it's not a threat, Stockton. It's a promise." He glared at Cross, who chuckled.

The door of the restaurant burst open and an excited Mikman entered with a Winchester in his hands. "*Ach du lieber*! I *haff* found Miss Mary!"

A step behind him came Mary Tressian. In her hands was the Colt she kept at her store. She stepped into the restaurant and pointed at Tatum. "That man and his henchmen tried to murder Mr. Dane. I was there. I saw it all." She wiped a tear seeking relief from her left eye. "Two of those awful men came into my home this morning and tied me up so I couldn't be here." She choked and swallowed. "They hit Tess and locked her up—sweet Tess—when she tried to stop them."

Behind her a few steps came a bewildered Tess. The side of her face was red. When she saw the Mexican and the Frenchman at the front table, she jumped and pointed. "That's 'em, Miss Mary. They hurt me. They tied you up. They did. They did."

From his far table, Lester Wilson sprang to his feet. "That's been enough of this nonsense. Jericho Dane's been an outstanding citizen, and an excellent marshal. He rented a buggy from me to take Miss Tressian for a picnic. She was with him." He focused on Cross's back. "I helped him from that buggy when they came in. He was all beat up. Had a rope burn on his neck. Those good-for-nothing Cross cowboys tried to kill him."

Holding his big Colt, Reicker declared, "I've dun heard 'nuff. My rulin' is self-defense, pure an' simple. Mr. Dane's innocent." He pointed the gun in the direction of the rattled foreman. "Mr. Tatum an' them other six riders are hereby charged wi' assault an' attempted murder. They'll be held for trial."

Cross was on his feet. Spit flew from his mouth as he yelled, "You old goat! You aren't holding my men. I run this county."

From behind them, Mikman declared, "*Du* do *nicht* own this town, *Herr* Cross. Those men are under arrest as Judge Reicker has ruled. *Ja*."

Both the mayor and Mary pointed their guns at Cross and waited. Grabbing the cowboy's gun on his table, Reicker tossed it in Dane's direction. The blacksmith caught the weapon, drew back the hammer and held it ready.

Slowly pushing his chair back to the table, Cross walked toward the door without looking back or saying a word. Several of his men followed, including Hollis Walker. The cowboy paused and turned to look back at Dane.

"Damn," Walker muttered and walked on.

As Cross reached the door, Marshal Anthony hurried over to tell him that he had a fine new suit made for him, a gift. Cross snorted, shoved him away and left.

When Lecaunesse and Big Juan casually stood, Reicker barked, "Hold it ri't thar. The six o' ya—an' Tatum hyar—stay put. 'Member I know'd who ya be. I'll shoot any o' ya tryin' to leave my court."

Stockton stood, nervously grasping and ungrasping the back of his chair. He found the courage to ask the judge where the men were going to be held until the trial. Reicker didn't hesitate and declared they would be tied to the corral outside the livery. He looked back at Lester Wilson, who nodded his approval.

"I declare this hyar hearin' adjourned. It's over." Reicker waved his gun for emphasis.

"Judge, wait a minute," Dane said. "Tess pointed at the men who tied Mary—and hurt her. Who were they?"

Mary pointed at Lecaunesse and Big Juan. "Those two. They did it."

Glancing at Mary, Tess began jumping and pointing.

His eyes full of fury, Dane moved toward them and only Mary's words stopped him. "Don't, Jericho. Tess and I are all right. I promise."

Reicker said, "We'll add assault to their charges."

On the way to his ranch, an enraged Rudolph Cross began barking orders. He wanted his men to take over Kill Pond and hold it, no matter what. He would lead the attack himself. He would also send a rider to Waco to find the noted gunfighter, Greystoke Matson.

Cross had talked about it before. He looked around and his eyes settled on the young, bucktoothed rider. He told him to get a fresh horse and supplies when they got to the ranch.

"Find Greystoke Matson. Tell him I'll pay anything he wants," the big rancher said, then corrected himself. "No, I'll give you a note for him. I'll pay him five hundred dollars to shoot that damn blacksmith." He wiped his hand across his mouth to remove the spittle. "I'll pay him the same to get rid of Clell Edwards, too. And that idiot mayor. And that damn old judge. I'll give you some money to take along to pay for his expenses." He glared at the riders. "It's way past time we took control, boys."

The bucktoothed rider proclaimed, "Hell, boss, I'll get rid of that blacksmith for a hundred."

"Yeah, and Stockton was gonna whip his ass—an' then he was gonna hang him," Cross declared, yanking on the reins to keep his horse from lowering its head. "No. We're gonna turn Kill Pond into the Cross Pond." He smiled and looked around for support. "Greystoke Matson will do the cleaning up."

Positive remarks erupted as he viewed each rider. Even Stockton muttered his agreement through swollen lips.

"Stockton, you're gonna get with that idiot town marshal, the clothes-makin' bastard," Cross growled. "My boys aren't gonna stay tied to no goddamn corral. Get 'em loose. I don't care how you do it, but do it." He pushed against his cheek with his tongue. "Send 'em to the north-line shack. Tell 'em to stay there until I say different."

XI

Two weeks later, the town was still buzzing over the escape of the seven Cross men from the jail-corral. It had happened a week ago, at night. Marshal Anthony claimed no knowledge of the situation and refused to form a posse to look for them, stating he had no jurisdiction outside of town. Reicker and Mikman were furious, but the town council stood behind Anthony. Sheriff Stockton hadn't been in town since the Dane hearing.

But a new subject for town gossip had just arrived. Greystoke Matson stepped off the morning stage and changed everything with nothing more than the implied threat of his presence. People up and down the main street chattered about the dashing appearance of the well-known pistol fighter. The so-called jailbreak was forgotten for the moment.

They were fascinated by his long blond hair resting on his shoulders, set off by a wide-brimmed, flat hat; his matching pearl-handled pistols stuck in a red sash under a fashionable cutaway coat; his knee-length boots with the inlaid leather tops and the big Mexican silver spurs making sweet music as he sauntered around the coach to get a first look at the town.

No one seemed to notice Greystoke Matson carried a Bible in his left hand.

Mostly, though, the town talked about the reason for Matson being in Torsmill. It seemed obvious enough: Rudolph Cross had hired him. On the day before the corral escape, Cross's men had taken control of Kill Pond, and now guarded it night and day with armed men. They had also taken control of all the grazing land around the water. Attempts by the small ranches to drive them off had been futile.

The flamboyant gunfighter stretched and accepted his valise from the driver, who was exceptionally polite. The sideburned driver spat a long stream of tobacco juice and recommended the Vander Hotel.

Matson handed the driver a coin and asked him to take his luggage to the hotel, and that he would be along shortly.

"Ah, sure. Sure thing, Mr. Matson," the driver said, spat again. "Soon as I get the rest of this luggage out."

"I see. Where can one get a reasonably good meal?" Matson asked, setting the valise beside the driver and adjusting his wide-brimmed hat to shield the aggressive sun. He was a precise man, priggish, speaking with the high-pitched steel of growing up in northern Maine.

"Ah, Carter's restaurant. Over there. Most folks speak kindly of it."

"I will let you know if your recommendation was worthy." Matson walked away without looking at the driver.

The other passengers exited the coach and watched Matson head for the restaurant, and waited for their baggage to be lifted down. One passenger in a wrinkled suit noted that Matson had read the Bible most of the way.

Matson entered the restaurant, strutting like a grand duke. He paused and took in the nearly full establishment and headed for the farthest table, which was occupied.

"Good morning to you, sir," Matson said politely, standing beside the table.

"Same to you," came the annoyed reply from Gerald McCormick, who had just begun eating.

"This is my table, sir," Matson said in the same tone.

"Naw, it's mine." The town's lumber company owner shoved a large forkful of eggs and ham into his mouth, ignoring the cold-faced gunfighter.

Without further comment, Matson grabbed McCormick's shirt with his right hand and yanked him from his chair and onto the restaurant floor. The wooden chair sailed backward and banged against the far wall. Landing with a thud, the lumberman choked on his mouthful of food, then finally spit it out. Gerald McCormick stared up at Matson, a mixture of shock and infuriation on his face. Until he noticed the guns and realized who he was looking at.

"A-are you t-the one t-they call t-the P-Preacher?" he asked without moving from his sprawled position. "T-the s-shootist?"

"I have been called that, among other names," Matson said shrilly.

"Oh my, I didn't realize," McCormick said.

"Waiter, this man wants his food moved over there." Matson pointed at the paunchy waiter and then at a table halfway to the front. "He wants it moved now."

Hearing the noise, Henry Carter peered through the ajar kitchen door of his restaurant at the newcomer and the stunned townsman on the floor. Carter didn't know who the stranger was and didn't care. Carter swung open the door and went to the downed McCormick.

"How did this happen, Mr. McCormick?" Carter said, looking at Matson, who had retrieved the chair and was seating himself at the table.

Matson's smile was like that of a wolf. "I don't really know. One minute he was moving to a new table, the next he was down there. Clumsy, I suppose."

"Yeah, sure," Carter said.

"It's all right, my friend. Time for me to be going to work. I'm not hungry anyway." McCormick placed a hand on Carter's arm.

Carter told the lumberman that he would bring him a new meal, at no cost to him. McCormick declined and hurried toward the door.

Matson removed his hat and laid it on the table over the Bible he carried. "Are you the owner of this establishment?"

"Yeah, I am."

Carter told the nearest waiter to bring a wet towel to wipe up the regurgitated food. Matson pointed to McCormick's plate of food and asked that it be removed immediately. The mustached waiter handed the towel to Carter and stepped to the table and removed the plate, utensils and mug. Carter took the offered towel and picked up the food in it with one deft motion.

"I will expect this table to be available at all times—for me," Matson declared.

"What?" Carter frowned and studied the gunfighter.

"I said, 'I will expect this table to be available at all times—for me.' " Without waiting for any response, Matson said, "I want hot tea, freshly brewed. Two eggs. Poached. As soon as the whites coagulate, remove them. Toast lightly buttered. Crusts removed." He rubbed his chin. "If you have some good ham, I would like a slice. Not too thick. Some potatoes would be nice. If they're thinly sliced and crispy." Matson waved his hand to assist in his order without looking at the exasperated Carter.

The waiter whispered into Carter's ear and the owner frowned. He left and returned immediately with a cup brimming with hot tea.

"Your breakfast will be ready shortly, Mr. Matson," Carter said, rubbing his hands nervously.

"I am certain it will." Matson reached for the sugar bowl and scooped a spoonful from it into the hot brew.

He sipped his tea, decided it needed more sugar. He lifted his spoon again and was securing a heaping spoonful, appearing to not notice the frightful exiting of the other customers. He glanced at the good book beneath his hat. Reading it was a daily ritual, established by his mother. His older brother, David, did the same, and was a deacon in the church in the small town in Maine where they had grown up. He also owned a fine hotel.

Greystoke Matson didn't like attending church, but reading Scripture had become entwined in his habits, in spite of his deadly ways. Their mother had been a most righteous woman, who prayed often and thought Greystoke was earmarked for hell and David was a true blessing from God. She had died from pneumonia seven years ago, praying for Greystoke's soul to the very end. Neither brother ever knew their father, but had been told the man was an itinerant preacher.

Matson's skill with a gun had been evident at an early age; he killed his first man when he was fourteen. The man had been flirting with his mother, who took in laundry—and sometimes sold herself—to keep her family in food. She always asked God to forgive her afterward. The killing was the reason for his leaving Maine. In a hurry.

Since then, he had made a good living doing what he was good at—killing—and avoiding scrapes with the law. His eight known kills had been accepted by respective local law as matters of self-defense. He prided himself on that. He had also sold his gun to several ranches across Texas to help end land disputes. Even wore a badge once. His brother had written to him, offering a partnership in the hotel, but Greystoke wasn't interested.

Newspapers had spread his exploits, as had several DeWitt Ten Cent Romance books and a story in *Harper's New Monthly*. In those, he was presented as a hero with a gun. Several had him as a town marshal. He thought they were wonderfully funny.

Carter brought the steaming plate, waiting for Greystoke Matson's approval before retreating to the kitchen.

"This will do, sir," Matson declared. "Do you have any jam? Blackberry. I am not interested in anything else."

"Yes. I'll bring you some."

"I would have thought it would have already been on the table."

Matson ate slowly, chewing his food carefully and sipping his tea. It pleased him that his presence had created a stir. Finishing what he chose to eat, Matson returned his hat to his head, picked up his Bible and headed out.

Carter watched him leave, deciding it was better to let him go without paying than to confront him. He shook his head and turned to the thickset cook, working on an order of fried eggs and ham.

"Jesse, I'm going to go see the marshal. He should know this awful man is in town," Carter said, taking off his apron.

"You gonna let him eat here for free—all the time?"

Carter chose not to answer as he left through the back door.

At Anthony's Tailor Shop, Carter found the dapper part-time lawman working on a suit for Sheriff Stockton. Anthony looked up from his new Edward Ward Arm & Platform sewing machine from London. He volunteered that the clothes would be a gift to cement the friendship between the town and the county sheriff.

"That's real fine, Xavier," Carter said impatiently. "Did you know the killer, Greystoke Matson, the one they call 'the Preacher' is in town?"

Anthony looked up from his sewing. "Really? How interesting."

Carter explained what had happened in his restaurant, Matson's demands and his leaving without paying.

"Now surely, my good friend, you don't expect the marshal of Torsmill to interfere with what sounds like a simple case of misunderstanding." Anthony shifted the garment to continue his stitching. "Who knows if Mr. McCormick's falling down wasn't an accident? Or why he decided to leave? He's not been himself these days, you know." He looked away for an instant. "If you don't want to reserve a table for this Matson, tell him so. And go find him and ask for payment for his meal. I'm sure it was an oversight."

"The man is carrying two pistols. In violation of the town ordinance." Carter folded his arms. "What are you going to do about that?"

"At the moment, I'm busy, Carter, as I said." Anthony reached for a pair of scissors. "Why didn't you tell him of our town's ordinance and ask for his guns?"

"There's no way he would have given them to me."

"Did you ask?"

Carter waved his arm in exasperation. "Better get ready, Marshal. There's going to be trouble. A man like Greystoke Matson doesn't come to a town like Torsmill unless he's got a job to do."

"Really? And how do you know that?"

"Never mind." Carter swung around and left.

As he returned to the restaurant, he glanced in the direction of Jericho Dane's blacksmith shop. He wished the strong, capable blacksmith were still the law in town. He wouldn't let someone like Matson go without a proper confrontation. He just wouldn't. What in the world was the town council thinking?

By midday, two merchants had complained to Anthony about the gunfighter getting merchandise from them without paying. Of course, none had asked to be paid; they had either assumed he wouldn't pay or didn't want to run the risk of offending him. Nevertheless, they wanted the lawman to do something.

Strolling into the Tressian general store, Greystoke Matson touched his hand to his hat brim and acknowledged Mary's presence. "Good afternoon, m'lady. I am surprised to see so fine a flower in such a dismal settlement. Surely your stay is but temporary."

"I grew up in this town, thank you," Mary said sharply. "How may I help you?"

"I don't suppose your place would have any books on poetry. Shelley? Keats?"

Mary pointed toward the rear of the store. "Books are displayed in the back. I believe there is a book of Tennyson there,"

"Ah, yes, indeed, that would do, if none else is available. I wouldn't expect this town to have a taste for Shelley or Keats."

After watching her customers quickly leave the store, Mary noticed the gunfighter walking back through the store, carrying a small book along with his Bible.

"I see you found something," she declared.

Without slowing down, Matson nodded.

"You need to pay for it."

He grinned and paused. "I have not had to pay elsewhere. I thought Torsmill was being kind to a stranger."

"Don't know about 'elsewhere.' But you pay here—or leave the book."

The ominous sound of a gun's trigger clicking into place made him turn toward her. Slowly. She held a Colt in both hands, aimed at his midsection.

"Well, they tell me if you're in a gunfight, aim for the stomach. It'll put your adversary out of commission immediately," Matson said. "Most effective. They say."

"Glad to hear it," Mary said. "Are you buying the book—or leaving it?"

He chuckled. "I'm buying it. May I approach the counter?"

"Yes. You may also leave your guns here. They are not allowed in town."

His shoulders rising and falling, Matson shook his head. "I'll pay for the book. But I'll keep my guns. Thank you, m'lady." He withdrew coins and placed them on the counter. With a touch of his hat brim again, he turned and left the store.

Mary placed her gun on the counter and began to cry.

Laughing to himself, Matson walked across the street, watching the traffic coming and going without slowing down. He headed toward Dane's blacksmith shop; the steady pounding fascinated him. Rudolph Cross was clear about wanting this blacksmith dead, even though he was no longer the town's law. He also wanted the local judge and the mayor killed as well. And the most vocal of the small ranchers, Clell Edwards.

Matson smiled. Killing the townsmen would be easy. It didn't mean he would take less money, however. Killing the rancher would likely be more difficult since he would be surrounded by his cowboys most of the time. This blacksmith was alone, and the town—at least the town council—had rejected him. Matson decided he would get a handle on this blacksmith and then decide who would be killed first: Reicker, Mikman or Dane. It made good sense to get the tougher man out of the way first.

The pounding had stopped by the time the gunfighter crossed the street and drew near the shop. That silence bothered him. He didn't like surprises. But he told himself the blacksmith had simply stopped to do something else. Pushing aside the doors, he strolled into the work area. The forge fire was a deep crimson and a long-legged bay horse was tied, waiting to be shod. But no one was there.

Then he heard a noise inside a small storeroom. The blacksmith must be in there, he guessed. He laid the two books on a three-legged chest with open, empty shelves next to the entrance, folded his arms and waited.

"What can I do for you, mister?" Dane's voice came from behind the storeroom door, cracked slightly, enough for him to see through.

Matson's arms dropped to his side. "Ah, I wanted to see about getting iron for my horse."

"You just came in on the stage."

Matson frowned and his anger flared. "I'm going to buy a horse. That all right with you?" He motioned toward the shed. "Why don't you come out here so we can talk."

"Come back when you've turned in your guns."

"What?"

"You heard me. Torsmill is a peaceful town. We don't allow guns in town." Dane's voice was hard.

"Are you saying you aren't armed?" Matson's mouth curled at the right corner and his right eyebrow arched in support.

"I don't go around town with it. Just keep it here. In the storeroom."

Matson licked his lower lip. "Not sure I believe that, blacksmith."

"There's one way to find out."

Matson's hands came up and away from his body. "Hey, I wasn't looking for trouble. Just looking to see where I could get shoes for my horse." He looked at the ground for a moment. "I'll come back later."

"Sure. Bring your horse. Leave your guns."

After a few minutes, Dane emerged from the storeroom. His forehead was dotted with nervous sweat. It had just been happenstance that he needed more nails and they were in his shed. He glanced at his long coat hanging from the wall nail. His revolver was there; his new shotgun, at his house.

He grunted, went to the coat and retrieved the gun. He shoved it into his waistband under his work apron and went to the entrance to his work area and looked around. Matson was strolling down the sidewalk, swinging two books in his left hand; Dane watched him disappear into a saloon.

Touching the gun at his waist, the blacksmith knew the worst had come to Torsmill. Greystoke Matson wasn't here by chance. He was here to take care of some business for Rudolph Cross. He was here to help the rancher take control of the region.

Then it dawned on him that Matson had likely come from Mary's store. He hurried across the street, not stopping to remove his apron or put on his shirt.

Halfway across the street, Mikman hailed him. It was clear the mayor was coming to see him.

"*Herr* Marshal Dane, a word please." The gunsmith waved his arms and hurried to meet the concerned blacksmith in the middle of the street.

Dane gradually stopped, glancing in the direction of the general store.

A freight wagon lumbered past them and the driver swore his opinion of their being there.

"I *haff* come from *der* council meeting," Mikman declared breathlessly. "Dey vant *du* to be *der* marshal."

"I don't understand. Did Xavier resign?"

A buckboard rumbled past them headed the other way. The rancher waved and they returned the greeting.

"*Ja*, he did so," Mikman said. "*Der* three who voted him in asked him to do so. I told them *du* vould probably *nicht* vant this after *der* vay they treated *du*."

Dane didn't respond.

"I ask for this favor, *Herr* Marshal. Me. Personal it be." Mikman rubbed his hands together. "Torsmill needs *du*. More than ever. I fear for this town."

Dane nodded. "I will do it. For Torsmill."

Mikman handed him the tin badge.

From the door of the general store, Mary came running. She had seen the exchange and knew what it meant. Tears had welled in her eyes by the time she reached Dane.

"You can't do this, Jericho," she pleaded. "You can't. What about us? Doesn't our life together mean anything?'

Mikman stepped away, unsure of what to do or say.

Dane bit his lower lip. "Mary, you are everything I've ever wanted, and more. But what kind of life together will we have if we let Cross rule us? And that's what this is all about."

"But can't you wait? Maybe this awful man is just passing through." Mary's cheeks were lined with wetness.

"He will have a chance to leave."

XII

That night was a sleepless one. Torsmill slept fitfully after a day of fear. Back at his house, Dane admitted to himself the responsibility of confronting Greystoke Matson was his, regardless of the consequences. He had accepted that when he took the badge.

Unable to sleep, he went to his shop and worked for several hours. No one heard the pounding or gunshots muffled by a towel. Returning to his home to prepare for the encounter, he fixed a pot of coffee, but it didn't taste right. Pushing the cup aside, he wrote a note and placed it in an envelope addressed to Mary Tressian. Left it on his table. A farewell letter. And a statement of his enduring love.

His plan was simple. If he could catch Matson in his room, preferably sleepy, he might be able to talk him into leaving quietly. Of course, it could end in shooting. That was a risk he must take.

Certainly there was little chance the two of them could meet in public without one being forced to act. Facing him with others would only bring violence and good men would be killed. It had to be man-to-man. Dane had no intention of backing down from the likes of Matson, but he didn't want to provoke trouble either. He was counting on being able to convince the gunfighter that he wouldn't be able to kill him without getting hurt himself; he was counting on the hired gun being reasonable.

He was counting on a lot, he told himself. Buttoning his long coat and pulling his hat down on his head, he left his house. At his side was Mikman's shotgun. In his coat pocket was his .44 Smith & Wesson revolver. It carried five fresh cartridges as usual; nothing in the chamber where the hammer rested. Five extra bullets and five more shotgun shells jiggled in his other pocket. His left arm was awkwardly pushed against his coat as he strolled along the silent street. Stopping at his shop, he left five pieces of bread for the squirrel and went on.

No one was aware of his perilous undertaking. Certainly not

Mary. Or Judge Reicker. Or Fred Mikman. Mary would have talked him out of his crazy idea. Or tried to. Reicker and Mikman would have wanted to go with him.

Soon dawn would discover the same tenseness that tightened around the town.

"Sweet hour of prayer . . . sweet hour of prayer . . . that calls me from a world of care," he sang softly to himself, *"and bids me at my Father's throne . . . and escaped the tempter's snare. In seasons of distress and grief, my soul has often found relief . . . by thy return . . . sweet hour of prayer."* It seemed like the right song to sing. He had prayed at the table.

Pausing at the hotel's double doors, he took a deep breath and entered. Oil lamps split the lobby into ragged spaces of dark and yellow. He was glad to see there were five of them and walked to the registration desk. The young clerk was asleep, snoring forcefully.

Dane laid his shotgun on the counter, grabbed the clerk by both arms and lifted his upper body upright from its comfortable position.

Startled and disoriented, the clerk cried out, "Wha-a-a! I'm not asleep . . . honest . . . I . . ."

"Quiet, Johnny. It's me, Jericho. Jericho Dane. I need to talk to Greystoke Matson. What room is he in?"

"Ah, how . . . how can I help . . . you, sir?" the thinly built man, with acne controlling his face, said. He was flustered by the awakening.

Dane made no attempt to let him go and the clerk made no move to break the grip on his upper arms. The clerk's eyes darted around the room, trying to avoid looking at the lawman holding him seemingly with little effort.

"Johnny, I want to see Matson. Now."

"But, sir . . . but . . . that's against hotel rules, you see . . ." The clerk was shaking. "I . . . can't . . . I . . ."

"Johnny, I don't have time for this. Get me the key," Dane said, his voice graveled by impatience and tension.

"Y-yes-s-s . . . y-y-yes-s-s, s-sir," Johnny managed to answer, looking like he might vomit.

Dane released him. The frightened man searched wildly for the right room key. Room twenty-three. Johnny remembered because the gunfighter had specifically requested that number; it had something to do with a woman; the clerk couldn't remember what, though. Dane wasn't interested. He rubbed his hands to relieve the nervous tingling running through them and rolled his shoulders to momentarily ease their heavy burden

There was time to change his mind; no one would know. Only he would know. But that was enough, he told himself.

Turning around, the clerk held out the key as if a piece of treasure. Color had left the thin man's face. His eyes were watering. Dane declined; he only needed the room.

"Before you and I go up there, Johnny," Dane said, "I need something I can write on. I'll use this pen."

Jerkily, the young clerk pushed away his lodging book and lifted an odd-shaped sheet of paper from the drawer. Dane quickly wrote several sentences on the sheet using the ledger pen. Occasionally, he glanced up the stairway to his left, like a deer drinking water at an open stream. His mouth was dry, too dry to swallow. His shoulders and neck ached. His forehead was tattooed with sweat.

Dane wiped away the wetness with his coat sleeve as the clerk tried to regain his composure. A growing wet stain near the front of the hotel man's pants was evidence he had failed in that task.

"Johnny, I need your help for a minute up there. You won't be in any danger, I promise." Dane nodded toward the dark stairway. He picked up the shotgun and couldn't help recalling that he had planned on using the gun in the fall to hunt grouse. The revolver in his pocket felt like a boulder.

Four steps from the top of the stairs, Johnny vomited. Twice. Dane waited while the sweating clerk wiped his mouth with his shirtsleeve. At the door to room twenty-three, they stopped. Dane slid past it three feet, standing tight against the wall. His shotgun was pointed where Matson would appear. He motioned for Johnny to stay against the wall on the other side. As directed, the clerk knocked hesitantly, shivering like a wet calf in a January wind. His hand shook so hard he could barely make it hit against the wood; his first attempts were barely heard.

Dane scowled and urged him to knock harder, his waving shotgun giving the instruction.

Gazing up at the hallway's yellowed ceiling, Johnny swallowed hard and rapped loudly. Three times. Then twice more. Five, Dane thought. Good.

A sleepy voice with an arrogant edge answered. "What the hell do you want?"

"I-it's J-Johnny . . . f-from t-the front d-desk. I-I h-have, ah . . . a m-message . . . f-for you, M-Mr. M-Matson . . . ah, s-sir . . . pulesse, s-sir."

"Well, shove it under the door and then leave me alone."

Johnny responded with the request, pushed the folded sheet under the door and looked at Dane. After the marshal's nod, the terrified clerk ran down the hall. At the top of the stairs, he vomited again. Dane could hear the gunfighter get out of his bed and go to the message. Silence of a minute seemed longer. Then came a short rattle at the lock. The door swung open. Inside was black. No further sound was heard.

Wiping his sweaty palms on his coat, Dane made two quick strides to the side of the doorway opposite where he had stood. He reviewed his earlier decision: a shotgun made a more formidable entrance, but it was likely to make Matson use his gun immediately. He hoped to avoid that. Popping open the shotgun, he removed the slugs, closed it and slid the gun into the darkened room.

Silence followed the thud and then a soft chuckle.

"Goddammit, man, I know you have another gun. Probably another greener."

"Smith & Wesson."

"That what you had in your shed?" Matson's voice was indifferent.

"Didn't have a gun in there."

"Thought so." Matson's voice was annoyed.

"You have to watch us blacksmiths. We're a sneaky bunch."

A hearty laugh preceded Matson's invitation. "Well, either come in, open the ball—or go home where you belong. I don't like being jerked out of . . . my beauty sleep." Matson's voice was thick and smoky.

Dane took a shallow breath when he wanted more, inhaling to gather in all the courage loose in the hallway. Pulling the revolver from his pocket and cocking it, he stepped into the terrifying void. As he entered, he moved instinctively to his right, against the wall. He grunted slightly and was angry for it. His gun was held ready in his sweating hand.

"You have one strange way of saying good morning, blacksmith." Matson laughed, sitting on the edge of the bed in a new nightshirt. One of his silver-plated revolvers was pointed at Dane's stomach.

Across the room, fresh clothes were neatly folded on a scratched oak dresser. A small closet was partially opened, revealing the rest of his travel wardrobe. A cast-iron bed dominated the room. A night table was crowded against it. Next to the closest wall an overstuffed green chair stood sentry, more fashionable than comfortable. In the remaining open space, there was a narrow table with two high-backed chairs, as well as a dresser and mirror. A red vase was centered on the table, filled with what once were flowers. Faded red curtains completed the decor.

As Dane's eyes became comfortable with the blackened confinement, he could see a Bible, a two-thirds-empty bottle of Irish whiskey, and another pearl-handled pistol lying on the night table. What looked like a book of Tennyson poems was also there. And a half-folded letter.

"Suppose it was a mite showy," Dane replied, forcing himself to grin, and letting the gun drop to his side.

Matson responded by laying his weapon on the bed. The gunfighter didn't look as big as Dane thought he would be. A little scrawny even. Lanky for sure. Matson's face was drawn, his manner sleepy, but his piercing eyes looked like bright death, seeing right through the blacksmith's thin coating of resolve. His blond hair was uncombed and unruly.

Without any sign of concern, Matson watched him curiously. The sleepy gunfighter picked up Dane's message again and read it aloud: " 'Greystoke Matson. This is Marshal Jericho Dane. Outside. No one with me. Want to talk. No shooting. No arrest. You have my word.' "

Upon finishing, Matson motioned for Dane to sit down in the overstuffed chair a few feet from him. The lawman declined politely, saying he wouldn't be long. Dane showed no signs of fear or tenseness. That surprised Matson. Most men were on edge around him and he liked that. It always made him feel superior.

"So they made you the town law again," Matson snapped. "Blacksmith, instead of a tailor. What makes you qualified for the job? You good with that revolver?"

Dane looked down at the gun in his hand. "No one else wanted the job."

Matson chuckled. "What made you think I wouldn't start shooting when you came in the door, blacksmith? You don't look stupid." His eyes were bright now.

"Not sure. Just a feeling, I guess," Dane replied. "But then if it had to be shooting, it might as well be here and now, instead of in the street. Good folks could get hurt there. I didn't think you would play it that way. Didn't think you were that stupid either." He paused, grinned, and added, "Pretty hard to explain self-defense with a marshal in your room."

"A man could die with that kinda thinking."

"Yeah, he could. Or find a way to live."

The remark silenced both men. Dane glanced at his own shotgun on the floor, then at Matson. The nearly empty room seemed smaller than when he first entered. The gunfighter lit a dirty lamp, letting wobbly shadows loose to watch them. Dane sensed Matson considered shooting. Just for an instant. A flicker in his brightened eyes. Dane had seen that look before. A shiver ran through him, causing his shoulder to lift to let the tremor go free into the night. He pushed against his stomach with his free left arm to give him some relief from the weight at his neck.

Matson's inclination passed as quickly as it had come. A different one took over, a casual stare of genuine interest. Matson's revolver lay on the bed with his hand resting on its gleaming white handle.

Dane spoke first. "Most of these folks in town are friends of mine. Like me, most fought for the Stars an' Bars. Some were Federals, though. Long way from home, I am." He shook his head. "No, that's not right. Torsmill is home."

"I was with Meade at Gettysburg. The first one," Matson responded.

"That was a bloody mess. I was lucky. Wasn't close by. Colonel Hay's 7th Louisiana, part of Taylor's brigade."

Matson didn't appear to be listening. "Yeah, but if Meade hadn't been afraid, we would've ended the whole damn war right then and there."

"There were a few Dixie generals we could've done better without, too," Dane said, half smiling. He hadn't expected the conversation to head this way.

"Well, that idiot Meade could have swept Missionary Ridge. Should have come blazing right after Pickett, and smashed you Rebs before you could rethink the thing. Only Meade, he was pure an' simple afraid of Lee." Matson hit the bed with his fist for emphasis. The impact lifted the unprotected revolver slightly off the mattress for a moment. His voice was steel rubbing against steel.

"Yeah, ol' Marse Robert, he was . . . a real war chief, wasn't he?" Dane answered. "Did you get hurt in that one?"

"Spent awhile in a hospital near the Potomac. But I rode with Sherman. At the end. Atlanta and all." Matson's eyebrows lifted triumphantly.

"Glad I didn't see that either."

"Don't blame you, Dane. Don't blame you at all," Matson said, looking around the room as if searching for something. "Say, you didn't think to bring along some hot coffee for this morning war of yours, did you?"

"Should've brought some fresh donuts, too," Dane said and laughed. "Next time I'll know better."

Matson started to say something, then paused and chuckled. He spotted the bottle of Irish whiskey and leaned over to pick it up, his back turned toward Dane. Was that an accident or was he testing? Dane's eyes shot to the pistol on the bed. It was there. But the gunfighter's second gun was inches from the whiskey bottle, within easy reach. Dane didn't move, silently telling his fingers that they shouldn't either.

Jericho Dane thought to himself that anyone watching this conversation would have never guessed that here were two men who might be killing each other in moments. Taking a hearty swig, Matson held up the bottle toward Dane. The blacksmith accepted with his left hand, stepping toward him, and took a sip, then another. The dark fluid went down his throat like hot butter. He didn't drink much, but the feeling was good. He handed the bottle back to the gunfighter, who swirled the remaining contents and took another long swallow.

"Don't get me wrong, blacksmith—or should I call you Marshal? I don't usually start the day this way . . . or end it. Just seemed like a good idea right now," Matson said, returning the bottle to its place on the table. "So . . . what's on your mind this fine morning, Marshal Dane?"

Dane grunted softly in response to the question and declared, "I want you to leave Torsmill."

"Right now? I haven't had my breakfast. No coffee even. Your fault, remember?"

"There's a stage today. Before noon. Supposed to be at ten. Tends to be a little later. So you've got plenty of time to eat first."

"Where's it headed?"

"Ah, goes through Waco first. That's where you live, isn't it?" Dane said, his voice sounding a little nervous to his brain. He wished it didn't.

"What if I don't?"

Dane looked away briefly, then turned back to face the gunfighter. His eyes were probably giving away his sudden fear. Dane was reminded of a doctor he had met during the War. The man seemed in control of his words and thoughts all the time. Efficient. Cool. Able to assess a situation without becoming emotionally involved or letting feelings make the decision. Why couldn't he be like that, especially now?

He was counting on his assessment of Greystoke Matson to be right. If he was wrong, they would end up killing each other right here.

It was Matson who broke the crawling emptiness of the room. "You want me to leave. You think I'm a threat to this . . . this hole of a town? What is the name? Torsmill." He answered his own question, motioned with his left arm and continued, "You came here with a shotgun. You don't like the idea of facing me, do you? Why did you change your mind? About the scattergun."

"Who would want to face you? Yeah, I was going to come in with that, but you might've started shooting."

"I would have," Matson said, nodding. "What about a man? Ever kill a man facing you with a gun?"

"Lots of soldiers have. Nothing I'm proud of, though. Doesn't take much to pull a trigger."

Matson grinned through clenched teeth. "You and me. Hey, people would be talking about that fight around here for a long time." He cocked his head to the side. "You would be famous. Marshal Jericho Dane dies in gunfight with the great Greystoke Matson."

For once, Dane didn't respond with any grunts or sighs or trembles, not even to himself. It pleased him.

"Not my idea of making history," Dane said as casually as he could muster. "We both could die—or be hurt awful bad. Of course, it might keep this town out of Rudolph Cross's hands. He's the reason you're here. To kill some of us. Guess I'm willing to trade you an' me for that. Don't want to, but I will."

"Your face looks like you've already run into trouble."

"Yeah, some Cross men."

"Heard that. Heard you did some good shooting," Matson said, pursing his lips.

"Did what I had to do," Dane said.

Matson motioned toward him. "Say, you're welcome to shed that long coat. Warm in here. Or are you hiding another gun?"

"Naw, I'm not hiding a gun. Brought that along to give me something to toss." Dane pointed at the shotgun on the floor. "A hideaway gun wouldn't do me much good against you."

The gunfighter chuckled, acknowledging the truth in his assessment. No one was as good with a handgun as he was. Or if there was someone, he sure wasn't hanging around this hick town.

"So, let's take a look at this situation, shall we?" Matson picked up the pistol from the bed and spun it nonchalantly in his right hand. "I have never run from a fight. Am I really worth dying for? You're no match for me . . . not even with that scattergun. And you know it. You wouldn't get that Smith & Wesson halfway up before I stopped you. Forever."

"I didn't figure you would run, Matson," Dane said. "I'm not asking you to. Just decide on your own to leave. That isn't running. That's choosing."

"Why should I?"

Dane answered evenly, "Maybe because I asked nice-like. Maybe because the deal you made with Cross doesn't look as good now."

Dane's remark didn't set well with the gunfighter and it showed in Matson's tightened face. Rage was just behind the mask of indifference.

Moving his shoulders slightly to relieve the heavy pressure, Dane responded by telling Matson that his staying would only cause trouble. It would mean the deaths of others. Him, too. Stopping the problem now would be to everyone's advantage. No one would know the two of them had even met. It would simply look like Matson had decided to move on. That's what it would be, in reality. Matson could wire Cross later. Or leave him a note.

"What about that silly little clerk?" Matson's eyes were slits that seemed to carry the question with their stare. He motioned with his revolver toward the far wall to indicate downstairs.

"I'll tell him you and I were old friends. From the War. I'll tell him not to say anything about our meeting, that you were just passing through. To see me. He won't talk anyway. Too scared. Threw up coming and going."

"I've never gone short on a contract."

Dane grunted, in spite of himself. It came out as a rebuttal to the gunfighter's claim. Inside him, there was a sensation that made him feel more alive than he had ever been.

"The next move is yours, not mine. But I am marshal here—and you can't stay." Dane could feel the sweat from his hand trickle onto the revolver it held.

Matson saw the marshal's shotgun on the floor. He walked over, lifted it with his left hand, broke it open and examined it as a jeweler might inspect a ring. He laid the weapon back on the floor. His own gun rested at his side in his right fist.

"Nice gun," the gunfighter observed, stepping toward Dane. "Smart idea. Unloading it before you sent it in here."

Now Matson and Dane were only a few feet apart. Matson, in his nightshirt, standing close to his new acquaintance.

"That's a lot to ask of a man, in one short meeting," Matson said. "I don't think Cross would like that much—my leaving now. He seems like a cold-blooded bastard, doesn't he? Might make it harder to get my next job if he starts complaining."

"Cross can't say anything without serious risk of arrest for attempted murder," Dane said. "He may be mean, but he isn't thick between the ears."

Without responding, the gunfighter walked away to the lone window in the room. With his left hand, he pulled aside the faded red curtain to view the street below. It was barely dawn, but three people were already on the street. A dog greeted them. In the distance, Matson could see riders coming. He knew who they were and spun the revolver easily in his right hand.

"You know, a fellow listening to this conversation, well, he just might think you were scared." The gunfighter didn't turn from the window as he reversed the direction of his spinning gun and continued twirling it, counterclockwise.

Dane thought that talking with this man was like petting a wildcat. One never knew when his hand was going to be bitten, regardless of how nice the animal seemed at any given moment.

"A knowin' man should be scared," Dane acknowledged. "You're a man with a reputation. Of course, there are folks around here who'd be quick to tell you I'm not a knowin' man." He cocked his head to the side. "Who'd want to hammer on iron over a hot fire all day if he had his druthers?"

Matson laughed at the counterpoint and held the gun with both hands, still looking out the window. "You've got sand, Dane. Not many men would have done this. That other marshal—that tailor—was as yellow as they come. What you're trying to do makes sense, but it takes sand. I could've killed you when you came through that door."

"You could've tried."

Turning toward Dane, Matson's eyes brightened; his revolver pointed at the blacksmith's stomach.

Dane didn't move. Everything in him froze.

A noise in the hallway broke the tautness in the room. Sounds passed. Matson paused a moment longer to make certain the hallway was clear of noise. It hadn't occurred to him until now that Dane might not be alone, in spite of what he had said. He stared at the marshal, then at the door. When he was satisfied the sounds were unrelated, he grinned and stepped back.

"The note there, from Rudolph Cross, is the contract, Dane." The gunfighter motioned toward the bed table with his revolver. "I'm to be paid five hundred dollars for killing you. Another five hundred for killing that little rancher—what's his name? Yeah, Edwards. And the same amount to get rid of your mayor—and that old judge. Plus travel expenses. That's a lot of money."

"You like Tennyson, I see," came Dane's unexpected reply. Beads of sweat broke out along his forehead.

"Don't change the subject," the gunfighter snapped.

"Wasn't. Tennyson writes a lot about fighting and dying. And living. I like his writing. What I've seen of it, anyway." Dane watched the gunfighter.

"You mean like . . . 'Then said Earl Doorm: "Well, if he be not dead, why wail ye for him thus? Ye seem a child. And be he dead, I count you for a fool; your wailing will not quicken him . . ."'" He completed the recitation, tossed the revolver on his bed, and walked to his closet. He began looking through his hanging clothes, facing the closet.

"That's real nice. What's the name of that one?"

"'Enid.' It's about knights," Matson said. His hands moved to a hanging coat as he continued reciting, "'Forgetful of his promise to the kind, forgetful of the falcon and the hunt, forgetful of the tilt and tournament, forgetful of his glory and his name, forgetful of his princedom and its cares, and this forgetfulness was hateful to her . . .'" He finished, but didn't turn away from the closet.

"That's pretty, Greystoke. Wish I could recite like that. All I know are some words to a couple of church songs from when I was a kid." He rubbed the back of his neck and hunched his shoulders to relieve the fierce ache.

"You're a real piece of work, blacksmith. You and I could have been good friends somewhere else. Are you superstitious?" Matson fiddled with something inside the hanging coat.

Dane thought for a second. "Well, sort of. I kinda like things in five."

"Did you do anything in fives this morning?"

Dane didn't have time to respond as the gunfighter spun around, his fist holding a pistol that had been hidden in the coat; its black nose blossomed with orange flame.

The first two bullets hit Dane's stomach, slamming him against the wall; the third, right at his heart. The bullets tore through his coat, then startlingly richocheted from their intended targets.

Staggering, Dane fired. Three times. Matson screamed, more like a cougar than a human, and flew backward, crashing into the closet. A fourth bullet bit Dane's left arm, hard enough to force the weapon from his hand, in spite of its tenacious grip. A fifth hit the wall behind him.

Three black holes appeared heart-high on Matson's nightshirt. His shaking hands pulled at clothes as he fell. Blood spotted everything close. The smoking pistol floated into the air like a strange bird before hitting the floor.

Dane leaned against the wall for support. He didn't move. His head rested on his heaving chest. His shoulders ached from the weight they carried. He unbuttoned his long coat with black holes in three places and let it drop. Under it was a protective vest forged from two oversized, heavy shovels and a sheet of iron. He had made it last night at his shop. The makeshift bulletproof vest hung about his neck by a reinforced leather strap.

The blacksmith's fingers ran over the three deep indentations made by Matson's bullets. His gaze took in the dents made by his test firing last night. With a groan, Dane lifted the iron vest from his shoulders, using mostly his good arm, and let it clank on the floor. His stomach and chest throbbed where the lead had tried to strike. His left forearm pounded. But the liberation was considerable, letting energy and relief flow through him.

Remembering his revolver, he retrieved it and walked to Matson's twitching body. Crimson was creating a circle under the gunfighter. His chest was a bloody seep. Matson's blurry eyes fluttered open and Dane knelt beside the dying gunfighter.

"I didn't want this, Greystoke," Dane said quietly. "I truly wanted you to leave. My fight is with Cross."

"How . . . did I . . . miss?" Matson's eyes wouldn't focus.

"You didn't." Dane pointed at the heavy vest across the room. "By the way, you didn't give me a chance to answer your last question. I tapped on that vest five times before coming here."

He looked down at Matson. He was dead. A strange smile gripped the gunfighter's face.

Noise in the hallway indicated people were running toward the room. Walking to the bed table, he picked up Cross's note, turned and opened the door, uncertain of what to expect. His revolver was readied in his fist.

Mary rushed in, holding her Colt, and threw her arms around him. "Are you all right, my darling? You're hurt! Your arm! Why didn't you tell me?"

"You would've stopped me." He kissed her cheek as his right arm dropped to his side. "I'm fine, my love. Just a nick."

Behind her came Reicker with his big Navy Colt and Mikman with a new rifle. They stepped inside and took in the battle scene.

"Looks like that fancy boy dun run into the wrong lawman," Reicker said and shook his head.

"*Ja,*" Mikman answered, studying the iron vest and the shotgun. "A blacksmith lawman."

All of them spun toward new sounds at the doorway.

It was a shocked Rudolph Cross. His mind took a few seconds to comprehend what he saw. Instead of a dead Jericho Dane, it was a dead Greystoke Matson. The big rancher's face was full of disbelief.

Behind him came Sheriff Stockton and two Cross cowboys; the younger had carried Cross's note to the gunfighter. Gathering in the hallway were hotel guests, the young clerk and a few curious townspeople who had heard the gunfire.

"What's going on here, Dane?" the rancher, finding his poise, demanded. "You killing more innocent people?"

Mary turned toward the rancher, her teary eyes now filled with anger. Her hands slid from Dane's neck, the Colt pointed at Cross.

Dane ignored the question and asked one of his own. "What brings you to Torsmill, to this hotel room . . . at this hour, Cross?"

"None o' your goddamn business, blacksmith. I asked you a question. We heard gunshots in here."

"Your meeting with Greystoke Matson is . . . ah, canceled." Dane motioned toward the still body. "Acting as the town marshal, I asked him to leave town and he tried to kill me instead."

"What are you talkin' about? You're mighty uppity for a—"

"Blacksmith," Dane interrupted. "Or a marshal. Which?"

"Quit playin' games, Dane. Everybody knows that tin star don't mean nuthin'. Stockton here is the real law."

Stepping away from Mary, the blacksmith-marshal stared at Cross. "This badge means something to me. To this town, too." He raised his revolver. "And you're under arrest for the attempted murder of Judge Reicker, Mayor Mikman, Clell Edwards—and me."

Pushing past Cross, Sheriff Stockton blurted, "You must be crazy, Dane."

Dane held up the note. "Maybe so, but I have Matson's word—and Rudolph Cross's letter to Matson. Five hundred apiece for killing the four of us. You wanted us out of the way real bad, didn't you, Cross?"

The bucktoothed cowboy to Stockton's left blurted, "Hey, that's the letter I dun took to Matson! See! Gave it to him when he were eatin' breakfast in Waco."

"Shut up," Stockton snarled, and turned to Dane. "You didn't give him much chance." He pointed at the protective vest.

"I gave him the chance to leave," Dane said, and added that Matson had explained that he had never gone back on a contract and that Cross would be angry if he left before completing his job.

The bucktoothed cowboy asked, "Who gets them fancy six-guns?"

Stockton told him to shut up once more. "You're going to have to answer for this shooting, Dane. I'll arrest you for murder—again. This time it'll stick."

Reicker barked, "Reckon not, Stockton. Dane was actin' under council orders. We all had 'nuff o' this crap from Cross. Now ya'll drop your iron. You, too, Stockton. Cross, unbuckle it. All o' ya are goin' to jail." He waved his gun.

"*Ja*." Mikman swung his Winchester toward the four men.

Mary cocked her Colt.

Turning red-faced, Stockton exclaimed, "I'm the sheriff of this county!"

Reicker growled, "Reckon this county's gonna have itse'f an election real soon. Yur gonna stand trial for helpin' prisoners escape."

Stockton bit his lower lip and unbuckled his gun belt. The two Cross cowboys followed. The bucktoothed cowboy asked, "If nobody wants 'em, can I have Matson's guns?"

"They'll be buried with Greystoke," Dane said.

Cross started to unbuckle his gun belt, then reached for the letter and Dane pulled it back.

"Let me see that!" he bellowed.

"Later. Right now, you're going to the shed. That's where we keep prisoners." Dane forced a smile. "Rest of you to the livery corral." He focused on a white-faced Stockton. "It'll go easier on you if you tell us where those escaped prisoners are. Cross can't help you now. Or hurt you."

"I said git rid o' that gun belt, Cross," Reicker growled. "I'm gittin' real tired o' waitin'."

Frowning, the big rancher unbuckled his gunbelt and let it fall near his feet. "I underrated you, blacksmith."

"Maybe so. Maybe so."

Lumbering past the crowd came Tess, still in her nightgown. She saw Mary and Dane and hurried to them as fast as she could. "Jerr-i-koo, Miss Mary loves you."

"I know." Dane smiled and reached out to hug the smiling general storeowner. "And I love her."

"Reckon this ol' judge'll be havin' a weddin' soon." Reicker grinned.

"*Ja.*"

The Desert Pilot

I
Pegasus and the Ox

One step beyond Billman lay the desert; young Ingram, minister of the Gospel, took the single step and sat down in the shadow of a rock amid the wilderness. Already one needed the shadow; for though the sun was barely above the horizon—had lost the rose and gold of dawn only the moment before—it was now white with strength and flooded the desert with a scorching heat. When the knee of Reginald Oliver Ingram projected into that heat, he withdrew it. It was as though a burning glass had been focused neatly on it. He looked down, half expecting to see the cloth of his trousers smoking. And this heat would increase until early afternoon, after which its power would diminish by almost imperceptible degrees. Until its face turned red, the sun would flood the desert with white fire.

Like shimmering snow was the face of that desert, except that snow is fixed and still, whereas the sands were covered with little wraiths and atmospheric lines. They quivered and throbbed, as a white-hot iron quivers and throbs. Mr. Ingram raised his eyes from the paper on his knee and took more careful stock of all that lay around him. He had been in Billman only a few days—not long enough to preach his first sermon, as a matter of fact—but he had come across the continent with a suitcase filled with books. From their well-studied contents he could name yonder gigantic saguaro, and the opuntias, surrounded with a halo of ivory sheen in the strong sunlight; and he knew also the deer-horn cactus not far off, the greasewood and mesquite on the sands.

To name all the living things in sight was to give an impression of companionable multitudes about him, but as a matter of fact all he observed was hardly more to the desert than is an occasional mist of white to the broad, pale bosom of the summer sky—nothing to give shadow, for the intense sun will look through the spectral clouds when it stands directly above them. So it was with this plant life—a few fantastic forms, looking like odd cartoons of animals, thrust in the sand with arms or legs extended foolishly—and yonder patches that looked like smoke against the sand.

But Mr. Ingram looked upon all these signs of desolation with an eye that was unafraid; for he carried about him a spiritual armor that blunted the edge of every danger and every painful instance. When he left the theological school, a wise, ancient and holy man had said to him: 'Now you are about to enter the world. Leave some of your books and bookishness behind you. Be a man among men; trust the angels a little less and man a little more!' The Reverend Reginald Ingram smiled as he thought of this speech. For, looking across the desert, it seemed to him that the hand of God was visibly revealed, and he penned hastily and strongly the first words of the sermon which he would deliver later that morning: 'Dear brothers and sisters whom I meet here at the edge of our civilization, we have gone very far from our old homes and we have left many of our old ideas behind us; we even have stepped beyond the reach of the law, I suppose; but we have not passed beyond the reach of God, and I wish to speak to you today concerning the signs of His loving Fatherhood, which are scattered about us, though the signs are unregarded by most of us, I fear.'

Having finished this burst, he paused, knitting his brows with the farseeing effort of a poet or a prophet. He glanced then to the tall forms of the San Joaquin Mountains far to the north and east, now washed with tides of light through air so pure and thin and dry that he could see the shadows which the boulders cast and almost pick out the individual trees which straggled up to the timber line. Beyond that line was a band of purple, and above the purple lay the glittering caps of snow and eternal ice, which, like a cup of haunting coolness, were offered forever to the sight of the parched desert beneath. A gleam of wings nearby drew his attention to the fluttering butterfly which wafted aimlessly up and down close to the sand, all jeweled and transparent in the powerful sun.

The rapid pencil of the Reverend Reginald Oliver Ingram ran again over the paper:

'Here, beyond the law, conscious of our own strength, and aware of the apparently cruel face of nature, we prepare ourselves for battle. But our Father in heaven permits life without battle, and sends out unarmed multitudes, who persist and give the earth gentleness and beauty. Consider the butterfly that flutters softly over the desert, harmless, soft, brilliant in the sun—'

He looked up for inspiration to complete his sentence, and noticed an active little cactus wren, balanced on a hideous thorn of the deer-horn plant.

'—or the wren,' dashed on the swift pencil of the minister, 'spreading his wings that the sun may flash through them and make of him a double jewel—'

He looked again, and saw almost at his feet a little yellow beetle looking as hard and glittering as a piece of quartz.

He touched it with the eraser of his pencil; it was, indeed, like pressing on a rock.

'—or the beetle,' went on the writer in glad haste, 'like a nugget of gold on the face of the desert. But these defenseless ones which can harm nothing and which give joy to the world teach us that we, also—'

Something whirred through the air; the butterfly was clipped in two by the long, wicked beak of the wren. The quivering halves tumbled almost at the feet of the watcher, but since he had sat quietly so long, the bird seemed to accept him as a part of the landscape, and, pursuing its prey, gobbled up the feast and was gone.

Mr. Ingram looked down at his page and puckered his lips in thoughtful regret. However, he continued: 'Teach us that we, also, have been placed in the world to make it beautiful with the work of the heart and not terrible and dangerous with the work of the hand. Gentleness is mightier than pride—'

He paused again, and saw that the golden beetle had encountered a smaller insect. Whatever it might have been, it was now unrecognizable. For the yellow beauty, beating its shardlike wings with joy or anger, was already tearing the weaker thing to bits.

'Gentleness is mightier than pride,' insisted Mr. Ingram's pencil, 'and the triumphs of the strong are, in reality, not triumphs at all; they are soon avenged.'

He completed the sentence rather grimly, and another whir in the air attracted him once more to the wren, which had dropped like lightning from its bower of thorns and attacked the golden beetle.

There was no battle. The beetle depended on the toughness of its armor, and depended in vain, for soon Ingram could hear the crackling of this natural coat of plate, and the beetle presently disappeared. Thereafter, the wren flitted onto a stone, and sat there opening its beak wide, pulling in its head, and ruffling its feathers as though it found its recent tough meal very hard to digest.

'I hope you choke on it!' said the minister sternly to the bird. And he wrote: 'Vengeance is near at hand, and we are being watched by a higher power. The victories which we win are always just around the corner from defeat!'

So wrote the man of God, and he had barely finished this sentence when new ideas forced themselves upon him, and he added fluently: 'Put off your guns and knives! The God who rules heaven and earth is a God of peace. Trust to Him, and He will lead you out of your troubles. What blow can threaten you that He will not ward away?'

He felt a glow of triumphant conviction as he finished. At that instant he heard a hiss like a volley of arrows whirring above him; a shadow slanted with incredible speed past his head; the wren was blotted out; there was a shrill scream, and away winged the big hawk which had dropped from the blue—and now sailed back into it, carrying a little tuft of crimsoned feathers in one set of talons.

Ingram watched the bird of prey rising gracefully and rapidly, climbing the sky in great spirals. It reminded him of the men he had seen in Billman since his arrival—lean, quiet men, who, when they were roused to action, struck with a sudden and deadly stroke. And all at once he felt more than a little helpless, for it seemed to him that he could hear the chuckles of his audience when he told them later that morning that there was no value in might or in the strong hand.

What lessons of gentleness could he derive from that nature where the smaller beetle was eaten by the larger, the larger by the wren, the wren by the hawk which towered in the sky, and the hawk, in turn, perhaps struck down by the soaring eagle? However, he would not be downhearted at once.

He followed the flight of the hawk past the cold summits of the San Joaquin range, and as he did so, the glory of the great Builder possessed his imagination. New ideas crowded upon him and drove his pencil at breakneck speed until he had covered several sheets; and when he stood up from the shadow of the rock and faced the glare of the sun, the sermon which had haunted him since his arrival at Billman was completed.

He glanced at the pages from time to time as he wandered back into the town; and before he reached his shack, he knew that the thing was firm in his memory. At his door he stood for a moment and watched the wind roll a cloud of dust up the street more swiftly than a horse could gallop. So let the idea which had come to him on this morning sweep through the minds of his auditors, and freshen in them the almost obliterated image of their Creator!

He entered his little house and was startled by the figure of a Dominican monk, whose fat body was covered with a gown of not overclean rusty black, girded with a long cord. The monk turned and grasped the hand of Ingram.

'Good morning, Mr. Ingram,' said he. 'I am Brother Pedrillo. I've come to welcome a fellow-worker to Billman.'

Ingram did not like the use of the word 'fellow-worker.' Young Mr. Ingram had been bred to a faith which does not look kindly upon the Roman Catholic creed; but in addition, he felt in himself so much aspiring vigor, such a contempt of the flesh, that to be yoked with Brother Pedrillo was like harnessing an ox in the same team with Pegasus.

So he turned away, busied himself putting up his notes for the sermon, and revolved swiftly in his mind the attitude which he should assume. However, the Lord works His will in mysterious ways. The Reverend Reginald decided that he would force himself into friendliness with the Dominican. Humility is ordained very early in the Gospel.

II
A Kindly Buzzard

He invited Brother Pedrillo to take a chair, and so became aware of the shoes of his visitor. They were made of roughest cowhide, but even that durable material was worn to tatters. The fringe of his robe, too, was worn to rags, and the bald head of the monk had been burned well-nigh black. At least this was a man who was much in the open air. The heart of young Ingram softened a little.

'You read philosophy, I see,' remarked the monk.

'Don't you?' queried Ingram, rather sharply.

'When I was just from school, yes,' replied the Dominican. 'But afterward, I let the thing slip. It was quite useless to me in my work.'

'Ah!' said Ingram coldly.

'Not,' added the other, 'that philosophy cannot be translated into the language and the acts of the man in the street; but I haven't the time nor the intelligence to do the translating. My work takes me long distances,' he explained more fully, 'and my tasks are placed far apart.' He pointed to his battered shoes.

'You don't live in Billman, then?' asked Ingram.

'I live in a district a hundred miles square.'

'Hello! Do you walk that?'

'Sometimes I get a lift in a buckboard. But my people are very poor. I must walk most of the days.'

'A frightful waste of time,' suggested Ingram.

'For those who live or for those who die,' said the Dominican, 'time is of little importance in this part of the world. Have you watched the buzzards?'

'Buzzards?'

'They wait on the wing a week at a time, without water, sailing a hundred leagues a day, perhaps; but, if they are watchful, finally they find food. It is that way with me. I go from village to village, from house to house. But if I find one good thing a month to do, I am satisfied. The rest of the time, I wait on the wing, as you might say.'

He looked down at his round stomach as he spoke, and laughed comfortably, until he shook from head to foot.

'I should think that you could settle down here,' said Ingram with enthusiasm. 'There are scores of Mexicans here. The number of their knife fights, you know—I beg your pardon,' he added, 'I don't want to appear to give advice.'

'Ah, but do it! Do it!' said Pedrillo. 'As we grow older we find little advice to take; and a great many occasions for giving. So say what is in your mind.'

Ingram looked at the other a little more closely, for he feared that he was being mocked; but he met an eye so transparent and a smile so genuine and childlike that he could not help laughing in return.

'There is nothing I can say,' he declared at last. 'Except that it seemed to me that there was enough in Billman to keep you busy every moment of your time.'

'In this little town,' said Pedrillo, 'my people shift so fast—up to the mines and back again, in and out—that I can do little except marry or bury them as they pass. If it were a settled place, then I could take a house here and live among them until I became really a brother to them. But as it is, the mines fill their pockets with money. They have plenty to spend on food and tequila, and something left over to gamble and fight for. Their minds and their hands are so filled that they have no need of me except when they are about to marry or to die. If I were to settle among them now they would forget that I am here. I would be a shadow to them. But since I come from a distance, at rare intervals, I am something more. They listen to me now and then. That is all I can expect. I am not ambitious, Mr. Ingram. But you have your own people, and they are not mine. All of mine will hear me—at least two or three times in their lives. Some of yours will never hear you at all. But a great many of them may take you into their everyday lives. That is the greater good. Unquestionably, the greater good. Ah, well, I must accept my destiny.'

His words were a good deal more serious than his manner, for he smiled as he spoke.

'But,' he added, 'I have never had gifts. Unless it is a gift to listen to people's sorrows. You, however, can mix with your kind and command admiration among them.'

'Why do you say that?' asked Ingram, frowning a little, as one who did not like to receive idle compliments.

'You are big,' said the Mexican, 'you are young, and you are strong. The men here are rough; but they cannot afford to scorn you.'

He pointed, as he spoke, to a little silver vase which stood on top of the bookshelf, a pair of boxing gloves chased on its side.

Young Ingram smiled faintly and shrugged his shoulders.

'That was before I had any serious purpose in life,' said he. 'That was before I found myself. Now I'm a man.'

'How old are you?'

'Twenty-five, almost,' said Ingram.

Brother Pedrillo did not smile. 'And how did you come to find yourself?' he asked gently.

Ingram found it strangely easy to talk about himself to this brown, fat face, these inactive but knowing eyes. He rested his elbows on his knees and looked into the past.

'I was smashed in a football game, and played too long afterward. It put me in the hospital. I had the germs of a fever in me at the time, and that gave the sickness a galloping start. It was a long struggle. But in the intervals, when I was not delirious and when I realized how close to death I lay, I wondered what I had been doing with myself for twenty years. Twenty long years, and nothing done, nothing worthwhile! A few goals kicked. A few touchdowns. Some boxing. Well, I determined that if God spared me I would give something to the world that was worthwhile. And when I could call my life my own, I began studying for the church.'

He checked himself and looked rather suspiciously at the Brother.

'I seem to be chattering a good deal,' he suggested.

'Talk is good,' said the older man with conviction. All at once he began to whistle a thin, small note. Ingram turned and saw a little yellow-backed lizard lying in the burning sun upon the threshold. It lifted its head and listened to the music. 'Talk is good,' added the friar, with a nod of surety.

He stood up.

'We begin to know each other,' he said.

'I want to ask you the same question that you asked me,' said Ingram. 'How did *you* happen to select your vocation?'

'But I had nothing to do with it,' answered the friar. 'My mother gave me to the church. And here I am,' he added, and smiled again. 'Whatever I can do, ask of me. I have little power. I have little knowledge. But I know something of the strong men who live here.'

'These ruffians!' cried Ingram rather fiercely.

Brother Pedrillo raised a brown hand.

'Don't call them that. Yes, call them that if you will. It is always better to put it into words than to leave it buried in the mind. But except for a rough man's act, would there be a church here now? Would you yourself be here in the desert, my brother?'

Ingram bit his lip thoughtfully.

'I don't know what you mean,' he replied frankly.

'You don't know?' asked Pedrillo, his smile fading. And for a single instant his eyes were keen and cold as they searched the face of his companion. 'Perhaps you don't,' he decided. 'You have not heard how your own church was built?'

'By a man named William Luger. I've been here only four days, you understand.'

'Do you not know how he came to leave the money for it?'

'No. Not yet.'

'So, so!' murmured the friar.

He sat down again and rolled a cigarette, whistling the small note to the enchanted lizard at the door. He made the cigarette like a little cornucopia, for such is the Mexican fashion. And Ingram saw, with a little disgust, that the fingers of the holy man were literally painted orange-yellow by the stain of nicotine.

'Let me tell you,' said the friar, beginning to blow smoke toward the rough beams of the ceiling. 'Billy Luger was a man typical of this part of the world.'

'A little better than that, I hope,' said Ingram, turning stiff.

'No,' replied the Dominican. 'He was just that. He had spent thirty years branding cattle—his own or ones he borrowed for the occasion. Finally he dipped into mining, when the rush started toward the San Joaquin silver and the Sierra Negra gold. He made a few thousand and was celebrating a trip to town one evening, when he got into a card game with "Red Jim" Moffet. Moffet shot him, and it was while Billy lay dying that he made up his mind to leave his money for the founding of a church. That's the story. And that's what brought you here.'

'And the murderer?' asked Mr. Ingram hotly. 'He was hanged, I trust?'

'You are a sanguinary young man,' smiled the Dominican. 'But these people are fond of killing with guns; they rarely kill with a rope. No, Moffet was not hanged. He's still alive, prosperous and well. You'll meet him around the town.'

'A most extraordinary tale,' said Ingram, breathing hard. 'Was no attempt made to bring his killer to justice?'

'The fact is,' said the friar sympathetically, 'that Moffet accused Billy of having a card up his sleeve during the game. And I believe that the bystanders agreed with Red, after the smoke blew away.'

Brother Pedrillo rose again.

'You are going to exercise much influence from the start, I know,' said he.

'And on what do you base that?' asked Ingram, again antagonistic.

'Where the ladies of the town go, the men are sure to follow—though sometimes at a little distance,' said Pedrillo, and he stepped out into the blast of the sun.

It glistened on his bald head as upon brown glass.

Once more the friar waved adieu, and trudged down the dusty street, leaving Ingram of two minds as he stood in the doorway. He could not quite make out the import of that last remark. It sounded suspiciously like a touch of sarcasm, but he could not be sure. At length he turned to complete his sermon. It was not easy. He had to set his teeth and force his pencil on. Because from time to time across his mind came the vision of a card game—and one man with cards up the sleeve!

III
With Tears in Her Eyes

Women? He had not guessed that there were so many in the entire town, aside from the Mexican section across the creek. They filled more than half the front part of the church, whispering, buzzing, and then settling down to watch his face with a curious insistence, until he began to feel that they were hearing not a word.

He lifted his eyes from them and directed the strength of his little oration toward a dozen men who remained as far back as possible on the benches, huddling themselves into the shadowy corners.

They were listening, and they did not seem convinced by this talk about peace. Now and then they looked gravely at one another. Once or twice the Reverend Reginald Ingram thought he saw a faint smile. But he could not be sure. Only he knew that the church now began to seem extremely small; and that the sun beat upon it with a terrific force. It was hot, very hot; and he wanted a cooling wind to pour in and bring him relief.

Well, that small miracle was denied for his gratification, and Ingram centered his attention fiercely on his sermon—bulldogging it through, as he often had done on the football field. Yardage on a football field, however, is chalked off with convenient white lines. Yardage in a church is a different matter. One may be under the goal posts one instant, and fighting to keep from being scored on the next.

However, he drew his parallels. The yellow beetle and the gay little wren were called upon to furnish a metaphor apiece. The cruel hawk was not mentioned at all. And gradually he established his own conviction in the picture he was drawing of peace on earth, and good will among all of the men living upon it. He felt that he was drawing his audience together a little more. As for the hulking men in the rear—let them rise and sidle with creaking boots toward the exit. Not one of the feminine heads before him turned to watch them go. No, all were feverishly concentrated upon him. They were brown faces, indubitably Anglo-Saxon in spite of their color. And the eyes seemed strangely blue and bright by contrast. He began to feel that never before had he seen so many intelligent women gathered together. For, if the truth must be known, Mr. Ingram looked down upon the other sex. They rarely bothered him. No woman can talk football, and few can talk of religion with much conviction.

The minister ended his sermon, and the organ responded in squawks of protest to the organist who was trying to furnish music to close the service. However, the little crowd did not depart, and Ingram, descending from his throne, was softly enveloped in a wave of organdies and lawns that brought a fresh, wholesome laundry smell about him.

The ladies introduced themselves, and he listened gravely and earnestly to their names. If he was to work with such material as this, then it behooved him, by all means, to come quickly to the knowledge of it.

They had enjoyed his sermon, it appeared. They had enjoyed it, oh, so much! Everything he said was *so* true. If one only stopped to think! How well he understood the desert, and their problems! Someone was asking him to come home to lunch. And then another, and another.

A girl with very pale, blonde hair and very blue, blue eyes seemed to brush all the others aside with her gesture—though she was a little thing—and stood directly before him, smiling up.

'They have no right to you,' said she. 'My poor mother couldn't come, and she wanted me to remember every word you said. As if I could do that, in my silly head! So you have to come home to lunch with me. Go away, Charlotte! Don't be foolish! Of course Mr. Ingram is coming with me!'

Even among the others it seemed to be taken for granted that Mr. Ingram would, of course, go with her of the pale hair and the extraordinarily blue eyes. They gave up. And she carried him off from the church.

Indeed, he had a distinct impression that he was being carried. He could remember her name by a little effort; in fact, it was a very odd one. She was called Astrid Vasa.

As they came from the church, a tall man, who looked compressed by his store clothes and nearly strangled by his necktie, approached them, with a red-faced grin for the girl.

'Come along, Red,' said she. 'This is Red Moffet, Mr. Ingram.

Red, this is Mr. Ingram. You know. He runs the church, and everything. Don't you, Mr. Ingram?'

She looked up at Mr. Ingram at the conclusion of this infantile question, and shut out the view of Red Moffet with a parasol which slanted over one shoulder, and which she was spinning with a very delicately made little hand. Ingram wanted to frown, but he couldn't help smiling, which made him more determined than ever to frown. And so his smile grew broad!

'Red works in a mine, or something,' explained Astrid Vasa, shrugging a shoulder in the direction of Mr. Moffet.

'I *own* a mine,' said Red. 'It's kind of different.'

He was offended, of course. It occurred vaguely to Ingram that Mr. Moffet seemed *very* offended. For his own part, he wondered what his attitude should be toward the man who had killed the founder of the church over which he now presided. But after all, it was said that the other cheek must be turned. Ingram, concentrating on the thought, set his teeth.

They reached a picket fence in front of a little unpainted house. Few of the houses in Billman were painted, for that matter. 'I dunno that I'll be comin' in,' said Red Moffet gloomily.

'You better come along,' said Astrid. 'We gotta couple of the best-looking roosters that you ever saw for dinner.'

'I'm kind of busy,' said Red, more darkly than ever. 'So long!'

And he rambled down the street with a peculiarly awkward leg action. It reminded Ingram of the stride of a certain tackle of his college team, a fellow uncannily skillful in getting down the field under a kick, and marvelous in providing interference. He was more interested in Red Moffet from that instant.

'He's got a grouch on,' confided Astrid. 'He always wants to be the whole show since he got his silly old mine. C'mon in!'

The screen door screeched as it was kicked open from within. A burly gentleman in shirtsleeves stood before them.

'Hello; where's Red?' asked he in a pleasant voice.

'Dad, this is Mr. Ingram, the minister, and he's just been persuaded to—'

'Hullo, Ingram! Glad to see you. Where's Red, sis?'

'I dunno. He got a grouch on and beat it. I can't be bothered—all his notions.'

'You little simp,' said the inelegant Mr. Vasa, 'you'll be havin' him slide through your fingers one of these days.'

'Dad, what *are* you talkin' about?' exclaimed Astrid, very pink.

Her sire looked from her to her companion and grunted.

'Humph,' said he. 'Is that it, eh?'

'Is that what?' asked Astrid, furious.

'Aw, nothin'. C'min and sit down and rest your feet, Ingram. Lookit—ain't it like a fool girl, though? Shufflin' a boy like Red around? Know Red, I guess?'

'I've barely met him,' said Ingram, with reserve.

'Have, eh? Well, he's all right. Kind of mean, sometimes. Yep, mean as hell. But straight. Awful straight. Why, that kid's got a half million dollars' worth of mine up in the San Joaquin. Wouldn't think it, would you, to look at him? But I've seen it. Make your mouth water. Lord knows how deep the vein runs. Maybe take out a hundred thousand a year for a hundred years. Can't tell. And here's our Astie with a gent like that in her pocket, and chucking him away over her shoulder. Finders, keepers! Sis, you're a simp. That's all!'

'Father!' cried Astrid, dividing the word into two distinct parts, each concealing a world of meaning. 'D'you know that you're talkin' to a minister, with all your profanity, and—and talking foolishness about Red Moffet? Who said I had him in my pocket? Who wants to have him there? I'm sure I don't. And—what do you *mean* by talking like this to a perfect stranger?'

'Aw, don't step on your own toes to spite me, sis,' suggested her father, grinning. 'Besides, maybe Ingram ain't going to be a stranger for very long. How about it?'

This extreme directness embarrassed Ingram. He searched his mind—and found nothing with which to respond except a smile which might have received varying interpretations. Astrid retreated to regain her composure and let her blushes settle down to a normal pink.

'She's a good kid,' pronounced Mr. Vasa, 'but careless. Doggone careless. Far as that goes, though, this here is a land of carelessness and accidents. Billman's an accident, you know.'

'An accident?' said the polite Ingram.

'Sure. You know how it started?'

'No. Started?'

'Sure. A town has to start, don't it? Aw, you're fresh out of the old States, where a town put down roots so long ago that there ain't any story left about it except a legend that's a lie. Well, things ain't that way out here. We ain't scratched many wrinkles on the desert yet, and the only ones we've made are all new. Take Billman. Old Ike Billman was started for the San Joaquin range when the mines opened up there. Had a string of wagons loaded with stuff to sell for ten prices, the old hound! But he busted down here. Broke a wagon wheel. Before he got it fixed the boys were rushing through on the way for the San Joaquin on one side and for the Sierra Negra on the other. They wanted supplies, and wanted 'em so bad that price was no object. So Ike, he piled out his stuff and sold it out here just as good as he could have done if he'd marched all the way into the mountains. Then he put up a shack, and began freighting more stuff—not to the mines, but here. Other folks followed the good example. Then some of us have got interests in both places—San Joaquin and Sierra Negra—so we live in this halfway station. Y'understand? That's how Billman started growing. Just plain accident.'

'You're a mine owner also, then?' said Ingram in a polite attempt to discover the interests of his host.

Astrid returned. She had studied her smile before the mirror and felt that it would do.

'Sure, I'm a mine owner. I mean, I got shares in a couple of mines. I was a blacksmith when I come out here to—'

'Dad,' put in Astrid, 'I don't see why you have to rake up all the old family history. I'm sure Mr. Ingram isn't interested.'

'Why not?' asked Vasa. 'Ain't it honest to be a blacksmith? I never was in jail—except overnight. I got nothing to be ashamed of. It's a darn good trade, Ingram—blacksmithing. The money that I made out of it was honest. But this mining game—just luck! I took a couple of flyers at it. And they both connected with the bull's-eye. There you are. I'm gunna be pretty well off. I could sell out now for a hundred thousand. Maybe more. Not so bad, eh? But I guess I was just as happy hammering iron, hot or cold. It's the thing that you're cut out for that counts. Luck ain't apt to make you happy, Ingram. I'll never be worth shucks as a miner. But I could lay a shoe on the hoof of a horse so fine it would make you stare. You come and watch me some day. I still put in a few hours in the old shop now and then, just to keep my hand in.'

Mrs. Vasa, as small as her husband was large, rather withered but still good-looking, stood in the doorway. She was flushed from her work in the kitchen, and wiped her hands on her apron before she greeted the minister.

'Astie says that the sermon was just wonderful. I'll bet it was,' said Mrs. Vasa. 'Now you come along in and have a bite of lunch with us, will you? I'm mighty glad to have you here, Mr. Ingram. I was just too busy to get to church this morning. Church is kind of new in Billman, you know. And it takes a body a time to get into the run of going again. But my folks were mighty regular; they never missed a Sunday hardly. I always think it does you sort of good to go to church. Cools you off, you know, and it's restful. D'you think that you're gunna like Billman, Mr. Ingram?'

This was poured out effortlessly, rapidly, as they got to the table and sat down. Mr. Ingram could have made a quick answer to the final question, but it was not necessary to answer questions in this house. Between the head of the house and his wife there was no room left for silent spots.

Afterward they had music. Ingram sat down to supper, and remained to listen in amazement.

'Astie, she sings like a bird; doggone me if she don't!' said her father.

And that was exactly what she did. She accompanied herself on the piano. As smoothly as speech flowed from the lips of Mrs. Vasa, so song poured from the throat of her daughter, and the accompaniment bubbled delightfully in between.

'Dragged that doggone piano clean out from Comanche Crossing,' declared Vasa. 'And I never regretted what it cost, derned if I have. Now ain't it a treat to have a girl that can sing like that? She ought to be on the stage, where thousands could enjoy her. Honest, she should. But she'll never get there.'

'Why do you say that, Dad?' asked Mrs. Vasa.

'Because she's got her career all mapped and laid out for her right here in Billman,' said the head of the house.

'Career?' asked Astrid. 'What sort of career?'

'Humph!' said the ex-blacksmith. 'Breakin' hearts, or tryin' to!'

'Dad, you're just—' cried Astrid.

'You might let the poor girl—' began Mrs. Vasa.

'Aw, be still!' said Vasa. 'Ingram's gunna know about you pretty quick, if he don't already. I tell you what, Ingram. If that girl hadn't been born with a pretty face, she would have amounted to something. But she's got just enough good looks to spoil her. Her heart's all right. But her mirror keeps tellin' her that she's Cleopatra.'

'I hope you don't pay no attention, the way that he keeps on about his own flesh and blood,' said Mrs. Vasa to her guest.

Ingram smiled. But it was with an effort.

'Tune up, sis,' commanded Vasa. 'Go on and tune up, will you, and stop shaking your head at me. It ain't gunna change me. I'm too old to change. Take me or leave me. That's my motto. Maybe there's rough hammer marks on me, but the stuff I'm made of is the right iron, I think. Go on and sing, will you? Gimme some of the old ones, where you don't have to listen too hard. "Annie Laurie," that's about my speed. Somethin' nice and sad. Or "Ben Bolt." Doggone me, if that ain't a swell song, Mr. Ingram. What you say? "Ben Bolt," sis. And make her nice and sobby!'

They had 'Ben Bolt' and 'Annie Laurie,' also.

And afterward Mr. Vasa went to sleep in his chair and snored. And Mrs. Vasa announced that she would go and close her eyes for a minute. Such a warm afternoon! Mr. Ingram was glad to excuse her. He sat in the shade of the house with Astrid.

'I guess you think we're terrible people,' said Astrid sadly, 'the way that Dad carries on.'

'No,' said Ingram earnestly. 'I don't think so at all. I like him. He doesn't pretend. He's honest. I like him a great deal, you know.'

It was pleasant to see her face light. Her smile was like her singing, charming beyond words. And Ingram wondered how such a flower could have grown in such rocky soil. It made him feel, too, the value of that background of culture which enables one to appreciate the great and the simple, the complex and the homely.

'He thinks I ought to go on the stage,' said Astrid. 'But I'll never get there. No, I'll have to stay here in the desert.'

'Do you want to go?'

'I don't know,' said she. 'Only—I'm so lonely here.'

She looked up at him with sad eyes.

'Poor child!' said Ingram, melting. 'Lonely?'

He leaned a little toward her. Charitable kindness is commanded directly.

'Oh, lonely, lonely!' sighed Astrid, still looking into his face with suffering eyes. 'Do you know—but you wouldn't want me to tell you—'

'I think I would,' said the gentle minister.

'You know such a lot, and you're so wise and clever,' said Astrid, 'you would laugh at me!'

'I'm none of those things. And I won't laugh.'

'Really you won't?'

'No.'

'Well, of course I know a lot of people here. But though there are lots of them to chatter to—well, perhaps you won't understand—there's really not a soul for me to talk to.'

'Poor child!' said Mr. Ingram. He felt that he had said that before, but it was so true that he could not help repeating it. 'Poor child, of course I can understand!'

'Until you came, Mr. Ingram. And I really think that I could talk to you.'

'You shall, my dear. Of course you shall, whenever you please.'

'And you won't laugh at me?'

'Certainly not.'

'And when I tire you, you'll just send me away?'

'We'll see about that,' said he, tolerantly.

'Ah, you could understand!' said Astrid. 'The others—they just think that I'm always gay. They never guess, Mr. Ingram, how close the tears are sometimes!'

Yes, yes! But he could guess! He could see the tears now, just welling into her eyes. And he dropped a large, strong hand over her little one.

They sat in silence. He felt prepared to face the world. He felt the ability to endure, to suffer. And some day, when he had children, he was sure that he would be able to raise them tenderly, and well.

IV
Around the Corner from Nowhere

There followed for Ingram several days of severe labor, for he was establishing his parish, enlisting the interests of various people, and accepting sundry contributions which poured in with amazing speed for the first public work which he attempted. This was the establishment of a little hospital.

Sick men came down constantly from the mines in the San Joaquin, or in the Sierra Negra, and from Billman they were in the habit of taking the long stage journey overland to Comanche Crossing, where they could get medical attention of a kind. Ingram saw the possibility of putting up something which would be more than a way-station for the sick. And his idea was taken up enthusiastically. Mexican labor made the adobe bricks rapidly on the banks of the creek, and the terrible sun dried them to the proper strength; after that, skilled Mexican workers raised the walls of the hospital. There were three main rooms, and they were built of generous size, with lofty ceilings and thick walls, so that the sun's heat would not turn the place into an oven. For bed equipment there were various improvisations, and many donations were made after Ingram set the example by giving up his own cot. If he were willing to sleep on the floor, others would be equally brave in facing uncomfortable nights on the boards. For doctors there was no want; for several of them were among the men who had tried their luck in the gold rush and had run out of funds. They returned to their professional work and supplied the hospital with a competent staff. The Mexicans made excellent nurses, assisted from time to time by volunteers from among the ladies of Ingram's congregation. As for the funds to pay for all this necessary labor and expenses of various kinds, the inhabitants of Billman willingly dug deep into their purses, and in addition came contributions from all the mines.

The work of the hospital filled Ingram's hands for some time, and won for him a great deal of friendly recognition. In the meantime, a building of another kind went on to completion; a sure sign that the old days of Billman were drawing to a close, and that civilization was gathering the wild little town into its arms. For one day a thin, small man came to Ingram, a being so withered and lean that he seemed like a special product of the desert environment, equipped by nature to live for a long time without moisture of any kind. His skinny neck projected from a collar that would have girt in comfort the throat of a giant. His footwear was not neat. And when he fixed his melancholy eyes upon the minister, the latter was sure that this was another one of the race of hobos who pestered him from time to time.

Said the little man: 'I'm Sheriff Ted Connors. I came over to fix up a jail in this town, because it looks to me like this would be a handy place for a jail to stand. It wouldn't never have to be empty. And I'd like to know from you, how you get the folks in this town to fork over the money for a good cause?'

The two spent a long hour going over ways and means. And the very next day the foundations of the jail were established by the running of a shallow trench through the surface sands. The jail was completed in very few days. And the withered little sheriff jogged out of town, leaving his work to be carried on by a younger, bigger, and much more formidable-looking deputy, Dick Binney.

'Now that there's a church and a jail,' said big Vasa, 'it looks like Billman was pretty well-collared, eh?'

Ingram agreed. It was, he felt, only a matter of waiting a few weeks for the lawlessness and roughness of the town to subside. He had had a taste of that lawlessness before the town was very old. For one night—the hospital had been opened that day and the first patients, the wrecked victims of a mine explosion, installed—masked men entered Ingram's shack and bade him come with them.

They led him down the main street, which was singularly deserted, and out from the town to a point where a crowd was gathered under one of the few trees of the neighborhood. Beneath that tree stood a man whose hands were tied behind him; around his neck was the noose of a rope which had been flung over a limb above his head. Ingram realized that he was in the presence of a crew of vigilantes.

A gruff voice said to him: 'Here's Chuck Lane, that wants to talk to you, kid, before he swings. Hop to it and finish the job pronto. We're sleepy!'

'Do you intend to hang this man,' asked Ingram, 'without the process of law?'

'Ah!' said the leader of the crowd, 'is that your line? Now look here, kid, if there's gunna be any arguin' about that out of you, you can turn around and go home. Chuck swiped a horse, the skunk, and he's gunna swing for it. There's been too much borrowin' of horses around these parts lately. And he goes up as example number one. If you got any talkin' to do, do it on Chuck, will you?'

Ingram considered briefly. After all, he was quite helpless before these armed fellows. A protest would accomplish no good; it would merely deprive the victim of whatever spiritual comfort he might desire.

As he stepped up to the man who wore the noose, the others, with an unexpected sense of decency, made a wider circle around them.

'It's all right, boys,' said Chuck Lane cheerfully, noticing this backward movement. 'All I got to say can be heard by you gents.'

'Chuck,' said the minister, 'are you guilty of the crime of which they accuse you?'

'Crime?' echoed Chuck. 'If borrowin' a horse when a man's in a hurry is a crime—sure, I'm guilty! Well, kid, that ain't why they sent for you. Fact is, I want to know something from you.'

'Very well,' said Ingram, 'if you are a member of any church—'

'I was took to church once when I was a kid,' said the thief. 'Otherwise I ain't been bothered about them. But now when I come to stand here, around the corner from nowhere, it seems to me a pretty good time to find out what's on the other side. What do you say, Ingram?'

'Do you mean that you have doubts?' asked Ingram.

'Sure! Doubts about everything. Is this the finish—like going to sleep and never waking up? You're a smart young feller. No matter what lingo you're paid to sling in the church, you give me the low-down out here, man to man. I won't tell nobody what you've said.'

'There is a life to come, surely,' said Ingram.

'Will you gimme a proof, then?'

'Yes. The beasts have flesh and sense. Man has something more. He is born with flesh, mind, and spirit. Mind and flesh die, but the spirit is imperishable.'

'You say it pretty slick and sure,' remarked Chuck Lane. 'You really mean that?'

'Yes.'

'Well, then, the next thing is: What chance have I to slip through without—without—'

'What chance have you of happiness?' asked the minister gently. 'That I cannot tell. You know your own mind and life.'

'What difference does the life make, really?' asked the horse thief. 'Ain't it what's in the head that counts most?'

'Yes,' said Ingram. 'Sin is more in the mind than in the body. Have you anything on your conscience?'

'Me? Well, not much. I've taken my fun where I've found it, as somebody has said before me. I knifed a gent in Chihuahua, once. But that was a fair fight. He'd taken a pass at me with a chair. I shot a fellow up in Butte, too. But the hound had told everybody that he was going to get me. So that don't count, either. Otherwise, there ain't been nothing important. This little job about the horse—that's nothing. I was just in a hurry. Now, kid, the cards are on the table. Where do I go?'

'You are young,' said Ingram. 'You're not much more than thirty—'

'I'm twenty-two.'

The minister stared, aghast. Much, much of life had been scored on the face of this young man in his few short years.

Chuck seemed to understand, for he went on: 'But the wrinkles don't set till you're forty,' he remarked, 'and you can change your face up to that time. Y'understand?'

'Did you intend to take up some other way of—'

'I was always aiming to be a farmer, if I could get a stake together. Nothin' wrong with my intentions, but the money was lackin'.'

'And how did you try to earn it?'

'Cards was my chief line.'

'Gambling?'

'Yes.'

'You were honest, Chuck?'

'I never had the fingers for real crookedness,' admitted Chuck frankly. 'I could palm a couple of cards. That was all. And I generally met up with somebody a good deal slicker than I was. So my winnings went out the window.'

Ingram was silent.

'Does that make it bad for me?' asked Chuck ingenuously.

It was a grim moment in which to play the judge, but Ingram

answered slowly: 'You've been a man-killer, a thief, and a crooked gambler. And perhaps there have been other things.'

'Well,' said Chuck, 'I suppose that closes the door on me?'

'I don't know,' said Ingram. 'It depends, in the first place, upon your repentance.'

'Repentance?' echoed the other. 'Well, I dunno that I feel bad about th' way I've lived. I've never shot a man in the back, and I've never cheated a drunk or a fool at the cards. I tried to trim the sharks, and the sharks always trimmed me.'

'Is that all?' said Ingram.

'That's about all. Except that I'd sure like to get with the right crowd of boys on the other side. I never had no real use for the tinhorns, thugs, and short sports that must be crowded into hell, Ingram. But you think I got a mighty slim chance, eh?'

Wistfulness and manly courage struggled in his voice.

'No man can judge you,' said the young minister. 'If you believe in the goodness of God, and fix your mind on that belief, you may be saved, Chuck. I shall pray for you.'

'Do it, old-timer,' said Chuck. 'A prayer or two wouldn't do me any harm, and it might do me a lot of good. And—look here—hey, boys!'

'Well?' asked someone, coming closer.

'I'd like Ingram to have my guns. It's all that I've got to leave the world.'

'Are there no messages that I can take for you?' asked Ingram.

'I don't want to think about the folks that I leave behind me,' said the thief. 'I got a girl down in—well, let it go. It's better for her never to hear than it is for her to start grievin' about me. Better to think that I run off and forgot to come back to her. So long, Ingram!'

'Gentlemen,' said Ingram, turning on the crowd, 'I protest against this unwarranted—'

'Rustle the kid out of the way,' said someone, and half a dozen strong pairs of hands hurried Chuck suddenly away.

Behind him Ingram heard a groan, as of strong friction, and, glancing back, saw something swinging pendulous beneath the tree, and writhing against the golden surface of the rising moon.

V
A Gent With a Gun

The death of Chuck Lane caused a good deal of excitement in the town, for he was no common or ordinary thief, and the minister overheard one most serious conversation the next day.

He had stopped at Vasa's house to talk over the choir work with pretty Astrid, for she led the choir for him, and a thorough good job she made of it. There he met Red Moffet, and Red, with an ugly glance, rose and strode away, barely grunting at the minister as he passed.

'I think Red doesn't like me very well,' said Ingram. 'He seems to have something against me. Do you guess what it is?'

'I can't guess,' said Astrid, with the strangest of smiles. 'I haven't the least idea!'

But now the gallant form of the deputy sheriff, Dick Binney, swept down the street, and Red Moffet hailed him suddenly and strongly from the sidewalk.

'Binney! Hey, Binney!'

The deputy sheriff reined in his horse. The dust cloud he had raised blew down the street, and left him with the shimmering heat of the sun drenching him. So terrible was the brightness of that light, and so great the radiation of heat from every surface, that sometimes it seemed to the young minister that he lived in a ghost world here on the edge of the desert. All was unreal, surrounded by airy lines of imagination, or radiating heat.

Unreal now were those two men, and the horse which one of them bestrode. But very real was the voice of Red Moffet, calling: 'Binney, were you there last night?'

'Was I where?'

'You know where.'

'I dunno what you mean.'

'Was you one of them that hung up poor Chuck Lane?'

'Me? The sheriff of this here place? What you take me for, anyway? Are you crazy?'

'I dunno what I take you for. But I've heard a yarn that you was with the rest of them cowards and sneaks that killed poor Chuck.'

Dick Binney dismounted suddenly from his horse.

'I dunno how to take this here,' said he. 'I dunno whether it's aimed at the boys who hanged Chuck last night, or at me!'

'I say,' declared Moffet, 'that Chuck was an honester man than any of them that strung him up. And if you was one of them, that goes for you, too!'

It seemed that the deputy was willing enough to take offense, but he paused and gritted his teeth, between passion and caution. Certainly it would not do for him to avow that he had been one of the masked men.

So he said: 'What you say don't bother me, Red. But if you're out and lookin' for trouble, I'm your man, all right!'

'Bah!' sneered Red Moffet. 'It wouldn't please you none to make trouble for any man in town, now that you got the law behind you! You can do your killings with a posse now.'

'Can I?' replied Binney, equally furious. 'I would never need a posse to account for you, young feller!'

'Is that a promise, Binney?' asked Moffet. 'Are you askin' me to have a meetin' with you one day?'

'Whenever you like,' said the deputy. 'But now *I'm* busy. I ain't gunna stand here and waste time with a professional gunfighter like you, Moffet. Only, I give you a warning. You got to watch yourself around this part of the world from now on. I'm watchin' you. I'm gunna give you just enough rope to hang yourself.'

He jumped back into the saddle, and galloped down the street, leaving Red Moffet shaking a fist after him and cursing volubly.

Mr. Vasa, coming home, paused to listen with a judicious air to the linguistic display of Red. Then he came into his yard, shaking his head gravely.

'I'll tell you what it is,' said Vasa, greeting his daughter and the minister, 'things ain't what they used to be around these parts. There's a terrible fallin' off of manhood all around! There's a terrible fallin' off! There's been enough language used up by Red and Dick Binney, yonder, to have got a whole town shot up in the palmy days that I could tell you about.'

'Dad!' cried his daughter.

'Look here,' said the ex-blacksmith, 'don't you make a profession of being shocked every time I open my mouth. You live and learn, honey! I tell you, there was never no fireworks in the way of words shot off before the boys reached for their guns in the old days, Ingram. No, sir! I remember when I was standing in the old Parker saloon. That was a cool place. Always wet down the floor every hour and sprinkled fresh, wet sawdust around. Made a drink taste a lot better. It was like spring inside that place, no matter how much summer there might be in the street. Well, young Mitchell was in there, drinking. Same fellow that shot Pete Brewer in the back. He was drinkin' and yarnin' about a freighting job that he'd come in from. He ordered up a round.

' "I'll buy one for the boys," says he.

' "No, you won't," says a voice.

'We looked across, and there was Tim Lafferty that had just come through the swingin' doors.

' "Why won't I?" asks Mitchell.

' "You ain't got time!" says Tim.

'They went for their guns right then, and as I stepped back out of line two bullets crossed in front of my face. Neither of 'em missed. But it was Mitchell that died. Well, that was about as much conversation as they needed in the old days before they had a fight. But now, look at the way that those two have been wastin' language in the street, and nothing done about it. I say, it's disgusting!'

'Do you think that Red's a coward?' asked the girl sharply.

'Red? Naw! He ain't a coward. And he can shoot. But what's important is that the fashion has changed now. A gent with a gun that he wants to use feels that he's got to write a book about his intentions before he can burn any powder. They didn't waste themselves on introductions in the old days. Well, those times will never come back.'

The minister asked gravely: 'Is it possible that the deputy sheriff could have been at the lynching the other night?'

'Well, and why not?'

'Why not? The representative of the law—'

'Why, old Connors made a terrible mistake when he up and appointed Dick for the job. Dick is all right some ways. But he's got an idea that the law is to be more useful to him than to the rest of the folks. He hated Chuck. I got an idea that he *was* at the hanging. And that's why Red is mad. He loved Chuck. Good boy, that Chuck Lane.'

'Did you know him?' asked the minister, with some eagerness.

'Did I know myself? Sure, I knew him!'

'He was a gambler and—a horse thief?'

'That was careless—swiping the horse. Matter of fact, though, if he'd got to the other end of the line, he would have sent back the coin to pay for the horse as soon as he got enough money together. But you got to judge people according to their own lights, and not according to yours, young man!'

Thus spoke Mr. Vasa, with the large assurance of one who has lived in this world and knows a good deal about it.

'It's a brutal thing to lynch any man, no matter how guilty,' declared Ingram.

'Hey, hold on!' cried the blacksmith. 'Matter of fact, there ain't enough organized law around here to shake a stick at. Not half enough! And I don't blame the boys that hung up Chuck. Can't let horse stealing go on!'

This double sympathy on the part of Mr. Vasa amazed and silenced Ingram.

'You're lookin' thin,' went on Vasa. 'Tell me how you're likin' the town. You run along into the house, Astie, will you? I got to talk to Ingram.'

Astrid rose, smiled at her guest, and went slowly toward the house.

'She's got a sweet smile, ain't she?' was the rather abrupt beginning of the blacksmith's speech.

'She has,' said Ingram thoughtfully. 'Yes,' he added, as though turning the matter in his mind and agreeing thoroughly, 'yes, she has a lovely smile. She—she's a fine girl, I think.'

'Pretty little kid,' declared the father, yawning. 'But she ain't so fine. No, not so fine as you'd think. Wouldn't do a lick of housework, I don't think, if her life depended on it. Y'understand?'

'Ah?' said Ingram, vaguely offended by this familiarity.

'And she's fond of everything that money can be spent on. Look at that pony of hers. Took her down to look over a whole herd at the McCormick sale. Nothin' would do for her. "I'll take that little brown horse, Dad," says she.

'"Now, Astie," says I, "don't you be a little fool. That little brown horse is a racer, out of blood more ancienter than the doggone kings of England. For a fact!"

'"All right," says she, and turns her shoulder.

'"Look yonder at that fine chestnut," says I. "There's a fine, gentle, upstanding horse. Half-bred. Strong, not a flaw in it anywhere. Warranted good disposition. Mouth like silk. Footwork on the mountains like a mule. Go like a camel without water. Now, Astie, how would you like it for me to give you that fine horse—and ain't he a beauty, too?"

'"I don't want it," says she. "It'll do for that cross-eyed Mame Lucas, maybe!"

'"Astie," says I, "what would you do with a horse that would buck you over its head the minute that you got into the saddle?"

'"Climb into the saddle again," says she.

'"Bah!" says I.

'"Bah yourself!" says she.

'It made me mad, and I bought that doggone brown horse. Guess for what? Eleven hundred iron men! Yes, sir!

'"Now, you ride him home!" says I, hoping that he'd break her neck.

'He done his best, but she's made of India rubber. Threw her five times on the way, and had half the town chasing the horse for her. But she rode him all the way home, and then went to bed for three days. But now he eats out of her hand. Wouldn't think that she had that much spunk, would you?'

'No,' agreed the minister, amazed. 'I would not!'

'Nobody would,' said the blacksmith, 'to look at the sappy light in her eyes a good deal of the time. But I'm tellin' you true. Expensive! That's what that kid is. If there was ten pairs of shoes in a store window, she'd pick out the most high-priced pair blindfold. She's got an instinct for it, I tell you!'

Ingram smiled.

'You think that she'd change, maybe,' said the blacksmith. 'But she won't. It's bred in the bone. God knows where she got it, though. Her ma was never an expensive woman.'

He rolled a cigarette with a single twist of his powerful fingers, and scratched a match on the thigh of his trousers. A hundred more or less faint lines showed where other matches had been lighted on the same cloth.

'This ain't a blind trail that I been followin',' he announced. 'I'm leadin' up to something. D'you guess what?'

'No,' said Ingram. 'I really don't guess what you may have in mind.'

'I thought you wouldn't,' said Vasa. 'Some of you smart fellows couldn't cut for sign with a five-year-old half-wit. Matter of fact, what I want to know is: Where are you heading with sis?'

'Heading with her?' said Ingram, very blank.

'Where d'you drift? What's your name with her? Does she call you deary, yet?'

Mr. Ingram stared.

'Has she held your hand yet for you?' asked Vasa.

The blood of a line of ancient ancestors curdled in the veins of Mr. Ingram.

'She does all of those things to the boys,' said the blacksmith. 'There is even two or three that may have kissed her. I dunno. But not many. She gets a little soft and soapy. But she's all right; I'd trust Astie in the crowd. I wondered where you'd been sizin' up with her?'

'I don't know what you mean,' declared the minister.

'Aw, come on!' grinned the other, very amiably. 'Everybody has to love Astie. Some love her a little. Some love her a lot. Even the girls can't hate her. How d'you stand? Love her a little? Love her a lot?'

Ingram began to turn pink. Partly with embarrassment, and partly with anger.

'I have for Astrid,' he said with deliberation, 'a brotherly regard—'

'Hell!' said Vasa.

The word exploded from his thick lips.

'What kind of drivel is this?' he demanded.

At this, Ingram narrowed his eyes a little and sat a bit forward. More than one football stalwart who had seen that expression in the eyes of Ingram had winced in the old days. But the blacksmith endured this gaze with the calm of one who carries a gun and knows how to use it. Who carries two hundred and thirty pounds of muscle, also—and knows how to use it!

'Don't give me the chilly eye like that, kid,' he continued. 'I aim to find out where you stand with Astie. Will you talk?'

'Your daughter,' said the minister, 'is a very pleasant girl, and I presume that that closes this part of the conversation?'

He stood up. The blacksmith rose also.

'Well,' said Vasa, glowering, 'suppose we shake hands and part friends on it?'

'Certainly,' said Ingram.

A vast, rather grimy paw closed over his hand, and suddenly he felt a pressure like the force of a powerful clamp, grinding the metacarpal bones together. But pulling a good oar on a powerful eight does not leave one with the grip of a child. The leaner, bonier fingers of Ingram curled into the plump grip of Vasa, secured a purchase, and began to gather strength.

Suddenly Vasa cursed and tore his hand away.

'Sit down again,' he said suddenly, looking at his splotchy hand. 'Sit down again. I didn't think you was as much of a man as this! It's what comes of layin' off work. I'm soft!'

The minister, breathing rather hard, sat down as invited. He waited, silently.

'You see, Ingram,' said the blacksmith, 'I've watched sis with the other boys, and I've watched her with you. She's always been getting a bit dizzy about some boy or other. But with you it's a little different; I guess she's hard hit. Now, that's the way I see it for her. How do I see it for you? And mind you, she'd take my head off if she thought that I was talking out of school.'

Mr. Ingram looked at the wide blue sky—the sun dazzled him. He looked at the ground—it was withering in the heat. He looked at the fat face of the blacksmith, and two keen eyes sparkled back at him.

'I didn't think—' he began.

'Try again,' said Vasa with a chuckle.

The blue eyes and the smile of Astrid flashed into the mind of the minister. Her smile was just a little crooked, leaving one cheek smooth, while a dimple came covertly in the other.

'I don't know,' said Ingram; 'as a matter of fact—'

'Only holding her hand?' said the blacksmith with a smile. 'Well, Ingram, I ain't throwin' her at your head. I'm just telling you to watch yourself. It don't take more'n five minutes for a girl like that to make a strong man pretty dizzy. And if she ever gets the right chance to work on you, I know Astie! She'll hit you with everything she's got, from a smile to a tear. She'll either have you on your knees worshippin', or else she'll have you comfortin' her. God knows what she would need comfort about! But that's the way she works. You understand? And one thing more—Red Moffet is wild about her. Red is the closest to a real man that's ever wanted to marry her. And he's got everything that her husband ought to have—money, grit, and sense. You've got sense. I guess you've got grit. But I know you ain't got money. Mind you, I'm just talkin' on the side. But, whichever way you're goin' to jump, you better make up your mind pretty quick. Because Red, if he don't hear something definite, is gunna lay for you with a gun one of these days!'

With this remark, Mr. Vasa arose.

'Girls are hell to raise,' said he, confidentially. 'Hell to have 'em and hell to lose 'em. Come on in, Ingram!'

'I'm busy at the church,' said Ingram, rather stunned.

'Has this here yarning cut you up some?'

'No, certainly not. I thank you for being so frank. I didn't, as a matter of fact—'

'Maybe I shouldn't have told you. Well, it's out now, and it'll bring matters to a head. Whichever way you jump, good luck to you!'

They shook hands again, more gingerly. And Ingram turned out the gate and went up the street, his head low, and many thoughts spinning in his mind, like the shadows of a wheel. It was, of course, ridiculous that Ingram should think of marrying a silly little Western girl.

And still, she was not so silly. File off a few rough corners of speech—she would learn as quickly as a horse runs—and—

He came to the church and stood before it, hardly seeing its familiar outlines. He had received counsel. But, oddly enough, what he wanted to do now was to go back and see Astrid and find out, first of all, if she really cared for him.

Suppose that she did; and that he was not ready to tell her that he loved her? He made a sudden gesture, as though to put the whole idea away from his mind, and with resolute face and firm step, he went into the church.

VI
Talking Was His Business

A little chill went through Billman next day, for it was known that Red Moffet had discovered the name of at least one member of the posse that had hung Chuck Lane. Mr. Ingram heard the story from Astrid when she stayed a few moments after choir practice. It was a large choir, and though it was impossible to obtain enough male voices to match the sopranos, it was pleasant to hear the hymns shrilling sweetly from the throats of the girls.

Astrid stayed after practice and told the exciting tale. Mr. Red Moffet, by some bit of legerdemain, had secured the very rope with which Chuck Lane was hanged by the neck until dead. And, having secured that rope, Mr. Moffet had examined it with care and promptly recognized it. For, at the end, there was a queer little knot such as only a sailor would be likely to tie. And in Billman there was a cowpuncher and teamster who had been a sailor before the mast—one Ben Holman, a fellow of unsavory appearance. And worse reputation.

Red Moffet had, first of all, searched wildly through Billman to find the owner of that rope. But it was said that Mr. Holman heard that he was wanted and decided to look the other way. He slipped out from the village into the trackless desert. Mr. Moffet started in pursuit in the indicated direction, but straightaway the desert became truly trackless, for a brisk wind rose, whipped the sands level, and effaced all signs.

Red Moffet came back to Billman, and the first place he went to was out to the cemetery, carrying the hangman's rope with him. He visited the most newly made grave and sat for a long time beside it. He himself had paid for the digging of that grave and for the headstone, which stood at one end of it, engraved in roughly chiseled letters:

'Here lies Chuck Lane. He was a good fellow that never played in luck!'

Men said that the inscription was Red's contribution also.

Whatever were the thoughts that passed through Moffet's mind s he sat there alone in the graveyard, Billman did not have the lightest hesitation in describing them as fluently as though Red ad confided his ideas to the world in general.

'If you know what he was thinking, tell me,' suggested the young ninister to Astrid.

'Oh, of course. Red was swearing that he would never give up he trail until he had Ben Holman's scalp.'

'Does he intend to murder that man for being one of the mob?' sked the minister.

'Murder?' echoed Astrid. 'Well, it isn't murder when you stick y a pal, is it?'

'This pal, as you call him, is already dead. And though the means ised were illegal, I must say that it seems to me young Lane was not vorthy of much better treatment than he received.'

At this, Astrid, who was sitting lightly on the back of a chair, swinging one leg to and fro, frowned.

'I don't follow that,' said she. 'You've got to stick by things, I suppose. Death doesn't matter, really.'

'But, Astrid—'

'I wonder,' broke in this irreverent girl, 'what folks would say if they heard me call you Reginald, or Reggie, say!'

'Why do you laugh, Astrid?'

'Why, Reggie is really a sort of a flossy name, isn't it?'

'It never occurred to me,' said that serious young man. 'But to return to what you say—about death not mattering—'

'Between a man and his pal, I mean,' said Astrid. 'Why, you live after death, don't you?'

'Yes,' said Ingram. 'Of course.'

'Then,' said she triumphantly, 'you see the point. Even after a pal is dead, you'd want to do for him just what you'd do if he were living. That's pretty simple, it seems to me!'

'My dear child!' exclaimed he. 'What service is Red performing to Chuck Lane by chasing Ben Holman out of Billman and murdering him if he can?'

'Why, Reggie,' said the girl, 'how would you serve a friend, anyway? Suppose you're a friend of mine and you want music for your church. Well, I'd sing in your church, wouldn't I?' And she wrinkled her nose a little and smiled at him. 'Or suppose that I was a friend and that you wanted a new wing built on the church,

I'd build it for you if I could, wouldn't I? Same in everything. Yo serve a friend by doing what he would do for himself if he coul but which he can't—'

'I don't exactly see how you relate this to Red's murderous pu suit of Holman.'

'You don't? You're queer about some things, Reggie. Suppos that Chuck Lane could come back to earth, what would he war to do except turn loose and chase down the boys that strung hir up? And first of all he'd want to get the fellow who loaned hi rope to do the job. I think that's pretty clear!'

'Astrid, Astrid,' said Ingram, 'do you excuse a murder with murder?'

'But it isn't murder, Reggie! Don't be silly! It's just revenge!'

' "Vengeance is mine, saith the Lord!" '

'Oh!' said she. 'Well, wait till the time comes, and I'll see hov long you'd sit still and let a partner be downed by thugs or yegg or something! You'd fight pretty quick, I guess!'

'No,' said he. 'Lift a hand against the life of a fellow? Astrid, w expressly are commanded to turn the other cheek!'

'Sure,' said Astrid. 'That's all right. But you can't let peopl walk over you, you know. Isn't good for 'em. Would make 'en bullies. You got to trip 'em up for their own sakes, don't you?'

'My dear Astrid, you are quite a little sophist!'

'And what does that mean?'

'A sophist is one who has a clever tongue and can make the worse way appear the better, or the better appear the worse.'

She grew excited.

'Suppose, Reggie, that you were to stand right here—you see? And a gun in your hand—'

'I never carry a gun,' said the minister mildly.

'Oh, bother! Just suppose! You're standing right here with a gun in your hand, and your best friend is standing in the doorway of the church, and you see a greaser come sneaking in behind him with a knife—tell me, Reggie—would you let the greaser stick that knife into his back, or would you shoot the sneak—the low-down, yellow—'

'Such a thing could never happen here in the house of God,' said Ingram.

'Oh, but just supposin'! Just supposin'! Can't you even do a little supposin', Reggie? You make me tired, sometimes! I pretty nearly believe that you haven't got any real pals! Tell me!'

'Pals?' He echoed the word very gravely. And then his face grew a bit stern with pain.

'Hold on!' cried Astrid. 'I didn't mean to step on your toes like that. I see that you *have* got 'em, and—'

'No,' said he. 'There was a time when I had a good many friends. They were very dear to me, Astrid; but when I took up this new work, why, they drifted away from me. So many years—a very closed life—books—study—a bit of devotion. No, I'm afraid that I haven't a single friend left to me!'

'That's terrible hard!' said the girl, sighing. 'But I'll bet you have, though. Look here, it makes you feel pretty bad, doesn't it, I mean the thought of having lost 'em?'

'I trust that I have no regrets for the small sacrifices which I may have made in a great cause which is worthy of more than I could ever—'

'Stop!' cried Astrid. 'Oh, stop, stop! When you get humble like that, I always want to either cry—or beat you! I want to beat you just now! I say, you feel terrible bad because you've lost all those old friends. Then you can be sure that they feel bad to have lost you. So they still *are* your friends, and they would come jumping if you just gave them a chance! Tell me about them, Reggie.'

He shook his head.

'It is a little sad,' said he, 'to think of all the men who've been—well, I think I prefer to let it drop.'

'But I want to know. Look! I've told you everything about myself. And I don't know a thing about you. That's not fair. But the whole point is, that any real man would go to hell and back for the sake of a friend. Now wouldn't he?'

The minister was silent.

Astrid went on, innocent of having given offense: 'I'll tell you how it is, then, with Red. He and Chuck were old pals. Chuck's lynched. Well, Red wouldn't be a man worth dropping over a cliff if he wouldn't try to do something for his old partner. Isn't that clear and straight? I want to make you admit it.'

'I can't admit that,' said the minister slowly.

'By jiminy!' said the girl. 'I *do* believe that you've never really had a hundred-percent friend—the kind that they raise in this part of the country, I mean. A fellow who would ride five hundred miles for a look at you. Never write you a letter, most likely. But fight for you, die for you, swear by you, love you dead or livin', Reggie. That's the kind of a friend that I mean!'

The minister had bowed his head. He was silent; perhaps the torrent of words from that excited, small, round throat was bringing before his eyes all the men he had ever known.

'What are you seeing?' she asked suddenly.

'I'm seeing everything from the stubble field where the path ran to the swimming pool,' said Ingram sadly, 'to the empty lot behind the school where we used to have our fights; and the schoolrooms; and the men at college. Boys, I should say. They weren't men. They can't be men until they've learned how to endure pain!'

'Look here!' she snapped. 'Does a fellow have to suffer in order to be the right sort?'

'Would you trust something that looked like steel,' asked he, 'unless you knew it had been tempered by going through the fire?'

'Now you're getting a little highflown for me,' said the girl. 'It isn't only the men that have been your friends. But suppose I were to say that a girl you've known was in danger—the very one that you liked the most—suppose that she were standing there in the doorway, and a sneak of a Mexican was coming up behind—what would you do? Would you shoot?'

'No, I would simply call: "Astrid, jump!"'

'I—' began Astrid.

Then the full meaning of this speech took her breath away and left her crimson. Ingram himself suddenly realised what he had said, and he stared at her in a sort of horror.

'Good gad!' said the Reverend Reginald Ingram. 'What have I said!'

'You've made me all d-d-dizzy!' said Astrid.

'I—as a matter of fact, the words—er—were not thought out, Astrid!'

'Of course you didn't mean—' began Astrid.

'I hope you'll forgive me!' said Ingram.

'For what?' she said.

'For blurting out such a—'

'Such a what?' she persisted.

'You're making it hard for me to apologize.'

'But I don't want you to apologize.'

'My dear Astrid—'

'I wish you'd stop talking so far down to me!'

'I see you're offended and angry.'

'I could be something else, if you'd let me,' said she.

'I don't understand,' said Ingram miserably.

'I could be terribly happy, if you meant what you said.'

He looked hopelessly about him. A daring blue jay had lighted on the sill of the open window. Its bright, satanic eyes seemed to be laughing at him.

'You see—Astrid—'

'Don't!' cried she and stamped her little foot.

'Don't what?' he asked, more embarrassed than ever.

'Don't look so stunned. I'm not going to propose to you.'

'My dear child—the friendship which I feel—which—so beautiful—most extraordinary—fact is that—I don't seem to find words, Astrid.'

'Talking is your business,' said the girl. 'You've *got* to find words.'

'Do I?' asked Ingram, wiping his hot brow.

'You can't leave me floundering like this, unless it's because you have some sort of a doubt about me. I want to know. Tell me, Reggie!'

'What?' asked he, very desperate.

'You make me so angry—I could cry!'

'For heaven's sake, don't! Not in the church, when—'

'Is that all you think about—your silly old church? Reginald Oliver Ingram!'

'Yes, Astrid!'

'Do I have to tell you that I love you?'

Mr. Ingram sat down so suddenly and heavily that the chair creaked beneath his weight.

'Stand up!' ordered Astrid.

He stood up.

'You don't really care!' she cried.

'Astrid—I'm a bit upset.'

'Are you sick?'

'I'm a bit groggy.'

'Reggie, cross your heart and tell me—have you ever been in love?'

'Not to my knowledge.'

'Never really been in love?'

'No.'

'Are you a little giddy and foolish and—'

'Yes.'

'You *are* in love!' said she.

'Do you think so?'

'Have you never proposed?'

'Never!'

'Never in your whole life—to any girl?'

'No!'

'Then you'd better begin right now.'

'Astrid, the thing is impossible!'

'What is?'

'To marry. You understand? I'm a minister. A poor man. Nothing but my salary—'

'Bother the silly salary! Do you want me?'

'Yes.'

'Honestly?'

'Yes.'

'More'n all the world?'

'Yes.'

'More'n all your old friends—almost as much as your church and your work?'

'I think so,' said he.

'You'd better sit down,' suggested Astrid.

She took the chair beside him, and leaned her shining head against his shoulder.

'Heavens!' said Astrid.

'What's wrong?'

'How terribly happy I am! Why, Reggie, you're all trembling!'

'Because I'm trying to keep from touching you.'

'Why try?'

'We sit here in the house of God and in His presence, Astrid.'

'He would have to know some time,' said she. 'Gracious!'

'What, dear?'

'How hard you made me work!'

VII
They Didn't Need Him

The ideas of Astrid about the practical problems of the future were extremely simple and to the point. They could easily live on his salary. How? All she wanted would be some horses for riding, and a few Mexican servants—

'I have just enough,' said he, 'to support one person on the plainest of fare, with no servant at all.'

'Oof!' said Astrid.

But after a little thought she arrived at another solution. She would simply tell her father that she needed enough money to marry on. And, of course, her father would give it to her.

'I couldn't marry you on another man's money,' said Ingram.

'But he isn't another man. He's my father.'

For answer, Ingram raised her hand to his lips, and felt it quiver as he touched it.

'I can see,' said Astrid, 'that I'll never be able to call my soul my own in our house! You're going to be a bully, Reggie!'

He smiled.

'But what *shall* we do?' she asked.

'Work—and wait—and I'll hope,' he began.

But she broke in: 'Of course it'll be arranged. You could go up in the hills and discover a mine or two, the way that Father did. Reggie, that's a glorious idea! Because I'd really like to be rich. Wouldn't you? You could build such a wonderful big church then!'

Ingram studied her, half in awe and half in amusement, for heedless child and wise woman blended so oddly and unexpectedly in her that he never knew just how to take her.

However, having suggested that he take a flying trip to the mountains to make himself rich, she next felt that it might be better if no word of their engagement were given out for the moment.

'Chiefly because of Dad,' said the girl. 'The minute you showed up, he said that I would throw over Red and marry you if I could. The silly old thing!'

'Has Red a claim on you?' asked Ingram.

'Red? Not a bit!'

'But you spoke of throwing him over?'

'Oh, right after the rodeo, you know. When Red had the prize both for riding and roping. Well, just about that time I saw a good deal of him, and I said that I'd marry him, some day, maybe!'

'As a matter of fact, you were definitely engaged to him?' asked Ingram sternly.

She turned and stared at him.

'What terrible rows we're going to have!' said Astrid Vasa. 'I hope we'll love each other enough to get through them safely. Sure—maybe you can say that I was engaged to him.'

'But you said before that he didn't have a whit of claim on you!'

'Oh, Reggie, don't pin me down. It's not fair, is it? You'd never doubt that I love you, Reggie? What did any other man matter to me after I once saw you?'

'Did you break your engagement with him?' asked the minister, clinging grimly to the point.

'You're going to be mean, I see,' sighed Astrid.

'Did you?'

'Of course, it's broken to tiny bits!'

'Before today?'

Her eyes were wide open, like the eyes of a child.

'Reggie—don't!' she begged.

'Then I'll go to tell him myself,' said Ingram.

'No!' screamed Astrid.

'No?'

'Don't go near him! He'd—he'd kill you, Reggie!'

'Would he murder me if I told him that you had become—'

'Don't even speak about it! It makes me see you lyin' dead! He told me he'd do it!'

'Told you that he'd do what?'

'He told me that he'd kill the other man, if I ever turned him down after once being engaged to him!'

'Did he actually tell you that—the ruffian?'

'Before he even proposed to me!' said Astrid.

'Ah?'

'He told me to think things over. Because he was going to ask me to marry him. He knew that I'd been engaged to other boys. He said that he wasn't a boy, but a man. And that he didn't expect to fall in and out with the girl he hoped to marry. It was to be all of him or none of him. And he said that if I ever drifted away from him, he'd stop me by putting a bullet into the gent that I was drifting toward. You understand, Reggie? Don't go near him, because he's a terrible fighter!'

Ingram made no promise. He watched Astrid walk down the street from the church, and he heard her gay voice sing out to a friend as she passed.

It left him to grave reflections. Old Vasa's first suggestion had utterly stunned him; but this dénouement, following so suddenly and unexpectedly, seemed to him most mysterious. It had been a matter of the moment. There was no reflection or planning. Words had burst from his lips of their own accord. And now he had placed himself in the hands of a little bright-haired girl of the desert, the daughter of a rude blacksmith and a simple household drudge.

He thought of the people among whom he had moved in other years, and his heart failed him. But when he thought of Astrid, his courage returned. For he felt that there was the right stuff in her. She had the right ring, and only bell metal makes the bell.

As for Red Moffet, he did not give that gentleman a serious second thought. Ingram returned to his little office beside the church and sat there for an hour, casting up accounts, going over papers, and with a mighty effort forcing out of his mind every concern except that of the church which he served.

Boxing teaches one to concentrate in a crisis; so does football; and the minister felt grateful to both sports as he worked in his little private room, with only the ghost of Astrid floating somewhere in the back of his brain.

It was very hot. But he had compunctions about taking off his coat while he was in any part of the sacred edifice. In fact Mr. Ingram was hopelessly medieval in many respects. And he kept himself stiffly incased in the armor of outworn ceremony. However, the robes in which an idea is clothed are often essential to it; remove a man's manners, and you are apt to remove the man; and very few think of their prayers before they are on their knees. The gesture provokes the word, the word provokes the idea, and the idea may finally lead again to an act. So the young minister in his office kept himself rigidly in hand and would have been the last to guess that he did not use the formalities, but that the formalities used him.

In the midst of his labors, a tap came at his office door. He opened it and found himself facing Mr. Red Moffet. A dark scowl was upon the face of that gentleman, and according to the classic advice, he struck at once into the middle of his tale.

'Ingram,' said he, 'Billman don't need you. Astrid don't need you. I don't need you. You better move on before sunset!'

And with that brief remark, he turned and walked away, leaving the minister to stare after him blankly.

He had already heard of such warnings. Men who disregarded them usually fought for their lives before the next morning came—or else they accepted the advice and moved on.

What was he to do?

He had done his share of hunting; he had worked with a revolver at a target in his time. But all of this was years ago and he was hideously out of practice, of course. Besides, he could not possibly use violent measures, even in self-defense. He could not imagine a more un-Christian proceeding.

What, then, was he to do?

He turned the thing backward and forward in his mind. Of course, he could not flee from the town. Of course, he could not ask for help from—from Vasa, say. But then, what remained to him to do?

He had felt that this was the very brightest and most joyous day in his entire life. But the brightness had been snatched away. No, not altogether! A thrill of happiness remained in his heart and never could be snatched away, save by her who had given it.

So, in a dark mood, indeed, he left his office and went back to his shack, where he paced up and down, wondering, probing a mind in which he knew he could find no suggestion of a solution for his difficulties. A great bitterness against Moffet swelled in his heart. For certainly it was unfair to attack one who was consecrated to peace and to peaceful ways. At another time—a few years before—when the clerical collar was not yet around his neck, he would not have been troubled by such a threat as he had received today. But those old days were gone, and his hands were tied!

But there was something of the ancient Roman in the minister. He had been placed at his post, and at his post he would stick, like those sentinels at Pompeii, who stood on guard until the ashes and the lava of Vesuvius buried them.

'Ah,' said a voice at his door, 'we still have our little yellow friend, eh? You've made him at home, Mr. Ingram, I see?'

He looked up and saw the black-robed Dominican before him. There was something so comfortable and reassuring in that brown, fat face that Mr. Ingram fairly jumped from his chair to take the hand of the Mexican.

'Come in, Brother Pedrillo,' said he. 'Come in and sit down. I'm glad to see you!'

'Thank you,' said the other, and settling himself in the largest chair he turned to the lizard and whistled a thin, small note. Then he laughed, as the little creature lifted its head and listened.

'Look!' said the friar. 'You'd never think that he could move as fast as a whiplash, to see him now stiffened with the sun and a whistle, eh?'

Ingram made no comment. Small are the troubles of the man who can lose himself in the contemplation of a yellow lizard on a doorsill!

The friar turned back to him.

'I thought I could possibly be of help,' said he.

'Help?' asked Ingram, utterly at sea.

'Yes,' said the Dominican. 'I thought that I could help you pack.'

VIII
In the Hands of the Lord

It brought Ingram bolt upright.

'What do you know?' he asked.

'Know?' said the other, as though surprised by such a question. 'Oh, I know everything. I have to!'

'Will you tell me how?' asked Ingram.

'We Mexicans,' said the friar, 'are not like you Anglo-Saxons. Our tongues are connected directly with our hearts and our eyes. And so everything that we see or hear or feel must overflow in words—even the smallest things, you understand?'

'I don't see how that applies,' murmured Ingram.

'Think a moment, and you'll see the point,' replied the brown friar. 'You don't know of the Mexicans in this town. You don't have to, because your work takes you to the Americans. But the Mexicans know you. For instance, some of them have been treated in your hospital—'

'It isn't mine,' said Ingram. 'I only suggested—'

'And planned, and begged and superintended, and collected the staff, and raised the money. Ah, we know, dear brother! All of those brown-skinned fellows who have been in the hospital have thanked the doctors, but they haven't forgotten you!'

Ingram stared. He had not foreseen such an eventuality when he planned the hospital.

'Those men are curious about you, of course,' said the friar. 'So they ask questions, they talk about you, and they find a few who can answer—a few of their own kind. The servants at the house of Señor Vasa—they are Mexicans, you understand? And though you have no Mexicans in your congregation, you have an old man to take care of the garden beside the church, and another to clean the place—well, they see! They have eyes and they know how to use them as quickly—as that lizard, say.'

'Well, what do they tell you?' asked Ingram impatiently.

'They tell me,' said the Dominican, 'that you, also, have eyes, brother, and that you know well how to use them.'

'That I don't understand,' replied Ingram.

'Ah,' said Pedrillo. 'Shall I be more open? The señorita is charming enough, surely. Can we not compliment you on—'

He paused, smiling.

'Oh, well,' said Ingram. 'There are no secrets in this town, I presume.'

'Also,' said the friar, 'a voice carries far in the silence of the desert. So I heard that perhaps you would be in a certain hurry today!'

'Will the whole town know what Moffet said to me?'

'The town? Perhaps. The brown part of the town will, to be sure! You need not doubt that!'

'Tell me. What would you do if you were in my place, Brother Pedrillo?'

'I would not hesitate. I would pack at once and leave town before the sun set. I would be a comfortable distance away before the sun set, as a matter of fact.'

Ingram shook his head.

'You don't mean that,' he said. 'Having been assigned to a post, you wouldn't desert it!'

'That's a very harsh way of stating it,' said the friar. 'Suppose that I had no care about myself, still I would go.'

'Ah?'

'Because it would seem to me very wrong to allow another man to commit a mortal sin in raising his hand against me. If you remain, Red Moffet must attack you. He has promised to do so. Nothing under heaven could keep him from fulfilling the obligation. That is the code by which he lives, of course. I understand it and, therefore, I should never place temptation in his way!'

'Run away from him?' asked Ingram. 'I couldn't do it!'

'Why?' asked the Dominican. 'Is it because you think it's wrong, or because you're a bit concerned about public opinion?'

Ingram raised his head.

'Public opinion? No!'

'I am afraid that you mean yes,' said Pedrillo.

'Well, perhaps I do. I don't want people to call me a coward!'

'Ah,' said the other, 'it's a hard time with you, I can see. To my more supple nature, the way would seem perfectly clear. But to you—no, that is different! I understand, however. Pride is a stubborn passion. And will it keep you erect in the face of this storm?'

'I trust that it will,' said Ingram.

'Well—then tell me what I can do for you, brother?'

'Nothing,' said Ingram. 'What *could* you do?'

'A great many things. Suppose that I let a word fall to a few of my compatriots in this town?'

'What of that?'

'A great deal might come of it. For instance, a number of them might call on Mr. Moffet in the middle of the night and urge him out of the town—'

The minister's nostrils flared with a burst of wicked passion, which he controlled with a strong and instant effort.

He recalled the powerful form of Moffet, his long, mighty arms. A gun sagged at either hip in a well-worn holster, polished not by hand, but by use.

'If they went to Moffet like that,' he said at last, 'some of them might be killed.'

The Dominican was silent.

'Some of them surely *would* be killed. Moffet would never go with them alive!'

'Perhaps not,' said Pedrillo. 'There is such a thing as duty which has nothing to do with pride, you see. Their duty would be to take him away so that he might be a danger to you no longer. His pride would force him to fight. What would come of it, who can tell? But much, for instance, may be done by a soft approach, and by the use of the rope. A rawhide lariat in the hands of one of my countrymen can be a knife, a club, or a tangling spider's web, strong enough to hold a struggling lion. Perhaps you had better let me send word to my friends!'

Ingram shook his head, more fiercely decided.

'This is my own fight,' said he, 'and I must see it through by myself. No other shall lift a hand on account of me!'

'You are familiar with guns, then?' asked the Dominican.

'I have been. But now I carry no weapons.'

'Here,' said the friar, 'is a chance for me to serve you. I shall bring you a revolver—'

'No,' said Ingram. 'The Gospel tells me what I must do in a case such as this. *Resist not evil!*'

'Our Lord,' said the Dominican, 'taught us by parables and seldom spoke directly. But He knew that He was not speaking to angels, neither was He speaking to devils. He wished us to interpret Him as a human being speaking to other human beings.'

Suddenly Ingram smiled.

'If you had twenty tongues,' said he, 'you couldn't persuade me! Thank you for coming.'

'I have failed then?'

'No, not failed. You have done what you could for me!'

'Then what will you do?'

'Pray,' said Ingram.

'Pray for Moffet, also,' said the friar. 'Because he is in danger of a frightful crime! Ah, brother, you have come very close to happiness in this place, and now I fear you are coming even closer to sorrow!'

'I am in the hands of the Lord,' said the minister, with a stern composure.

'And in the end,' said the Dominican, 'perhaps He will reveal to you the right way.'

He departed, wandering slowly from the door, pausing two or three times to turn back to his young friend as though there were still new arguments swelling up in his throat; but he seemed to decide that none of them would be of any avail, so stony had been the expression of Ingram.

After the friar had disappeared, Ingram looked across the roofs of the houses, with the heat waves shimmering up from them like steam, to the broad and burning plain of the desert.

He was seeing another picture in his mind's eye—of the bug eaten by the beetle, the beetle eaten by the wren, and the wren destroyed by the hawk. He began to wonder vaguely what order was maintained in this corner of the universe, and what topsy-turvy expression of the Divine Will was represented in it.

Then he turned from the doorway, flung himself on his blankets on the hard floor, and was presently asleep.

He wakened with a singing in his ears, for it had been very hot.

He staggered to the door. It was still breathless, no wind was stirring, and the ground and the houses poured out as from the mouths of ovens the heat which they had been drinking in all day. Twilight had thickened and the night was coming on rapidly, but a dim band of fire still circled the horizon as if with an ominous promise that, as the day had been, so would the morrow be also.

Ingram washed his face and hands. Supper was not thought of. He had been warned to leave the town that day before sunset, and the sun already had set!

Now what would happen?

He forced himself to go methodically about his business. He

was conscious of a vast, craven desire to flee from the house and hide in some dark corner, but he fought back the impulse sternly. He lighted a lamp, trimmed the wick, saw that it was burning brightly and evenly, and then sat down with a book.

The print blurred and ran togther. He could not make sense of the thing that lay before his eyes.

Then he mastered himself again, with such a vast effort that sweat not brought on by heat poured down his forehead. The words cleared. He began to take in the author's meaning.

And then a voice called strongly from the street: 'Ingram!'

He recognized it at once as the voice of Red Moffet. Yonder he stood in the dark of the public way. Perhaps others were gathered covertly to watch the tragedy.

The minister stepped into the doorway.

A lamp was burning at a window just across the street, and against that lamp he saw the silhouette of the horseman.

'I am here,' said Ingram.

Then something whistled over his head. He was gripped by the powerful clutch of a slip noose, and jerked from his feet as Red Moffet began to ride down the street, dragging his victim through the thick dust behind him.

IX
Keeping the Secret

Ie was half stifled when the dragging ceased, and suddenly he vas trundled by skillful hands in a net of stout rope. He could not nove hand or foot, and was brought by main force and tied to a apling.

No one was near. Billman was lost in darkness. The town was at s evening meal, and Moffet had chosen the most convenient our to work without interruption.

Deftly Moffet removed the minister's shirt.

He stepped back.

'I'm gunna give you a lesson that ought to last you a while, you kunk!' said Red Moffet. 'If you was a man, I'd shoot daylight out f you. But bein' only a minister, I got to do this!'

And a riding quirt sang in his hand and branded the back of he minister with fire.

A dozen strokes, but not a sound from the victim.

'Fainted, eh?' grunted Moffet.

He lighted a match.

Blood was trickling down Ingram's white back. He walked round and by the light of the match Moffet stared into such eyes s he never before had seen in any human being.

He dropped the match with an oath.

Then he said in the darkness: 'That'll teach you. But if I catch ou in Billman tomorrow, I'll handle you worse'n this!'

And he rode away, the thick dust muffling the sound of his orse's hoofs.

Against that tree the minister leaned all night. Exhaustion overame him; but the cutting ropes which bound him held up the veight of his body; and burning rages of shame and hate sustained im until, in the crisp chill of the desert morning, men found him here and cut him down.

He fell like a log, unconscious. They carried him back to his house nd gave him a drink of whisky. One grim-faced cow-puncher said

to him, half sneering and half in pity: 'You better get out of town, Ir
gram, before Moffet does worse'n this to you!'

Ingram made no reply. His nerves were so completely sha
tered that he dared not open his lips for fear anything from a so
to a scream might come from them.

He lay trembling until the mid-morning.

Then he got up, stripped away his tattered clothes, and washe
his swollen, wounded back. He remembered suddenly that it wa
Sunday morning, and that a sermon should be preached in hal
an hour.

So he walked to the church with a steady step—and found no
a soul there!

Not even the Mexican to ring the bell! He rang it himself, lon
and loudly, and then went back into the church and waited.

No one came. The little church through its open doors dran
in some of the sultry heat of that bitter day, but no human bein
crossed its threshold until long after the sermon should hav
begun.

Ingram wondered if it was a sense of delicacy which held back
the crowd of women who should have been there.

And then into the church walked no woman, but the tall, lumbering giant, Vasa. He came up to the minister and sat down beside him.

Pity and wonder were in Vasa's glance, but withering scorn
predominated over them.

'I got a note from sis for you,' said he, and tendered an envelope.

It was amazingly brief and to the point.

It merely said: 'How could you lie down and let any man do
that to you? I'm ashamed and I'm sick. Go away from Billman.
No one will ever want to see your face here again!'

No signature even. The words were enough. And the splotches and smudges which covered the paper—well, they were a sign of tears of bitterest shame and disgust, no doubt. He folded the paper carefully and put it into his pocket.

'I'd better be going,' said Vasa.

And he stood up. He added suddenly: 'Darned if I ain't sorry, Ingram. I didn't think you were the sort that would let any—'

He stopped himself, turned upon his heel and was gone. Ingram closed the church and went home again.

Delicacy which had kept the women from the church that

morning? There was no more delicacy in Billman and its people than there was in the birds and the insects of the desert around them. They were walled away from him now by the most profound contempt.

By the middle of the afternoon, he knew what he must do, and he walked down to the telegraph office. He met a hundred people on the way, but not a single pair of eyes. They turned away when they saw him coming. They slipped this way and that so that they might not have to encounter him. Only a pair of boys ran out of a gate and after him, laughing, yelling, calling out words suggested to them by the fiend that inhabits boys.

At the telegraph office he wrote a telegram:

> My usefulness at Billman ended; suggest that you send a new man and an old one for this post; will wait till his arrival if necessary.

He signed that message and directed it to those who had dispatched him on this distant mission. Then he walked back down the street toward his shack once more.

He wanted to hurry, but he made himself walk with a deliberate step. He wanted to skulk around the backyards to get to his destination, but he checked himself and held on his way through the thick of men and women. More boys came out to mock at him. And he heard a mother sharply scold her offspring.

'Let the poor, good-for-nothin' creature alone, can't you, boys?'

That was for him!

He got to his shack again, and remembered suddenly for the second time that day that it was the Sabbath. So he took up his Bible and began to read, forcing his eyes to consider the words until a shadow fell through the doorway and across the floor to his feet.

It was the Dominican.

He came in and held out his hand. Ingram failed to see it.

Then Brother Pedrillo said: 'I guessed at a good many things, brother. But this thing I didn't guess at. I thought that it would be simply a matter of guns. I didn't imagine that it could be anything worse!'

He added, after a moment: 'Brother, I understand. The rest have not seen the truth. You hate them now. Afterward, you will remember that they are like children. Forgive them if you can. Not today. It would be too hard. But tomorrow.'

This he said, and afterward withdrew as quietly as he had come, and went down the street with a fat man's waddling step.

In due time, he passed Vasa's house, and found the busy matron in the garden, snatching a moment from her housekeeping to improve the vegetables. He leaned on the picket fence to talk with her.

'And how's Astrid?'

'That girl's in bed,' said Mrs. Vasa. 'Pretty sick, too.'

'Sick?' queried the friar. 'What does the doctor say about it?'

'Oh, it ain't a thing for doctors to know about. Doctors ain't much help sometimes, Brother.'

Pedrillo wandered on down the street. He passed the hotel, where he was hailed jovially by the idlers, and drinks of various kinds and sizes were suggested. He refused them all, not that he was above having a glass of beer—or pulque as the case might be—but because he drank in a house, not in a saloon. And at the farther corner of the hotel he fairly ran into Red Moffet.

Red hailed him. The friar walked on in silence, and the tall cow-puncher instantly was at his side.

'Look here, Pedrillo. What's the matter? Didn't you see me?'

'I don't want to talk to you, Red,' said the friar. 'Because if I start talking, my temper may get the best of me.'

'You mean Ingram, I suppose,' said the big fellow.

'I mean Ingram.'

'Well, what would you have me do? Use a gun on him instead?'

'May I tell you what I think, Red?'

'Fire away, old fellow. *You* can say whatever you please.'

'Then I'll tell you what I firmly believe—that if a scruple didn't stand in his way, Ingram could thrash any two men in this town!'

'What kind of a joke is that?' asked Moffet.

'It's not a joke, but the coldest kind of hard fact.'

'Why, Brother, the man's yellow!'

'Don't tell me that, Red. He's simply keeping himself in hand. He won't fight on principle—not for the sake of his own hide. And just now, you are on the crest and he's in the trough. But I shouldn't be surprised if he turned the tables on you one of these days!'

'He'll have to make it quick,' said Red. 'The quitter has had enough. He's wired to be taken from the town.'

'Has he done that?'

'Yep, he's hollered for help.'

And Red grinned with malicious content.

'Very well,' said the Dominican. 'He's asking to be relieved because he thinks he no longer can do good here—after the way you disgraced him. But I'll tell you, Red, that this is going to be no short story for you. It is apt to be a very, very long one!'

He went on without further words, and with a very dark brow, leaving Red Moffet deep in thought behind him.

On across the creek to the poorer section of the town went the friar, until he found himself in the quarters of his compatriots. There the theme was the same as that which occupied the Americans in the more prosperous section of Billman.

And a lame fellow fresh from the hospital said to the Dominican: 'Our friend, Señor Ingram, he is not much of a man, Brother?'

'Who has told you that?' snapped Pedrillo.

'Look! He has been whipped like a dog!'

'Shall I tell you a thing, my friend?'

'Yes.'

'It is a great secret, amigo.'

'Then tell me, Brother.'

'This Señor Ingram is a quiet man. But also when the time comes, it will be seen that he is *muy diablo.*'

There is no way to translate that phrase—*muy diablo.* It means 'much devil' or 'very devil.' And then it has other meanings as well. One can say that a maverick is *muy diablo.* Also one may use the expression concerning a stick of dynamite. The peon listened to the friar and opened his eyes. Never for a moment did it occur to him to doubt.

'I shall keep the secret!' said he. 'But when will Señor Ingram act?'

'That is with God and his conscience. He will act in good time!'

And he watched the peon hurry away. He knew that in half an hour the whole town would be apprised of the secret that Señor Ingram, the minister, in some mysterious way, was *muy diablo.* Brother Pedrillo was content.

X
The Mystery of Work

Rumor in Billman, as in all small Western towns, moved with the speed and the subtlety of a serpent. And so the tale rapidly went the rounds that Ingram, despite his fall at the hands of Red Moffet, was stronger than he seemed to be; that he was, in fact, *muy diablo*. He was biding his time. Before long, something would happen to reveal him to the people as he was in truth.

The cow-punchers, hearing the tale, shrugged their shoulders and were inclined to laugh. But afterward, they remembered and pondered the matter. There had been something in the unflinching manner with which big Ingram walked their streets the very day after his disgrace that gave them pause. They turned the matter in their minds and became more serious. The story came to the ears of Astrid Vasa and made her sit up suddenly in bed, her eyes shining.

Who could tell?

In five minutes she was dressed. In five minutes more she was on the street, hurrying to Ingram.

She found him in his shack, with a telegram in his hand, which told him that there was no possibility of replacing him at once in Billman, and that he would have to remain at his post for an indefinite period. In the meantime, he must write all details of what had happened.

When Astrid called, he came out into the sun and stood there with his head lowered and thrust forward a little, like a fighter prepared to receive a blow. She was abashed.

So she stood by the gate, guiltily hoping that no one would see her there.

'I only wanted to say, Reggie, that I wrote that note without thinking. I hope that I didn't hurt you—I mean—I thought—'

He lifted his eyes to her face. Astrid uttered a little cry.

'I should never have written it!' she pleaded. 'I'm sorry. And I didn't know that you would—that you—'

And she added suddenly: 'Won't you say something?'

No, not a word. She did not feel that his was the sulky silence of a child. Rather it was a considerate silence, as of a man who needs a quiet moment for thinking. But it was as though she were thrust away from him by a long arm. It was as though she never could have been near him.

Astrid began to regret, and to regret bitterly. Not that she knew just what was in the mind of Mr. Ingram, or what he was as a man—but that she felt he was something different from any other man who had ever been in Billman. And Astrid loved novelties!

'You won't forgive me!' moaned Astrid suddenly.

'Forgive you?' repeated the deep voice. 'Oh, yes, I forgive you!'

No passion in it. No more than if he were reading the words out of a book, and somehow that was more to Astrid Vasa than the bitterest denunciation. She shrank away down the street and hurried to her home.

Her father was not there.

She rushed to his shop, and there she found him. The forge was sending up masses of smoke, for the fuel had just been freshened; smoke wreathed all the shadowy cave in which the forge flame was darting like a snake's tongue. In the midst stood Vasa, his shirt off, the top of his hairy chest and his wonderful arms, loaded down with muscles, exposed. He had donned a leather apron. In one hand he swayed a fourteen-pound sledge tentatively.

'Dad!' cried Astrid, 'I want to speak to you!'

'Hey—you! Get out of here!' called her father fiercely.

She had walked into the grime and the heavy, impure air. And with the unceremonious wave of his arm her father sent her staggering back to the door.

She was furious, for no human being ever had treated her after this fashion. Not since she had first been called by her full name of Astrid.

She saw the two assistants bear the great beam of iron from the forge fire, each of them toiling with a pair of huge pincers. She saw the beam laid across the anvil. Then the sledge in the hands of her father began to sweep through the air in rapid circles, and at each stroke a thousand rays of liquid fire darted to every corner of the shop, lighting up all its cobwebbed angles and showing the smoke, thick as milk, which hovered against the beams of the roof.

The assistants winced under those showers of sparks and

shrank away; the blows fell more rapidly. She heard her father bellowing orders, and saw the iron being turned, moved here and there on the anvil according to his directions. And then, half disgusted and half afraid, she saw that all this noise and smoke and fury was merely for the sake of putting a bend in that massive bit of iron, a right-angle bend, and also to round the iron about the angle point.

Then she saw her father seize the iron beam with one pincer and with one hand plunge it into the tempering tub. With one hand—that burden for two strong men!

There was a frightful hissing, as though a vast cauldron filled with rattlesnakes had been threatened with death. A billow of steam rolled out and all within the shop was lost in fog. At length, parting the mist before him with his hand, Vasa came toward Astrid and towered above her.

'Well, honey, what you want?'

She did not answer. She only stared.

'I was kind of rough, Astie, dear,' said he. 'Don't be mad with me!'

It was not his roughness that amazed her, but his sudden gentleness. And Astrid began to guess at vastly new thoughts, and vastly large ones. That bending of the iron in itself was not so important, perhaps. The iron would become a part of a stupid machine. But what *was* important was that a man with fire and hammer to aid him had turned that strong iron as though it had been wax, melted and molded it, and given it a new shape!

So thought Astrid. And she could understand the roughness with which her father had greeted her. For she had come between him and his work—that mystery of work! She had been nothing—merely an annoyance! She had felt, before this, that nothing so important as herself could come into the life of some chosen man. But now she guessed that the more worthwhile the man, the more his work would mean to him, and the less the winning of a woman. Would she, then, be pushed into the background? Was it right?

Right or wrong, with terrible suddenness the girl realized that she never could care truly for any man save for one capable of elevating his labor into a god in this fashion. Even if it were no more than the shaping of iron beams. Yes, even that work could be great and important if it were approached in the right manner. And it was this which gave a certain surety and significance to her father. He was all that she had ever thought him—gross, careless, slovenly—but also worthy of respect.

So thought Astrid, and accordingly she greeted her father as she never had greeted him before, with a touch of awe.

'Can you spare me a minute, dear Dad?' she said.

'A minute?' he asked, amazed. 'Sure, kid! Or an hour; now what you want? What's botherin' you? You look sort of upset!'

He took her by the elbows and lifted her to the top of a great packing case. She would have cried out, at another time, because his hands were smudging her dress. But now she merely smiled down at him, a rather uncertain, frightened smile.

'You tell your old dad!'

'You remember that note you took to Reggie Ingram?'

'Aye, I remember.'

'I told him in that note—that I didn't have any more use for him!'

'Hello! That was kind of hard!'

'Dad, I'd got myself engaged to him before that.'

'You did!'

'And then I threw him over.'

'What else could you do? A gent that lets himself—'

'No!'

He was silent.

'You tell me, then,' he said at last.

'I want him back! Dad, you got to get him back for me!'

Mr. Vasa combed his hair with fingers covered with the black of iron.

'What am I gunna do, honey? Get down on my knees and beg him to marry you after all? Look here, I'll bring him to the house. You got to do the rest; but, sis, ain't you a little crazy to want to take a man that's been—'

'No!' cried she.

He was silent again. And she wondered that with all his force he should submit so easily to her desires. It was as though he felt that her intelligence was worth more than his in this affair.

'I can't talk to him!' said Astrid, with a sob. 'I've just been to see him and tried, but he only looked at me and said nothing until I asked him to forgive me, and then he said that he would; but he's put me out of his life—and I can't stand it! I can't stand it, Dad!'

'So? So?' murmured the big blacksmith.

He lifted her down to the ground and dried her eyes.

'I'm gunna do what I can,' said he. 'But I dunno! It looks pretty bad. Though there's a yarn going around the town that after all he's not what we think—that this Ingram is *muy diablo*, sis. Have you heard that?'

She answered fiercely: 'You wait and see! You wait and see!'

Vasa nodded, and she went slowly back home.

It had been a day of wreckage and disaster to her old idea, and the new idea was not yet firmly established in her mind, so she felt weak, and frightfully uncertain. She only guessed that there were such forces loose in the world of men as she never before had dreamed of.

And then, at the door of her home, she met Red Moffet, who was grinning, and looking both shamefaced and proud of himself, like a child who expects to be praised.

She shrank from him.

'I've got a headache; I can't talk to you, Red,' she told him truthfully enough. 'I've got to be alone!'

And she walked straight past him.

Now Red was a man among men, and he was intelligent enough to prospect for gold-bearing ore, and find it and work it. But he did not understand the ways of women. Men usually are like that. The more brave and bold and successful they are in their own fields, the more obtuse, clumsy and inept they are with the women who enter their lives. Perhaps there never was a universal favorite with women who was not a bit effeminate, or something of a charlatan. One needs a dainty touch with women. A conversation with them is like a surgical operation upon nerves. The slightest slip of the hand or a cut a shade too deep and the result is total failure. The light-tongued jugglers of words—they are the successful ones.

But poor Red did not know this.

All he was sure of was that he loved this girl, and that he felt he had eliminated from the competition his one dangerous rival. But instead of reaping the fruits of victory, he was received with open weariness and disgust.

So he followed her to the door and even touched her shoulder.

She whirled around at him, shrinking as if his touch were a contamination.

'I want to know,' began Red, 'what's happened to make you so very—'

'You bully!' she cried.

It staggered Red, and he fell back.

'Bully?' he said, amazed.

'You cowardly, great, hulking, worthless bully!' cried Astrid, following him.

He could not stand his ground. He retreated through the door, forgetting his hat.

She threw it after him.

'I hope I never see you again!' cried Astrid.

XI
'Without Losing No Dignity'

Nothing offends us so much as the illogical. We do not demand a great deal from the world. But we wish for our logical rewards—and a little bit more. If a child has cut up your best hat in order to make an ashtray for you, you must not scold him, no matter how your heart is bleeding. He expects a bit of praise, and praise he must have. Or if you point out to him, with care, that he has been in most frightful error and really deserves a whipping, then he is mortified, ashamed, shrinks from you, and presently hates the entire world.

This was exactly the frame of mind of young Red Moffet. He had seen an Easterner, a tenderfoot, a minister, walk into Billman and promise to carry away the prettiest girl in the entire town. He had stopped that proceeding with the might of his good right arm, and now all glory, all reward was denied him!

He jammed his hat upon his head and set his teeth. He was, indeed, furious enough to have torn out the heart of his best friend and thrown it to the dogs.

He was known in Billman, was young Red Moffet. And when he was in such a humor, it would have been hard to hire a man to cross his way. But Fate, who insists on shuffling the cards and dealing the oddest hands, now drew the worst deuce in the pack and presented it to Red Moffet.

For Ben Holman had come back to town that day. He had been angered by the wrath of Red Moffet; and since he was only one-third wildcat and two-thirds sneak, he had vowed to himself that never would he cross the path of that dreadful destroyer of men. There had been sundry killings in the past of Ben Holman himself, but always he had shot or knifed from behind. That allowed him to take better aim and keep a cooler head. Whereas when he stood confronting another puncher who wore a gun, he discovered at once that his heart was out of sorts.

But now the good news came to him that Red had put down the minister, for the reputed reason that the minister needed putting down if Red was to keep his girl, pretty Astrid Vasa. Ben Holman knew Astrid by sight and he felt that the man who had won her back would be so completely happy that he would forget all past enmities—even his hatred of those who had officiated at the killing of poor Chuck Lane.

At any rate, Ben was something of a gambler, the kind who always likes short odds. And what odds could be shorter than these? He determined to return to Billman and try his luck in appeasing Mr. Red Moffet before a gun could be drawn on him.

These were the reasons which drew Ben back to the town. They were good reasons; they were well thought out; they were well founded. If he had come half an hour earlier, all would have been well.

But at this very worst of moments, as he turned the corner of the street, young Red Moffet came straight upon Holman, riding toward him and not twenty feet away.

There was no time for thinking. Holman screeched like a frightened cat and whipped out his gun with the desperation of any cornered wild thing. He actually got in the first shot, and it lifted the hat of Red Moffet and sent it sailing into the air. Red Moffet got in the second shot. And he did *not* miss. His bullet struck Ben Holman in the throat, tore his spinal column in two, and dropped him in a shapeless heap on the farther side of his horse. Then Red Moffet went out with his smoking gun and saw what he had done.

He felt no pangs of conscience. He was merely relieved, and sighed a little, as though he had gotten something out of his system. Then he straightened out his victim, put the latter's sombrero over his face, and hired half a dozen passing Mexicans to carry Ben to the burying grounds just outside the village.

Perhaps twenty men had been interred there under similar circumstances. Red Moffet had sent two there himself. But since he had always paid the price of the ground and the price of the burial, nothing had been said, and this time he expected not the slightest trouble.

He had simply done his duty by Chuck Lane—that thorough, good fellow—and having eased his conscience, what call was there for any further excitement about the matter?

But Fate, as has been said, is a tricky lady who loves to mix the cards and deal the unexpected. There was hardly a soul in Billman who cared whether Ben Holman lived or died. His reputation was not much more savory than the reputation of a coyote, or any other sneaking beast of prey. And everyone knew that Red Moffet shot from in front, waited for the other man to fill his hand, and was, in addition, a hardworking and honest member of the community. However, it happened that Red had, in fact, turned this trick before. And there is nothing more annoying to an audience than to have an actor return to the stage to sing his song over again when there has been no applause to warrant an encore. Red's last shooting exploit was hardly three months old. And the news about Holman's death touched the nerves of Billman's citizens in a sensitive spot.

Killing in the cow-country is a diversion to be forgiven any man now and then. But it should never be allowed to become a mere habit.

It looked as though Red had formed the habit.

More than this, hardly twenty-four hours ago he had manhandled the minister. When you came to think of it, the said minister had done no harm. As a matter of fact, he had been a useful and quiet member of the community. Reputations die quickly in a mining town, as elsewhere. But Ingram had built that hospital very recently. And there were a number of convalescents around the town at that moment. They did not take kindly to the roughing of their benefactor. And now they listened somberly to this new tale of violence.

A Western town usually makes up its mind quickly. As a matter of fact, often it doesn't stop to make up its mind before it acts.

Now Dick Binney, the deputy sheriff, had no love for Red Moffet. But he knew Red and he knew Ben Holman, and he no more thought of arresting the former for the killing of the latter than he would have thought of arresting a man for the killing of a prowling wolf on the streets of the town.

Eight tall, strong, brown-faced men strode into Dick's office and sat down in his chairs, on his desk, and in the window.

'Dick,' they said, 'we reckon that maybe you better put Red up where he'll be safe to cool off for a while. He's runnin' up the death rate near as bad as smallpox.'

Dick Binney looked from one face to another, and after a few moments' thought he nodded.

'Boys,' said he, lying cheerfully, 'I was thinking the same thing.'

He got up and left his office, and the big men followed him at a distance. The deputy came on Red Moffet, cheerfully chucking stones at a squirrel which was up a tree.

'Red,' said he, 'I hate to do this, but I got to ask you to come along with me.'

While he spoke, he tapped Red lightly on the shoulder.

'Come along with you where?' asked Red savagely. 'What you talkin' about, man?'

'To jail, for a rest,' said the deputy sheriff.

'To jail?' said Red Moffet. 'What's the funny idea?'

And he added vigorously: 'For what?'

'For the killing of Ben Holman.'

'It's dirty work on your part,' said Red Moffet in anger. 'You know that Holman has been due to be bumped off for a long time, and the only thing that saved him was that nobody wanted to waste a bullet on an insect like him.'

'Sure,' agreed the deputy. 'You never said nothin' truer. Matter of fact, Red, I ain't been no friend of yours, but I would never have arrested you for killin' Ben. Only public opinion, it sort of demands this.'

'Public opinion can go hang,' said Red.

'Sure,' grinned Dick Binney. 'But when there's eight public opinions wearing guns, all of 'em, it's sort of different, don't you guess?'

He hooked a thumb in the proper direction, and Red Moffet became aware of eight good men and true, in various careless attitudes. Red had a practiced eye, and with one glance he counted eleven revolvers and three rifles. Those were the weapons which were displayed for public notice. Undoubtedly there were others concealed.

'Well,' agreed Moffet, 'it looks like you got some reason in what you say. Maybe I'll come along with you!'

Down the street they went.

'This is gunna be talked about, Dick,' said Red Moffet. 'It's gunna be said that I'm no good, if I let myself be arrested without strikin' a blow.'

Dick Binney, walking beside him, nodded in ready agreement.

'That's true,' said he. 'I hadn't thought about that.'

Red halted.

'I'm afraid,' said he, 'that I can't let you take me without shooting for the prize, old-timer.'

'Hold on, Red,' said the deputy sheriff, 'if I was to kill you just now—hatin' your innards the way I do and me being sheriff—it would be all right. But if you was to kill me—well, you know how things go with a gent that kills a sheriff?'

Red Moffet nodded gravely.

'I know,' said he. 'You sure are playing the part of a white man to me today, Dick. If I didn't hate you for a low skunk, I'd figure you to be one of the best.'

'I'll shoot your innards out, one of these days,' said Binney, 'but I ain't gunna take advantage of you now. I'll tell you what I'll do. I'll put a hand on your shoulder. You knock it off. I'll make a pass at you with my fist and we'll close and grapple and start fighting as though we'd forgot all about our guns. Y'understand? The rest of the boys'll think that you're resisting arrest. They'll come runnin' up and you can afford to give up to eight armed men without losing no dignity.'

'Sure,' agreed Red Moffet. 'Dick, I pretty near love you when I see what a wonderful head you got on your shoulders!'

With that, Dick clapped a hand upon the shoulder of his companion. The hand was promptly knocked off; and Mr. Binney made the promised pass at his companion with his fist. However, he did not merely fan the air. He had a hard and ready fist and he cracked it squarely along the side of Mr. Moffet's jaw. The hair rose on the crown of Red's head. 'You hound dog!' he grunted.

And with that, he lifted a hearty uppercut from his toes to the chin of the deputy sheriff.

It was only by good luck that the deputy did not fall on his back. If he had done so, eight good men and true who were rushing down the street toward the fighters would have shot Red so full of holes that he would have looked in death like nothing but a colander. But by happy chance the deputy sheriff fell in and not out. He pitched into the arms of Red, who caught and held him, and they pretended to wrestle back and forth, the deputy sheriff groaning: 'You hit me with a club, you sap!'

In the midst of this struggling, the rescue party arrived, and quantities of guns were shoved under Red's nose. He pushed his hands into the air with a reluctance which was only partly assumed.

'You seem to have the drop on me, boys,' said Red. 'What might you be wanting of me? A invitation to call, or something like that?'

'He ought to get what Chuck Lane got, the darned man-killer,' said one harsh voice. 'Resists arrest, and everything! Lucky that we were on deck!'

'Lucky nothing!' declared the deputy sheriff, who was able to walk without staggering at about this moment. 'I was beating him to a pulp for my own pleasure before lockin' him up. Come along to the jail, Red, or I'll knock your block off!'

So, with a volunteer guard of honor, Red was escorted down the street and installed in the jail of which Billman was so proud. He was given the most comfortable quarters that the little building could afford, and Binney sat down outside his door and chatted with him, tenderly rubbing his jaw the while.

'When you get out of this, Red,' said the deputy sheriff, 'I'm gunna beat you to a fare-thee-well! But in the meantime, I'll try to make you comfortable here!'

XII
The Seventh Day

It is so unpleasant to dwell on the miseries which beset the mind of young Ingram that we may skip to the moment when Vasa leaned against the post of his door, saying: 'Hello, Ingram! Here I am back again. Am I welcome?'

There was an uncertain murmur from Ingram in reply.

'No,' declared the unabashed giant, 'I can see that I ain't, but still I ain't downhearted. I can't afford to be. But the fact is, old man, that you've cut up my girl a good deal. I've had to come along and try to make peace with you for her sake. What chance do you think I have?'

'Peace? With me?' asked the minister bitterly. 'But of course, that's a jest. I am a man of peace, Mr. Vasa. I thought that I had proved that to the entire town!'

The blacksmith felt the bitterness in this speech. He could think of nothing better to say than: 'Well, Ingram, folks are getting pretty sorry for what's happened. I suppose you know what they've done to Red Moffet just now?'

'I don't know,' said the minister, turning pale at the mere sound of the man's name.

'They've locked him up in jail! For what he done to you—and for killing Ben Holman!'

'Did he kill a man?' asked the minister slowly.

'Shot him dead.'

'However,' said Ingram, 'it was in fair fight, I presume?'

'What made you guess that?' asked the blacksmith.

'Because I thought that he was that kind of a man.'

'As a matter of fact, you're right. It was a fair fight. And that Holman was a hound. But still—we've stood for too much from Red. He's got to have a lesson. But I thought that I'd ramble up here and ask you about sis. Are you through with her for good and all, Ingram?'

The minister was silent.

'Think it over,' suggested Vasa. 'That girl is all fire and impulse. She's probably got ten ideas a minute, and nine out of the ten are wrong. Think it over, and let her know later on what you decide.'

'Thank you,' said Ingram.

Mr. Vasa felt very uncomfortable. He began to perspire freely, and finally he stood up and left. He hurried down the street as though to leave a sense of unpleasantness as far as possible in the rear.

Reginald Ingram was not cheered by this embassy. He had fallen so far into the depths of shame that he felt nothing could bring him back to self-respect. But now he began to torment himself in a new manner. Red Moffet was in jail. Was it his duty as a Christian to go to see his enemy?

The thought made him writhe. And in the midst of his writhings, Friar Pedrillo appeared. He was filled with news and, in particular, he could detail all that had happened concerning the arrest of Moffet.

'The evil are punished,' said the Dominican. 'And now Red Moffet is crouching in jail in fear of his life.'

'Do you think that they would hang him for what he has done?' asked Ingram, half sad and half curious.

'Not by process of law,' replied the friar. 'They can't convict him with a Billman jury for having killed Ben Holman, who was a known scoundrel. But there is another danger for poor Red.'

'Another danger?'

'Yes, of course. There's the mob, you know.'

'I don't understand.'

'You will, if you go downtown this evening. There's a whisper going about the town, and I think that after dark there will be a good many people grouping around the jail and planning to take Red out and hang him up.'

'Wait a moment,' cried Ingram. 'I thought that Red Moffet was popular in this town?'

'Six days a week, he is,' said the Dominican. 'But on the seventh you may find his enemies in the saddle, and this seems to be the seventh day.'

With that, Brother Pedrillo left, and Ingram found himself plunged into a melancholy state in which he was lost for the remainder of the day.

But when the evening drew on, he knew what he must do. He must go to the jail and be near when the crisis came. Exactly what prompted him to go, he could not tell. He could not honestly say that he wished big Moffet well. And yet—

As he walked down the street, he told himself that he would, at any rate, try to do what he could for the prisoner, in case of mob violence. When he reached the vicinity of the jail, he found a swarm of people of all sorts and all ages. And every one of them had one topic on his lips—the name and the fate of Red Moffet, who was now waiting in the jail for his end.

The minister went through the crowd like a ghost; it seemed that no one had eye or ear for him. He was an impalpable presence, not worthy of being noticed.

It was a strange crowd, gathering in little knots here and there, talking in deep, grave voices. Now and again, Ingram heard some louder, more strident voice. When he listened, it was sure to be someone recalling some evil act on the part of Moffet, some episode in Red's past which had to do with guns and gore.

The minister went to the jail, where he found the door closed and locked. When he knocked, a subdued voice inside said: 'It's the minister. It's Ingram.'

'Let him in, then,' said another voice.

The door was opened just enough for him to slip through and, as he did so, there was a rush from the street behind him. But the door was swung shut with a crash, before anyone got to the spot.

Outside there were curses loud and long, and a beating on the door by men who demanded entrance at once.

Inside, Ingram found the deputy sheriff and two others, a pale-faced group, who looked gloomily at him.

'What you want here, Ingram?' asked Dick Binney. 'Have you come to crow over Red Moffet?'

'No,' said Ingram quietly. 'But I'd like to talk to him, if I may.'

'Go on straight down the aisle. You'll find him there.'

Down the aisle went Ingram, and behind the bars of a cell he saw, among the shadows, the form of a man, his face illumined faintly, now and then, by the red pulsation of light as he puffed at a cigarette.

'Moffet?' he asked.

'Yes. Who's that?'

'Reginald Ingram.'

'You've come over to see the finish of me, I suppose?'

'I've come over to pray for you, man,' said Ingram.

'What on earth!' cried Red Moffet. 'D'you think that I want prayers from a whining yellow mongrel of a sky pilot?'

Ingram lurched at the bars of the cell. He gripped them and hung close, breathing hard, a raging fury in his blood and brain. The man in the cell stepped closer to the bars, in turn.

'Why,' he said, 'it seems sort of irritatin', does it, when I call you by name?'

'God sustain me!' said Ingram. Then he added: 'A mob fills the street, Moffet. When they rush this place, I don't think that the sheriff and his two companions will stand very long against them. And now that you have come to this desperate time, Moffet, I want to know in what way I can serve—'

'You lie!' said Red Moffet. 'The fact is that you've come over to enjoy the killing of me!'

Ingram sighed. But in the little pause which followed, he asked himself seriously if the prisoner were not right. For what else had drawn him to the jail with such an irresistible force? Had he felt, really, that he could be of help to Moffet? Had he felt that he could control the crowd?

He said suddenly: 'I hope that you're not right, Moffet. I hope that I've come here from a better motive.'

'That's right,' said Moffet. 'Be honest; be honest, man, and shame the hypocritical devil that's in a good many of you sky pilots.'

There was a wilder burst of noise outside, and the wave of sound crowded up around the walls of the jail. Those inside could make out the voice of a ringleader shouting; and then they heard Dick Binney defying the crowd and swearing that the prisoner would never be taken except at the cost of a dozen lives.

The minister heard Moffet groan bitterly: 'Oh, God, for a gun and a chance to die fighting! Ingram! Ingram! Find me a gun, or a club! What's the matter with me, askin' a hound of a sky pilot for help!'

Ingram retreated to the farther side of the aisle, dizzy, his head whirling with many ideas. He was trembling from head to foot—as he had trembled in the old days when he waited for the signal which would send him trotting out upon the field with the team.

There was another roar and a wave of running feet, but this time it curled around the jail and there was a sudden crash against the back door.

'The back door, Binney! Dick! Dick! *The back door*!' shouted Moffet.

He rushed to the bars and shook them with his frenzy, but Binney was already running to the back of the jail, cursing. His two assistants had had enough. They were out of the fight before it began, and Binney had to face the crowd alone.

He was within a stride of the rear door when it was beaten in, and a swarm of men, leaping through the breach, bore him down and trampled him underfoot. Up the aisle of the jail they poured, their terrible masked faces illumined by the swinging light of heavy lanterns which they carried.

Then Ingram leaped into their path.

He raised both hands before them, looking gigantic in the strange, moving light.

'Friends and brothers!' he called to them. 'In the name of the Father of Mercy, I protest—'

'Get that yellow-livered fool out of the way!' called a voice, and half a dozen rude shoulders crashed against Ingram and beat him out of the path.

'A couple of you hold the sky pilot,' ordered another voice. 'Now, gimme those keys you got from Binney!'

XIII
Things in General

It was dreadful to Ingram to stand pinned against the opposite range of bars, held on either side by a stalwart fellow, while the leader of the mob jangled the keys and tried them rapidly in the lock.

'He's shakin' like a leaf,' said one of Ingram's captors to the other.

'Sure,' said the second man, 'he looks real, but he ain't. He's a make-believe man. Stand fast, Ingram, or I'll bash you in the head, you big sap!'

Ingram stood still!

He heard a voice snarling at Moffet: 'Now, Red, what d'you say about yourself? The shoe's on the other foot, ain't it?'

'I know you, "Lefty,"' said Red Moffet, his voice calm. 'You never heard of a time when I was part of a mob at a lynching. I've fought fair all my life, and you know it, you swine!'

'Swine, am I?' said Lefty. 'I'll have that out of your hide before you swing.'

'Shut up!' barked the leader. 'These keys don't fit. Hold on—by heaven, I've got it!'

And the next moment the door to Red Moffet's cell swung open.

Then Reginald Oliver Ingram found his strength, as he had found it on other days when the whistle sounded the commencement of the game. The grip of those who held him slipped away from his muscles, which had become like coiling serpents of steel. He thrust the men staggering back and sprang into the crowd.

A round half dozen had rushed into the little cell the instant the door was opened as the yell of the two guards rang out: 'Look out for Ingram! He's running amuck!'

The others whirled, hardly knowing what to expect, and as they whirled, Ingram plunged through them. They seemed to him shadows rather than men. He had known how to rip through a line of trained and ready athletes. He went through these unprepared cow-punchers and miners as though they had been nothing. Reaching the cell, he slammed the door with such a crash that the spring lock snapped, and the bunch of keys fell violently to the floor.

A hand reached instantly for those keys—Ingram stamped on the wrist and was answered by a scream of pain.

At the same time a pair of arms closed heavily around his body.

It would not be fair, of course, on a football field; but this was not a football field. Ingram snapped his fist home behind the ear of the assailant, and the arms which had pinned him relaxed. Others were coming at him, leaping, crowding one another so that their arms had no play; and, with his back to the cell door, which contained Moffet and his half dozen would-be lynchers, the minister stood at bay.

The nervous tension which had made him shake like a frightened child in the cold before the crisis, now enabled him to act with the speed of lightning. He struck not a single blind blow. He saw nothing but the point of the jaw, and into that charging rank he sent two blows that tore out the center of it.

Arms reached for him; a rifle whizzed past his head; but he brushed the reaching arms aside, and plucked the rifle from the hands which wielded it.

The men gave back before the sway of it with a yell of fear. Two or three lay crushed on the floor of the jail. He stepped over or on the bodies and struck savagely into the whirling mass of humanity.

The butt of the rifle struck flesh; there was a shriek of pain.

The rifle stock burst from its barrel as though it had been made of paper!

Then a gun spat fire in Ingram's face. He smote with the naked rifle barrel in the direction of that blinding flash of light, and there was a groan and a fall.

Panic seized the crowd in that narrow aisle. They had no room to use their numbers. Many of them had fallen before the onslaught of this inspired fighter. They shrank from him; he followed on their heels.

And suddenly they turned and fled, beating each other down, trampling on one another, turning and striking frantic blows at their assailant, who now seemed a giant. And half a dozen times a revolver bullet was fired at him, point-blank. Panic, however, made the hands shake that held the guns, and Ingram drove the crowd on before him, striking mercilessly with his terrible club and treading groaning men underfoot as he went.

So the mob of rioters was vomited from the back door of the jail. As they swept out, two or three frightened fugitives, who had dragged themselves from the floor on which they lay stunned, staggered past Ingram and into the kindly dark.

Into that doorway Ingram stepped. He shook the broken rifle toward the mob which was swirling and pitching here and there like water.

Those behind wished to press forward; and those who had been in the jail dreaded more than death to get within the reach of that terrible churchman.

'You yelping dogs!' called Ingram in a voice of thunder. 'The door of the jail is open here. Come when you're ready! Next time I'll meet you with bullets—and I'll shoot to kill. Do you hear?'

There was a yell of rage from the crowd. Half a dozen bullets sang about Ingram's ears. He laughed at the crowd, and strode back through the doorway.

On either side of the opening he placed a lantern, of which several had been dropped by the fleeing mob. Their light would bring into sharp relief anyone who tried to pass through that doorway; and it would be strange indeed if that cowed host of lynchers dared to attempt the passage.

From the cell where the foremost members of the lynching party were held safe with Red Moffet there was now rising a wild appeal for help. The men called by name upon their companions, who remained in the darkness outside. They begged and pleaded for the opening of that door which they had unlocked with such glee.

Now from the floor near the rear of the jail, a man rose up and staggered toward Ingram. It was Dick Binney, with a smear of blood on one side of his face, where he had been struck by the butt of a heavy Colt. He had a gun in either hand, and his lips were twitching. Ingram felt that he never before had seen a man so ready for desperate needs.

'Ingram,' he said, 'God bless you for givin' me another chance at 'em! Oh, the scoundrels! I'm gunna make 'em pay for this! I'm gunna make 'em pay!'

There was a litter of weapons on the floor of the aisle, where five men lay, either unconscious or writhing in terrible pain.

The sheriff and Ingram gathered the fallen and placed them in a corner, while the sheriff's two assistants now again appeared and offered to guard the prisoners. Their offer of help was accepted in scornful silence, and the sheriff went back to the main prize of the evening—the half dozen ringleaders who were cooped safely in Red Moffet's cell.

Then a strange thing happened.

For the six were well armed—armed to the teeth in fact—and yet they had not the slightest thought of resistance. They crowded against the bars and with piteous voices begged the sheriff to let them out. They promised, like repentant children, that they would be good hereafter. They vowed to the deputy sheriff eternal gratitude.

Dick Binney, his face stiff with congealed blood, grinned sourly as he listened. Then he opened the door and permitted them to come out, one by one. At the cell door they were relieved of their weapons, and held in check by Reginald Ingram. They were before him like sheep before a shepherd. For the Reverend Reginald Ingram was a much altered man.

A random bullet had chipped his ear, and sprinkled him with streaks of blood. His coat had been torn from his back. One sleeve of his shirt was rent away, exposing a bare arm on which the iron muscles were piled and coiled. And perhaps his chief decoration was a great swelling—already blue-black—which closed one eye to a narrow, evil squint.

This terrible giant herded the prisoners along the bars, the bent barrel of the rifle, more terrible by far than any loaded gun, still in his hand. He spoke to the crestfallen men with a cheerful contempt. They would be held for attempted murder, and they would be treated as cowards should be treated. He ripped the masks from their faces, and called them by their names. And they shrank and trembled before him.

When the sheriff had emptied Red Moffet's cell, he locked up the recent aggressors, one by one, in adjoining cells. A miserable row they made! With them went three of the stunned men whom Ingram had trampled in the aisle. Two other of his victims were better suited for the hospital than the jail, and Binney's assistants cared for them in the office as well as they could.

Outside, the noise of the crowd had ceased with mysterious suddenness. When Binney cast a glance through the open rear door, half suspecting that his enemies might have massed covertly for a sudden thrust, there was not a soul in sight. Apparently, on reflection, the crowd had decided that there had been enough done that night—or enough attempted! They had remembered other employments. They had scattered swiftly and silently.

A cell door had clicked shut for the ninth time, and nine men were cursing or groaning behind bars, when a hand was clapped on the bare shoulder of the minister. He turned and confronted Red Moffet, whose face was transformed by a magnificent grin of triumph.

'Old-timer,' said Red Moffet, 'of all the good turns that was ever done for me, the best—'

He was silenced by a lionlike roar from the minister.

'Moffet, what are you doing out of your cell? Get back inside it!'

'Me?' said Moffet, blinking, and then he added: 'Look here, Ingram, you've been playin' dog to a lot of sheep, but that don't mean that you can—'

'Get back in that cell, you—you puppy!' ordered Ingram.

'I'll see you there first!' began Red Moffet.

Feeling that words were not apt to have much effect upon this bloodstained, ragged monster, Red followed his speech with a long, driving, overhand right which was aimed full at the point of Ingram's jaw.

It was an honest, whole-hearted punch, famous in many a town and cow camp throughout the Western range. It was sure death, sudden darkness, and a long sleep when it landed. But this time it somehow failed to land. The minister's head dropped a little to one side, and Moffet's thick arm drove over his shoulder; then, while Red rushed on into a clinch, Ingram swung his right fist up from his knee, swung it up, and rose on his toes with the sway of it, and put the full leverage of his straightening back into the blow.

It struck Red Moffet just beneath the chin and caused his feet to leave the floor and the back of his head to fall heavily between his shoulder blades. When his feet came down again, there was no strength in his knees to support his weight. A curtain of darkness had fallen over his brain. He dropped headlong into the arms of Ingram.

Those arms picked him up and carried him into his cell, laid him carefully on his cot, and folded his arms upon his chest.

'You didn't kill him, Ingram?' asked the overawed sheriff, peering through the bars as Ingram came out of the cell and slammed the door.

'No,' said Ingram. 'He'll be all right in a few minutes. And,' he added, looking around him, 'I hope that everything will be quiet here now, Binney?'

'Partner,' grinned Dick Binney, 'nobody could start trouble in this town for a month—after what you've done tonight! And—suppose we shake hands on things in general?'

They shook hands on things in general.

XIV
Muy Diablo, After All

It would be impossible to describe all that passed through the mind of the Reverend Reginald Ingram when he released the hand of the deputy sheriff. For, with a shock, he was recalled to himself. And he realized that, no matter how else his conduct might be described, it certainly had been most unministerial!

He did not have time to reflect upon the matter in any detail, nor to decide how he could reconcile what his fists had done with certain prescriptions in the Gospels. For now there was a violent interruption on his train of thought. Horses were heard galloping up the street. They stopped near the jail.

'It's more trouble! Stand by me, Ingram!' cried the deputy sheriff, picking up a repeating rifle. 'If they try to rush that door open, I'm going to blow a few of them sky high! These are some of the friends of the boys in the cells, yonder! Ingram, will you stand by me?'

'I will,' said the minister. And, automatically, he reached for a weapon from the sheriff's stock. It was a great, ponderous, old-fashioned, double-barreled shotgun, loaded with buckshot, adequate to blow a whole column of charging men back through yonder doorway.

Voices were heard calling, crying back and forth. Then into the bright lantern light which flooded the doorway, a figure sprang. Ingram tilted his weapon—

'No!' cried the deputy sheriff.

And he struck up the muzzles of the shotgun just as the triggers were pulled, and a double charge blasted its way through the flimsy roofing and on toward the stars.

'It's a woman!' called Dick Binney.

Aye, it was a woman who ran toward them now, crying: 'Dick Binney! Dick Binney! Where's Reggie Ingram? What've you done with him?'

Astrid was as unconcerned as though a popgun had been fired at her. Behind, charging through the doorway, came Vasa and a few of his neighbors to protect the girl. She disregarded them utterly. She found Dick Binney and caught hold of his rifle.

'Dick! Dick! You've let the brutes murder Reggie, and I'll—'

'Hey, quit it, will you?' exclaimed Dick Binney, striving vainly to free his gun—for he was not quite sure of the intentions of the cavalcade which clattered up the aisle of the jail. 'I didn't touch Reggie, as you call him. Here he is to speak for himself.'

The girl looked across at the tattered giant; and at the second glance she was able to recognize him.

'Reggie!' she screamed.

And all at once Ingram was enveloped—subdued—dragged forward beneath the light—kissed—wept over—exclaimed about—it would be impossible to express all the storm of joy and grief and fury which burst from Astrid Vasa.

It appeared that the large minister was an innocent darling, and all other men were beasts and wolves; and it further appeared that he was a blessed lamb, and that his Astrid loved him more than heaven and earth joined together; moreover, the man who had made his eye so black was simply hateful, and she would never speak to that man again—

'But, oh, Reggie,' she breathed at last, 'didn't you just have a gorgeous, glorious, ripping, everlasting good time out of it?'

He hesitated. He blinked. The question touched exactly the center of his odd reflections.

'Yes,' he said faintly and sadly. 'I'm afraid that that is exactly what I have been having. And,' he added, 'I'm frightfully depressed, Astrid. I've disgraced myself and my profession and my—'

The rest of the sentence was lost. Astrid was hugging him with the vehement delight of a child.

She dragged him forth. She pointed with pride to his tatters and to his wounds.

'Look!' cried she. 'Look at him! And he's ashamed! Oh, was there ever such a wonderful, silly, dear, foolish, good-for-nothing in the world?'

They got Ingram out of the jail.

The town was up by the time they reached the street. It had not been very safe to venture abroad during the period when the would-be lynching party had possession of the streets, but now it was perfectly safe, and, therefore, all hands had turned out and were raising a great commotion. And in the forefront, nearest to the jail, were the families of sundry gentlemen who, it was rumored, were now fast confined within its walls. And heaven knew what would become of them when the law had had its way!

Ingram appeared, disfigured, vastly unministerial, with Astrid Vasa at his side, and a small corps of men, heavily armed, walking behind the couple.

The crowd gave way.

'Brother Pedrillo was right, after all,' said a bystander. 'This feller sure is *muy diablo.*'

'*Muy diablo*!' murmured Astrid, looking fondly up at her hero. 'Do you hear what they're saying about you?'

'Ah, my dear,' said the battered hero. 'I hear it, and I'm afraid it shows me that I have done my last work for the church.'

'Bah!' said Astrid. 'You can do better work now than you've ever done before. You can build hospitals over the whole face of the country, if you have a mind to. By jiminy, I'll make Dad give you the money for another one right away, if you'll have it!

The minister made no reply.

He was too busy thinking of various widely disjointed phases of this business, and most of all he was wondering what sort of report would go back to the reverend council which had dispatched him to this far mission in the West.

He said good night to Astrid at her house, and went on up the street toward his own little shack. And as he came, the crowd—which was returning from the region of the jail, where they had been picking up the detailed story of the fight—gave way around him, and let him have a clean pathway. He had been downtrodden, cheaper than dirt in their eyes. He was something else now. He moved among them like a Norse god, a figure only dimly conceived in the midst of winter storm and mist. So Reginald Oliver Ingram walked down the main street of Billman and entered his shack.

As he entered, the strong odor of cigar smoke rolled out toward him. He lighted the lantern, and saw Brother Pedrillo seated in his one comfortable chair, smiling broadly at him.

'These cigars of yours,' said Brother Pedrillo, 'are very good. And I thought that, after all, you probably owed me one, being *muy diablo*, as it appears you are!'

There was a change in the church affairs of Billman. Indeed, for the first time in the history of the town, the activities of the church had to do with something more than weddings and funerals. Men who were a little past the first flush of wild youth formed the habit of drifting into the church on Sundays. Because, for one thing, all the other best men in the community were fairly sure to be there. They came for the sake of talking business after the church session had ended.

But then they began to grow a little more enthusiastic about the church itself. The manner of the young minister was not that of one speaking from a cloud. He spoke calmly and earnestly about such matters of the heart and soul as interest all men, and with such a conversational air that sometimes his rhetorical questions actually drew forth answers from his congregation. No one could ever have called it an intense congregation, or one that took its religion with a poisonous seriousness. But, before the winter came, it was a congregation which supported two schools and a hospital. It acquired a mayor and a legal system that worked as smoothly as the system in any Eastern city. And it was noted with a good deal of interest that in the political campaigns there was one speaker who was always upon the winning side, and he was none other than the gentleman of the clerical collar—young Reginald Oliver Ingram.

'How come?' asked a stranger from Nevada. 'Might it be because he's got such a pretty wife, maybe, that he's got such a powerful lot of influence with people?'

'I'll tell you the real reason of it,' replied a townsman, drawing the Nevada man aside. 'You take another look. Now, what d'you see?'

'I see a big sap of a sky pilot.'

'Stranger, I'm an old man. But don't speak like that to one of the younger boys of the town, or they'll knock your head off. I'll tell you the real reason why Ingram runs this town. It ain't just because he's a parson. It's because he's *muy diablo*, and we all know it!'

"When you think of the West, you think of Zane Grey."
—*American Cowboy*

ZANE GREY

THE RESTORED, FULL-LENGTH NOVEL,
IN PAPERBACK FOR THE FIRST TIME!

The Great Trek

Sterl Hazelton is no stranger to trouble. But the shooting that made him an outlaw was one he didn't do. Though it was his cousin who pulled the trigger, Sterl took the blame, and now he has to leave the country if he wants to stay healthy. Sterl and his loyal friend, Red Krehl, set out for the greatest adventure of their lives, signing on for a cattle drive across the vast northern desert of Australia to the gold fields of the Kimberley Mountains. But it seems no matter where Sterl goes, trouble is bound to follow!

"Grey stands alone in a class untouched by others."
—*Tombstone Epitaph*

ISBN 13: 978-0-8439-6062-4

LOUIS L'AMOUR

TRAILING WEST

The Western stories of Louis L'Amour are loved the world over. His name has become synonymous with the West for millions of readers, as no other author has so brilliantly recreated that thrilling and unique era of American history. Here, collected together in paperback for the first time, are one of L'Amour's greatest novellas and three of his finest stories, all carefully restored to their original magazine publication versions.

The keystone of this collection, the novella *The Trail to Crazy Man*, features the courage and honor that characterize so much of L'Amour's best work. In it, Rafe Caradec heads out to Wyoming, determined to keep his word and protect the daughter of a dead friend from the man who wants to take her ranch—whether she wants his help or not. Each classic tale in this volume represents a doorway to the American West, a time of heroism and adventure, brought to life as only Louis L'Amour could do it!

ISBN 13: 978-0-8439-6067-9

COTTON SMITH

"Cotton Smith is one of the finest of a new breed of writers of the American West."

—Don Coldsmith

Return of the Spirit Rider

In the booming town of Denver, saloon owner Vin Lockhart is known as a savvy businessman with a quick gun. But he will never forget that he was raised an Oglala Sioux. So when Vin's Oglala friends needed help dealing with untruthful, encroaching white men, he swore he would do what he could. His dramatic journey will include encounters with Wild Bill Hickok and Buffalo Bill Cody. But when an ambush leaves him on the brink of death, his only hope is what an old Oglala shaman taught him long ago.

"Cotton Smith is one of the best new authors out there."

—Steven Law, Read West

ISBN 13: 978-0-8439-5854-6

ANDREW J. FENADY

Owen Wister Award-Winning Author of *Big Ike*

No mission is too dangerous as long as the cause—and the money—are right. Four soldiers of fortune, along with a beautiful woman, have crossed the Mexican border to dig up five million dollars in buried gold. But between the Trespassers and their treasure lie a merciless comanchero guerilla band, a tribe of hostile Yaqui Indians and Benito Juarez's army. It's a journey no one with any sense would hope to survive, or would even dare to try, except...

The Trespassers

Andrew J. Fenady is a Spur Award finalist and recipient of the prestigious Owen Wister Award for his lifelong contribution to Western literature, and the Golden Boot Award, in recognition of his contributions to the Western genre. He has written eleven novels and numerous screenplays, including the classic John Wayne film *Chisum*.

ISBN 13: 978-0-8439-6024-2

John D. Nesbitt

"John Nesbitt knows working cowboys and ranch life well enough for you to chew the dirt with his characters."
—*True West*

FIRST TIME IN PRINT!

Will Dryden picked the wrong time to ride onto the Redstone Ranch. He was looking for a job…and a missing man. But one of the Redstone's hands was just found killed, so tensions are riding high and not everyone's eager to welcome a stranger. The more questions Dryden asks, the more twisted everything seems, and the more certain he is that someone's got something to hide. Something worth killing for. Dryden just has to make sure he doesn't catch a bullet before he finds out what's behind all the…

TROUBLE AT THE REDSTONE

ISBN 13: 978-0-8439-6055-6

ROBERT J. CONLEY

FIRST TIME IN PRINT!

NO NEED FOR A GUNFIGHTER

"One of the most underrated and overlooked writers of our time, as well as the most skilled."
—Don Coldsmith, Author of the Spanish Bit Saga

BARJACK VS...EVERYBODY!

The town of Asininity didn't think they needed a tough-as-nails former gunfighter for a lawman anymore, so they tried—as nicely as they could—to fire Barjack. But Barjack likes the job, and he's not about to move on. With the dirt he knows about some pretty influential folks, there's no way he's leaving until he's damn good and ready. So it looks like it's the town versus the marshal in a fight to the finish... and neither side is going to play by the rules!

Conley is "in the ranks of N. Scott Momaday, Louise Erdrich, James Welch or W. P. Kinsella."
—*The Fort Worth Star-Telegram*

ISBN 13: 978-0-8439-6077-8
